Praise for *Death of a Schoolgirl*
A Mystery Guild Alternate Selection

"Everyone's favorite character, Jane Eyre, returns in a marvelous new adventure. Joanna Campbell Slan's *Death of a Schoolgirl* is a must for all her many fans as Jane Eyre searches for an elusive killer who has Rochester's young ward in his—or her—sights."　　—Charles Todd, *New York Times* bestselling author

"Charming, winning, mannered, and so genuine it seems like a long-lost Brontë original. . . . The Jane Eyre we know and love is revealed as a nifty detective, just as resolute, clever, and independent as her fans always knew she was."
　　　　　　　　　—Hank Phillippi Ryan, Agatha, Anthony and
　　　　　　　　　　　　　　　Macavity–award winning author

"*Jane Eyre* was always one of my favorite books and I'm delighted to be able to peek at her life as Mrs. Rochester. I always knew she'd make an excellent sleuth."
　　—Rhys Bowen, Agatha and Anthony Award–winning author of
　　　　　　　　　the Molly Murphy and Royal Spyness mysteries

"A terrific beginning to a new series. In *Death of a Schoolgirl*, author Joanna Campbell Slan has given us a fully fleshed sequel to *Jane Eyre*, as darkly gothic as the original, only this time Jane uses her insatiable curiosity to solve a murder. An intriguing new sleuth!"
　　　　　　　　　　—Jeri Westerson, author of the Crispin
　　　　　　　　　　　　　　　　Guest Medieval Noir series

"A wonderful book. It's the best sort of historical mystery—richly detailed, cleverly plotted, and filled with characters you'll not want to leave behind."
　　　　　　　　　—Stefanie Pintoff, Edgar® Award–winning author

"This tasty blend of well-drawn characters and unexpected plot twists has all the rich flavor of England in the early 1820s. One nibble and you won't be able to stop until the very last morsel is nothing but a memory. Thank goodness there are more Jane Eyre Chronicles to come!"

—Kathy Lynn Emerson, author of *How to Write Killer Historical Mysteries: The Art and Adventure of Sleuthing through the Past*

"A delightful chance for Brontë fans to expand their acquaintance with Jane Eyre, who continues her modest but strong-willed ways in an ingeniously contrived return to teaching . . . and sleuthing."

—Charlaine Harris, #1 *New York Times* bestselling author

"Layered with compound mysteries that unfold in a manner true to Brontë's style . . . A faithful and ultimately satisfying continuation of an English classic."

—*Ellery Queen Mystery Magazine*

"Captures the essences of Jane and Rochester . . . The mystery is entertaining fun, but it is what happened to Jane and Rochester since the classic ended that subgenre fans will enjoy."

—*The Mystery Gazette*

"Slan has woven in some nice bits of real history and knitted her new story almost seamlessly onto the end of the Brontë novel. If you have read the original, your enjoyment will be enhanced, but if you haven't you will still enjoy this involving tale."

—*New Mystery Reader*

Death of
a Dowager

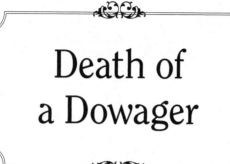

Joanna Campbell Slan

BERKLEY PRIME CRIME, NEW YORK

THE BERKLEY PUBLISHING GROUP
Published by the Penguin Group
Penguin Group (USA) Inc.
375 Hudson Street, New York, New York 10014, USA

USA / Canada / UK / Ireland / Australia / New Zealand / India / South Africa / China

Penguin Books Ltd., Registered Offices: 80 Strand, London WC2R 0RL, England

This book is an original publication of The Berkley Publishing Group.

DEATH OF A DOWAGER

Berkley Prime Crime Books are published by The Berkley Publishing Group.
BERKLEY® PRIME CRIME and the PRIME CRIME
logo are trademarks of Penguin Group (USA) Inc.

ISBN: 978-1-62490-437-0

PRINTED IN THE UNITED STATES OF AMERICA

Cover illustration by Alan Ayers.
Cover design by George Long.
Interior design by Laura K. Corless.

This is a work of fiction. Names, characters, places, and incidents either are the product
of the author's imagination or are used fictitiously, and any resemblance to actual persons,
living or dead, business establishments, events, or locales is entirely coincidental.
The publisher does not have any control over and does not assume any responsibility for
author or third-party websites or their content.

For my aunt, C. Shirley Helmly

Acknowledgments

First, I want to thank the many wonderful book clubs that have chosen to read *Death of a Schoolgirl,* the first book in the Jane Eyre Chronicles. Your emails to me are a source of great joy and encouragement. I am so very, very pleased that this new series has sent many of you back to read or re-read Charlotte Brontë's classic *Jane Eyre.* It certainly remains my favorite book of all time. For book club questions or more information about my other work, please visit my website at www.JoannaSlan.com.

Second, I offer my deep and humble appreciation to "Team Jane." My talented, perceptive, and devoted editor, Shannon Jamieson Vazquez, was actually editing this book while going into labor. I'm sure that little Sam was worth the interruption! While mother and son were bonding, the fabulous Michelle Vega stepped in. Meanwhile, my superagent, Paige Wheeler, continues to be my guiding light, and I adore her. Kayleigh Clark, my Berkley Publishing Group publicist, has done a great job of spreading the word about *Death of a Schoolgirl.* Maryglenn McCombs, my personal publicist, has always been my advocate and my cheerleader.

Last but not least, my sister, Jane Campbell, provided wonderful insight along the way. She's a fantastic plot-buddy who never lets me down. If you are lucky enough to write books for a living, better hope you have a sister as wonderful as Jane.

It is madness in all women to let a secret love kindle within them.

—Charlotte Brontë, *Jane Eyre: An Autobiography*

There is abundant evidence to prove that despite the wrong he did her in after years, she was always in his heart of hearts his "only real and true wife."

—William Henry Wilkins, *Mrs. Fitzherbert and George IV*

Prologue

Love has a transformative power, an alchemy that reshapes the most intransigent personality. I hear its magical intonations when my husband talks to our infant son, Ned. I see its thrilling ascendance when I watch my friend Lucy Brayton fuss over garments for her new son, Evans. I note its charming selflessness as our housekeeper, Mrs. Fairfax, anticipates our needs. I feel its strength coursing within me at night whilst I stare at the moon and count my blessings. In the still hours of the night, when the only sounds are soft snores of the sleeping persons who make up our household, I thank God for this familial harmony, this wondrous sense of belonging. Here, in the shelter of Ferndean Manor's leaking roof and crumbling walls, we thrive as a small tribe of like-minded souls. We are bound together by mutual affection as strong as any iron chain. It pleases me mightily to think how all of this is a result of our love, Edward's and mine.

What folly caused seekers of old to search for recipes to change base metal into gold? Far more potent is that emotion that transfers blissful ignorance into warm affection. For when we are surrounded by love, everything is tinted with a new hue of happiness. And that, I am confident, is the chemistry most worthy of pursuing. That transformation of the human soul! Love is more rare and treasured than any lump of gold. It is the prize that all of us seek, its end product is acceptance, and its denial is at the root of all sorrow.

To refuse a woman the chance to follow her own heart is cruelty beyond imagining. To force a man to marry a woman he can't love is to inflict misery. To brush aside the passions inflamed by love is to invite disaster. To underestimate the love of a parent for a child is folly.

This I have witnessed with my own eyes. It happened thus . . .

Chapter 1

Ferndean Manor, Yorkshire
May 15, 1821

"A nice day for a walk on the moors." My friend Lucy Brayton's sweet smile caused her blond curls to bounce becomingly under her bonnet. Halfway to her fortieth year, she could accurately be called handsome rather than beautiful, until she smiled. Then the sparkle in those summer sky blue eyes and the lilt of her lips proved transformative.

I agreed with her. "It is lovely."

White-as-wool clouds dotted the gray blue sky, and the freshly washed landscape glistened. Here and there, new green tree leaves served as a stunning background for the plum purple of the Northern Marsh orchids and the brilliant red of the poppies. She and I meandered along, watching out for puddles and picking posies to fill her trug.

"Lovely despite the standing water," I added.

"Here or there?" She nodded toward Ferndean Manor, and we both laughed, thinking back on the mess that last night's storm had made of the kitchen. Spring rains announced the changing of the seasons, and the fearsome storm had been exceptional. The elements had assailed us, blinding bursts of lightning and deep booms of thunder that put us all on edge. The combination of shocking sight and startling sound had produced a surreal counterpoint to our domestic tranquility as we gathered around the fireplace in the drawing room. After several hours, there had come a more intimate sign of the storm's fury—the clatter of rain hitting tiles. The roof in Ferndean's kitchen had buckled under the assault.

It was yet another sign of how the house, never meant for permanent inhabitants, had fallen into disrepair. Displaced from his family seat at Thornfield Hall due to fire, my husband, Edward Rochester, had decamped to his hunting lodge, and I'd joined him here. We made do with a small staff: John and Mary Harrigan, my husband's elderly manservant and his wife; Amelia Sands, my son Ned's nursemaid; Cook, a woman who came in from nearby Millcote several days a week; Leah, a maid of all work; and Mrs. Alice Fairfax, our housekeeper and distant cousin to my husband. Our household also included our son, Edward Rivers Rochester, who celebrated his first birthday on April 1, and Adèle Varens, Edward's eleven-year-old ward, home from school for the summer; as well as our houseguest Lucy Brayton, wife to Edward's good friend Captain Augustus Brayton, currently posted to India. I had been Lucy's guest in London the previous autumn, and we had quickly become close friends ourselves. The severity of the disaster demanded that all of us pitch in to help. The multitude of pots in our cupboards could not contain the water flowing through the ceiling at an alarming rate. Even little Adèle did her best to move jars of preserves and tins of spices. We spent much of the night and part of the morning trying to save what foodstuffs we could.

While we were elbow deep in the mess, John volunteered to inspect the roof. Someone needed to measure the size of the crater, determine what could be done, and send to Millcote for supplies. Neither Lucy nor I thought this a wise course of action. A glance between us confirmed our unanimity, our concern for the old man's safety. We managed to convince him to hold off at least until daylight. Then, early this morning, a rap on the back door announced John's grandson, Leah's husband, James. Hearing the howl of the wind and the pounding of the rain, the younger Harrigans had figured, quite rightly, that Ferndean would sustain damages. When he heard that his grandfather was set to climb on the roof, James quickly volunteered to go instead.

"Nay," said John. "I'll tend to it."

"Why not let the younger man prevail?" In a whisper, I expressed my worries to Edward, who shushed me, saying quietly, "John has always done for me, ever since I was a lad. I shall not shame him over his advanced age. If he thinks he can inspect the roof, I shall let him. He takes great pride in helping me." The fire that destroyed Thornfield Hall, his family home, had also taken Edward's left hand and right eye—leaving his other eye to suffer in sympathy for its lost companion—and rendering him more dependent upon John than he'd been in years.

Again, Lucy and I traded looks. This time hers was accompanied by a shake of her head and a suggestion for me. "After you see to Ned and Adèle, why don't we take a walk? We can gather wild roses from the bushes."

"Yes." I sighed. "I would rather be anywhere but right here. I have a bad feeling about John's adventure."

As I expected, Amelia had the children well in hand. Adèle was playing with a new set of paper dolls that Lucy had brought her from London, and Ned was busy chewing on a silver teething ring, yet another gift from my friend. I dispensed hugs and kisses all around before putting on my bonnet and meeting Lucy at the front door.

And so we found ourselves rambling in the surrounds, taking care not to step into standing water, and searching the bushes for signs that blackberries would follow. These we marked by tying white rags to them. The spring rains were harbingers of the onset of warmer weather.

Lucy showed me a branch of yellow blossoms. "Isn't the gorse lovely?"

"Gorse? The locals call it furze. The word means 'waste' as in reference to the vast lands before us." With a sweep of my arm, I directed her attention to the endless sea of heather purple moors, bracketed by pansy purple hills yielding to a bluebell-colored sky.

"Wasteland? Hardly. I thank you for bringing me here so I can appreciate this untamed beauty," Lucy said as she slipped her arm through mine. "How unlike my life in London, where I hurry from one social call to another, speaking of unimportant matters, staring at dusty interiors of overdecorated houses."

"Surely there is more to it than that. What do you talk about?"

A slight incline of her head served as an agreement. "The coronation of King George IV two months from now. That is all anyone thinks about. On and on and on. How much Prinny is spending. Who will be invited." She paused and then asked, "That reminds me: You still have the letter, don't you?"

I knew what she was referring to; due to an unusual series of events, I had in my possession a letter written by our sovereign to one of his paramours back when he was Heir Apparent. In this missive, he made several inopportune admissions, the most damaging one being his admission to bigamy—a union that could cost him the throne.

I hurried to assure her. "The letter is quite safe. Mr. Rochester had a strongbox installed in our bedroom wall."

"If the contents become known . . ." Lucy's voice trailed off as she bent to pluck a cluster of rose hips, their burnt orange hues vivid against her milky white skin. "Can you imagine the general anarchy that would follow? Already the people in the street despise His Majesty. Each day brings news of another extravagant purchase. Why just last week I heard he ordered a twenty-seven-foot-long robe of crimson silk velvet to be lined with ermine. Can you imagine? Did he learn nothing from the French? How can he go on and on spending money so freely while ignoring the fact that so many of his people are hungry?"

"Will you be invited to the coronation?"

"I have been presented at court. We often appear at the same fetes, levees, and other events. Will I be invited? Possibly. I don't know. I don't really care. Not much at least."

I smiled to myself. Although she could protest the desultory lifestyle she enjoyed in the heart of the city, Lucy Brayton's status there as one of the ton, the elite ten thousand that formed the uppermost crust of society in London, mattered to her more than she would admit. While her husband, Captain Augustus Brayton, protected the soon-to-be-crowned King George IV's interests in India, Lucy labored to raise her status among those who wielded a very different sort of power. I believe it had rather become a game to her, a challenge that kept her busy while Augie was away. But that pastime had recently taken on a new importance, because Lucy would soon have her heart's desire . . . a son. Though Evans Forrester could have brought Lucy much sorrow, being as he was the product of an illicit liaison between her husband, Augie, and another woman, rather than reject the infant because of his provenance, Lucy was overjoyed to "adopt" Evans when she learned that his mother had died. To her, Evans was not a burden or a sad reminder of her husband's unfaithfulness. He was the answer to a prayer—and she planned to transfer to this child the benefits she had accrued in her slow climb up the social ladder. She had yearned fruitlessly for children of her own, and now eagerly awaited young Evans's arrival from Brussels. His travel to England had been postponed until his nanny resolved certain family matters.

"Have a care, Lucy." Taking her by the elbow, I gently steered her away from a cluster of white sneezewort yarrow blossoms thick with industrious bees. "It would never do for you to return to London all swollen with beestings." What a pair she and I made! I was as ignorant of the social set as she was of our natural surroundings.

"Jane, you worry too much—"

A loud crack like the snapping of a large branch caused Lucy and me to turn toward the noise, which was followed by the sound of more wood cracking and splintering. Then a scream ripped through the morning calm. Next we heard a loud, resounding thump.

"John must have fallen off the roof!"

"Or through it!" Lucy said, as we picked up our skirts and started running toward Ferndean Manor. Our feet took us down the hillock, through a clump of elder trees and up a small rise, atop which sat Ferndean like a squatty brown teapot without a lid.

We heard a cacophony of voices shouting over one another trying to decide what to do. My husband's voice trumped them all when he ordered, "James! Ride for Carter! The surgeon! See if you can find him quickly. Tell him to come straightaway."

Was Edward sending James away because he didn't want the boy to know how badly his grandfather was injured? Or was my husband truly hoping that James could locate Mr. Carter in time to actually help John? Our seclusion would prevent medical assistance from coming quickly.

"Oh, Lord, please let him be all right!" I whispered as I pushed my way past John's wife, Mary.

As lady of the house, it was my responsibility to attend to the crisis. I saw John's right arm bent at an odd angle under him. His eyes were open, although his skin was a sickly greenish color and clammy to the touch.

"Lucy, could you fetch me a blanket from the stable? A clean one?" I asked.

A broken bone often caused a shift in the body's humors, and this, in turn, caused shivering and a general feeling of cold. A blanket would help allay these symptoms.

"John, please blink if you can hear me."

The old man did as I asked.

"He responded and he is breathing," I told my husband, whose damaged eyesight prevented him from seeing these things himself. "A bit of blood is trickling from his mouth and ear. There is some on his forehead as well." I stooped to lift the man's wrist. "His heart beats quickly but it is steady and regular. John? Can you speak?"

"Aye." The word leaked out from him.

"Where do you hurt?"

"Me arm." He spoke so quietly I strained to hear him. "Don't feel nubbit in me legs, either."

I recalled once having seen a girl fall out of a tree. The impact stunned her temporarily. I prayed that John just needed a few minutes to catch his breath. At least he was alive. Mary gently dabbed away the blood on her husband's forehead. The result showed that John was not as badly injured as we had thought at first. I could have cried with relief.

Lucy appeared with two wool blankets that smelled faintly of horse. She handed them to me then disappeared again. I tucked one under John's head and wrapped the other around him, trying to ease the fabric between the man and the wet ground.

Edward took his servant's hand in his and murmured encouragements until Lucy returned with a damp towel that she touched to John's mouth, urging him to suck a bit of the water.

Over the next four hours, Lucy and I took turns keeping watch over John. Mary held his hand while sitting as close as possible on a campstool.

James did not come back with Mr. Carter until nightfall. By then the old man was barely conscious. One look at Mr. Carter's face in the reflected light of the lantern and my worst fears were realized. The situation was very, very bad, indeed.

Chapter 2

Under Mr. Carter's direction, the men rolled John onto a blanket and carried him to his own cottage. Edward walked behind the impromptu stretcher, accompanying a crumpled version of Mary, a dazed figure at odds with the brisk woman who generally bustled around the manor. James brought up the rear, a solemn honor guard of one. While Lucy and I stood to one side and watched the procession.

"I suspect no one will want much to eat," said Mrs. Fairfax, looking after them, "but Cook and I managed to put together a pot of stew over the fireplace in the drawing room. She also baked a loaf of bread. Dear, dear. John had been failing of late, but he tried so hard not to let Master know. With Master's own health problems bothering him, John felt it was his place to serve, not complain."

"Was he ill? Or simply suffering from old age? Before the fall, I mean."

"A bit of both." Alice Fairfax sighed. "His teeth have been bothering him. He's lost weight. Mary begged him to slow down, but he refused to listen. Men can be so stubborn at times."

"But my husband would have understood. Mr. Rochester did not want him to climb on the roof. He cares a great deal for John," I said.

"Yes, I know that. And John also cares deeply for Master. After all, it was John who first set young Edward Rochester on a pony. John who gave him his first whipping for teasing the cat. John who told Old Master Rochester that Edward had been called out to duel."

"Pardon?" I was certain I had misheard her. "Called out to duel?"

"Yes. It happened long before I came to Thornfield, of course, back when Master's father was still squire. But from what I've heard, a man insulted the Young Master, and he responded in kind, then a letter came to the house calling him out." Mrs. Fairfax closed her eyes and shivered. "I'm told it was a near thing."

"What happened next? Did my husband meet him?"

"John handed the note to Old Master. Seems that Old Mr. Rochester had been corresponding with a family in Jamaica about their beautiful daughter and their fortune. John and two others went searching for Young Master. When they found him, they tossed a potato sack over his head, tied him up, and spirited him away aboard a ship bound for Jamaica. You know the rest of the story."

I mulled this over. "So in essence, John both saved my husband's life and was the instrument of his miserable first marriage."

"Yes. I know it took Master a long time to forgive John for that, but he did. John and Mary never reached above their station—they were far too loyal for such nonsense—yet they have always considered themselves part of the Rochester family. When Master was hurt in the fire, John nearly lost his mind with grief. Now John feels he must help Master feel independent. Why, he follows Mr. Rochester everywhere. He's especially mindful when Master goes outside."

Ferndean's surrounds were indeed full of unexpected dangers, from fallen tree limbs and rotting branches to the moors bordered by fields full of unpredictable farm animals. And, of course, there are always clumsy poachers, especially given the horrible winter of this past year; many locals struggle with hunger. Edward has given a sum to the church to be used for charity, and I planned to start delivering baskets of foodstuffs to the poor as soon as I mastered driving the dogcart.

On the other hand, where had all that worrying about Ferndean's hidden dangers gotten us? Edward was fine, but it was John who was badly hurt!

Shaking my head in discouragement, I hurried into the house and down the hallway to the nursery where my thirteen-month-old son, Ned, lay sleeping and Adèle was burrowed under her covers. I kissed my fingertips and transferred the affection to the children's cheeks before leaving them to their dreams.

Lucy and I joined Mrs. Fairfax in the drawing room for a quick bowl of the stew. The fragrance of lamb, rosemary, and carrots proved irresistible. There was no place to wash our dirty dishes, so Mrs. Fairfax piled them on a tray and carried them outside. "I'll tend to them in the morning," she told me before she retired to bed.

Edward had not yet returned. I feared the worst news possible as I paced the drawing room with its fireplace. The yellow red coals sent out a cheerful warmth that partially offset the chill I felt anytime I thought about John. Lucy sewed steadily on a little shirt she'd been making for nine-month-old Evans. "I wonder what color eyes he has," she said as she plied the needle.

Evans had a nanny, Mrs. Wallander, a Swiss woman who had been by his side since birth. Mrs. Wallander had written to say that she would happily accompany the boy to London and stay on at her post, but their departure from Brussels had been delayed when the nanny's own daughter was stricken with childbed fever.

"I am sure his eyes will be beautiful, no matter whether they are hazel or blue," I said, picking up my own project. Taking my inspiration from illustrated manuscripts, I had drawn a large version of the letter "E," followed by smaller letters "V"—"A"—"N"—"S." I was filling the surrounding space with all manner of vines, flora, and fauna. After I sketched everything in pencil, I would apply India ink, and finally use watercolors to complete the design.

Lucy set her work aside. "Jane, please, come stay with me in London. There is more than enough room for all of us! Come and stay for a good long time. Without Augie, the house on Grosvenor Square is far too big for me to live in alone. Find an overseer to repair this place, and come away with me, Jane. You'll be such a comfort when Evans arrives, and you know how I dote on Ned and Adèle. Besides, Edward is safer in London than he is here. Especially as this place crumbles around you."

"I know your generous invitation comes from your heart," I said. "Let me see what Mr. Rochester thinks of it. But first, we need to be sure that we've done all we can for John."

"It will do you good to get away," said Lucy.

Our conversation was interrupted by Edward's heavy footsteps. I met my husband at the door, and under the guise of an affectionate embrace, I lightly guided him to his favorite chair. Pilot, his faithful Newfoundland, trotted over to his master for a pat.

"How is John?" I asked after Edward was seated. Pilot pressed his nose into Edward's hand.

"Carter reckons the old man might never walk again . . . if he survives. The fall jarred him badly, so there's no telling what injuries he might have internally. We should count ourselves lucky if he makes it through the night." Edward shook his head. "I should have forbidden him from climbing up on the roof. I should have told him no."

"I believe I'll turn in for the night. You know, of course, that my home is always open to both of you." With that, Lucy excused herself, leaving my husband and me to talk in private.

I waited until the door closed behind her. "You cannot blame yourself. John is a proud man, and he refuses to accept his own limits. You have said as much." I slipped my arm around Edward's shoulders and he leaned his head against mine. After a moment in this awkward position, he pulled me onto his lap. There I stayed for a while. When the embers in the fireplace changed to gray and white as they cooled, I whispered, "Come, my husband. Let us go to bed."

Chapter 3

Edward slept restlessly, tossing and turning. At one point, he moaned in his sleep. Of late, his slumber was often interrupted by dark passages that set him thrashing and fighting the bedclothes.

"I am here, my love," I said as I wrapped my arms around him. "Edward?" I raised my voice enough to rouse him slightly.

"Wha—? Jane? Oh, my darling Janet." He called me by his favorite endearment. Soon he settled back into a regular pattern of breathing.

But I was wide awake. Slipping out of bed, I went to the window and threw open the shutters.

The thought of being here alone, surrounded by my young family, filled me with pleasure. Far from feeling isolated, I felt protected, as if by keeping it at bay, the world at large could not destroy the joy we found in one another.

And yet, was the world beyond these borders really so daunting? After Lowood Institution, the charitable school where I had been sent as an unwanted orphan, could any place be more hostile? And hadn't Lowood turned out for the best? Yes, at first it had been difficult, but eventually I'd gained my footing and found friends. And even at my lowest point, when I'd truly had nothing, I had managed to discover not only friends but family in unexpected places.

Surely I could do the same wherever we went.

A bat winged its way through the night sky, moving in silence against the mottled gray of a moonlit landscape. If only my husband could move through his darkness with such confidence!

A trip to London was in order. I had a sure friend in Lucy Brayton, and another in her brother, Bruce Douglas.

We couldn't remain in Ferndean any longer, not in its current condition, not with children and my husband's health to consider. Edward's melancholy and his vision grew worse each day. Ned could easily catch a fever. Adèle? Right now, with her school in Millcote closed for the summer, she was bored out of her wits. Without an outlet for her energies, she often chose misbehavior as a way to capture our attention. Certainly, Adèle would find the trip delightful, as she adored Lucy, or more correctly, she was agog at Lucy's well-appointed house and fashionable lifestyle. Moreover, my husband would have much-appreciated opportunities for entertainment and socializing in that friendly environment.

The next morning, while Lucy slept in, Mr. Carter joined my husband and me for breakfast and brought good news. Seeming blessedly oblivious of the disarray in our dining room, he took a place at our table. Once Leah served him hot tea, toast, a plate of sliced ham, cooked rashers of bacon, and cheeses, he gave us his full report. "The crisis seems past. If he is kept quiet, I believe your manservant will recover, Mr. Rochester."

"His full measure of health?"

"That I cannot say. He fractured his arm. I encouraged him to move his legs, and he was at last able to do so. But he did hit the ground hard, and at his age, such a blow can set off other issues. It's impossible for me to know what else might be amiss. A portion of his healing will depend on the sort of care and rest he gets now. To that end, I've inquired after the services of a healer, a Mrs. Pendragon, who lives several miles away, closer to Millcote. I hope you don't mind me taking this liberty."

"Not at all. John's recovery is my primary concern."

"Good. I thought you would feel that way." Mr. Carter looked relieved. "Mrs. Pendragon is of Welsh descent. More than a few of the locals actually fear her, but their reaction is born of ignorance. She has remarkable knowledge of the healing arts, and a vocabulary of herbal recipes that are unexcelled. As a matter of fact, I have learned much from the woman. I should like for her to stay here for as long as necessary. Mrs. Pendragon can instruct Mary in the preparations of certain tisanes and poultices. My biggest fear right now is that John will develop a fever or pneumonia. Both are common after an injury like this."

"Mr. Carter, is our help needed here? Perhaps my husband and I should repair to London. My husband and I had discussed going to the city, rather than staying here at Ferndean with all the repairs that need to be made," I said. "Is that wise? Or would it be best for us to wait?"

"I think you should go. If you stay here, John might try to hurry the mending process. If you are gone, he and Mary can devote themselves entirely to his recovery. He won't be tempted to move around before his bones knit."

"That reminds me," Edward said as he turned toward me, "before you came to breakfast, James scrambled up on the roof and took a look. The supporting beams have rotted through. The entire skeleton will have to be replaced. This is more than a simple patching job."

"I don't mind the inconvenience, nor am I put out by having to fend for ourselves, but I am worried about the damp.

We can't risk having Ned catch a fever. Especially living so far from Millcote. You saw how long it took James to fetch Mr. Carter."

"Yes, and you were lucky he managed to hunt me down." Mr. Carter put down his fork and looked at me sternly. "He happened upon me while I was on the road. Otherwise he'd never have found me going from door to door. I could have been too far away to be helpful. Of late, I've taken to making monthly visits to London myself, to meet with other like-minded men in the medical field. In fact, that's how I came to learn about Mr. Parmenter, the specialist whom I suggested you visit after I examined your husband several months ago."

"But you are still our local surgeon." Edward said this by way of confirmation. If Mr. Carter was not keeping his practice here, we would need to see what we could do about engaging another doctor for the people of our estate.

"I have been meaning to speak to you about that. This is a most inopportune circumstance, but well, I believe the time has come for you to engage another surgeon for your estate. Millcote and its surrounds are growing, and I am past my prime."

To this disclosure, Edward reacted with alarm, as did I. Mr. Carter seemed too young to retire, being only a few years older than my husband. However, we did not reply quickly enough to interrupt the surgeon's speech.

"More and more, I find myself arriving too late to be of maximal assistance. I spend more time in my carriage, riding from patient to patient, than I do at bedsides. Another doctor would lessen my load and assure your tenants of the sort of attention they need." I felt my husband relax—Carter merely wished for assistance, not to leave his position. "I've taken the liberty of mentioning this position to a young colleague of mine in London, a Samuel Lerner. There is another benefit you will find most interesting; he is a specialist in matters of the eye, having studied under Mr. Parmenter. He served me well for a short while when you were healing from your injuries after the fire. In fact, it was he who saved your one eye by his quick thinking and knowledge of ocular arts."

"Did he indeed?"

"Yes, I was delivering Mrs. Mulcahy of a child coming into this world breech, so I dispatched Lerner to your bedside. You were unconscious, and badly mauled, but he managed to spare you excess pain and to stabilize your condition until I could arrive. Believe me, his skills are astonishing, and you are living proof."

"Lerner? A Jew?" Edward asked.

"Yes, and one of the best minds for healing that I've met in my lifetime. Surely you won't hold his religion against him, if his skills are commensurate? Or exceptional?"

"Carter, remember to whom you are speaking. Of everyone you know, surely I am the most tolerant. Given the crooked path I've taken, how can I not be? Furthermore, I've met many of the Hebrew persuasion in my travels. I think they are ill-used as a people. Your suggestion surprises me only because I wonder if my tenants would accept him."

"I believe they will if I take him with me and introduce him around as my second."

"All in all, then, I believe it behooves us to take Lucy up on her kind offer," said Edward. "We can leave as soon as we pack. Some things should not be left unattended."

His words were straightforward, but they held a special meaning for me. He was suggesting that I bring along the letter.

I never meant to own it. Although I had thought about destroying it, as I had done the others, cooler heads than mine prevailed. I had sought the counsel of Lucy; her brother, Bruce Douglas; and my own dear Edward. My husband's argument had been particularly compelling: "That letter could change the course of history. If George IV slips into madness as did his father before him, it might prevent a bloody fight for control of the throne by pointing the way to a simpler solution."

And so we had kept it locked away. Now Edward was suggesting that I bring it along rather than letting it remain here at Ferndean. After all, there would be a myriad of workmen in and out of the house. The strongbox could easily be discovered, and a hammer applied to a chisel could force it open. Leaving it or any other valuables behind would not be prudent.

Mr. Carter interrupted my musings as he said, "If you would like, I can stop and speak with Thadius Farrell on my way home. He's a local builder well-qualified to see to your roof and kitchen. Mrs. Carter and I have engaged his services in the past, and we were well pleased. I'll send him round to talk with you."

"I believe your father once employed Thadius to make repairs to the stable," Mrs. Fairfax said as she carried a kettle of hot water to replenish our teapot. "I will stay here to direct the repair efforts and forward your mail."

"Excellent," said Edward.

"If you'll excuse me, I'm going to see if Mary needs anything," said the housekeeper.

"I will go with Mrs. Fairfax to look in on John one more time and then be off," said Carter. "As soon as I'm home in Millcote, I'll pen a letter to Lerner telling him to expect you. In fact, I am overdue for a visit to London myself, and I'd like to hear his opinion on your eye. Perhaps our visits will overlap."

"Yes," said Edward. "I think that would work nicely. I shall go with you to see John. While I cannot fix what is broken, I can reassure Mary that I will do everything in my power to aid her in his care."

Chapter 4

"I am warming to this whole scheme of running away to the city," confided Edward, later that day. "I believe I have been in need of a change of scenery. I promise you, Jane, that my mood will improve."

"If it pleases you, then it pleases me," I said. Yes, he had been rather low of late, although we both had tried to dismiss it. My husband had been a man of great physical prowess. He had often spoken to me of the pursuits he had hoped to teach our son, but even as Ned grew more and more adventuresome, Edward had come to feel his limitations accordingly. As a result, the restrictions of his missing appendage and poor eyesight weighed on Edward heavily.

An unruly thatch of his hair fell over his scarred forehead as he reached for my hand, lifted it to his mouth, and kissed it. "My darling girl, you are too good. We both know that London is anathema to you. You are never more pleased than when taking a long walk or curling up with a good book. Or even putting charcoal to paper and recording what fantastical images you conjure up in that busy mind of yours! Ah! Don't try to argue, Jane. You could have suggested that we rent another house out here in the country instead of decamping to the city. However, I know you have agreed to this for my sake, and I accept your sacrifice with good humor."

"Speaking of sacrifices, our ride in the coach should prove most interesting. Our son has become quite the explorer. Be forewarned that we will have our hands full trying to keep him out of the straw on the floor of the coach," I said with a scarcely contained laugh.

"Ned will find your efforts to curtail his activities most annoying! Perhaps poor Lucy would be better off to travel without us," Edward said.

"Oh, ho, ho, no, you don't!" Lucy's voice sang out as she entered the room, carrying a bouquet of snowy white daisies with egg yolk yellow centers. "This trip to London will give me a chance to practice my mothering skills."

"You will do just fine with Evans," I assured her, as I had been doing since the news first came of the boy's impending arrival.

"Jane is right, dear Lucy. There is no need for you to serve an apprenticeship at motherhood."

"That is kind of you," she said as she tapped him on the shoulder, "but I am determined to carry out my new responsibilities to the utmost of my abilities. My job is to provide Evans with every advantage. His life will be the apex of mine, and due to my efforts, he starts at a higher rung on the social ladder. All that I've endured for the sake of the beau monde will be worthwhile when my son is accepted into the fold. I shall call in all my outstanding chits, so that my son benefits from my arduous years of enduring hours of innocuous pleasantries in the name of greasing the wheel of social approval."

"You make it sound ghastly," I said.

"Most of the time, it has been," she admitted.

Her judgment on this subject baffled me. Lucy seemed to act as a barometer, with her needle fluttering first over one extreme and then the other. Now she was telling us how valuable she found society—and also how tedious. Which version was truer?

I proffered my own conclusion. "I believe you overvalue the worth of the ton and underestimate your own gifts. The ton matters not."

"I beg to differ," said Lucy. "The ten thousand have great power, even more so because our new King exhibits so little constancy of purpose. His mercurial nature is largely influenced by those around him, and what is fashionable at the moment. Therefore, the ton can make or destroy a person with their acceptance or denial—because as they lean, so bends the King's will."

"I cannot imagine such influence! To my way of thinking, anyone lucky enough to receive your affection has a tremendous advantage over his or her peers."

"My thoughts exactly." Edward nodded toward her. "Lucy, I bless the day that Augie married you. Thanks to his good taste, we are all a happy band of your beneficiaries."

"And I owe you a debt of gratitude for persuading him to ask for my hand. Oh, I do sincerely hope that you and Jane consider yourself fortunate to have me. I know I can be rather bossy at times. Toward that end, I have been doing some thinking. I suggest that we make good use of the three days we'll have in the coach. I have in my possession a listing of all the operas, concerts, and plays now appearing in London. Of particular note is Rossini's *Tancredi* at the Italian Opera House."

"*Tancredi*? Is that based on Voltaire's play *Tancrède*?" Edward wondered.

"Yes, the same. Fanny Corri-Paltoni has been reprising the principal role."

"That's capital!" Edward responded with more gusto than I'd heard in days. "Jane has never been to an opera, and I have longed to escort her. I heard Corri-Paltoni on the Continent a few years back."

"Yes," said Lucy, "and this piece is quite demanding, with two lengthy arias and no less than four duets."

Edward and Lucy began to discourse about music in a lively manner. Although I play piano (adequately) and sing (passably), my skills in this arena are, admittedly, lackluster. Edward was an accomplished singer, and he had a God-given beautiful tenor voice. Discussing the mezzo-soprano diva caused him to brighten with interest.

More and more, the timing of this trip fit everyone's needs. We could leave Ferndean to the efforts of the builder, offer companionship to Lucy as she waited for Evans to arrive, interview Mr. Lerner for the position here in the county, and get his opinion on Edward's diminishing vision.

Yes, it would be good for all involved, except . . . except that small still voice inside me that yearned for solitude and a simple life.

But Lucy had other plans. "Jane? You'll want a court dress for wearing to the opera. We need to discuss which styles and colors might look best on you. You can visit my mantua-maker so you have the proper accoutrements for any event."

"I have a lovely silk dress in claret that will be quite suitable."

Lucy's smile was indulgent. "No, my dear. It most certainly will not!"

I thought my friend mistaken but let the matter drop.

"To London!" Edward raised his teacup, and I followed his lead.

"To London!"

Chapter 5

Since the Rochester barouche had been lost in the fire at Thornfield Hall, James drove us in his dray to Millcote, where we could board the coach for London. The night we spent in that village would have been pleasant enough, except that Mr. Carter had insisted we take supper at his home. Edward had taken him up on his offer before I had the chance to share my concerns.

I knew from prior experience that Mrs. Carter thought our marriage shameful. Unfortunately, her opinions had been formed by ugly commentary provided by the Dowager Lady Ingram and her daughter Blanche.

At one time, the whole county had expected Edward to marry the beautiful Blanche Ingram. They were both superb equestrians, and their families had long been neighbors. Blanche was acclaimed far and wide for her great beauty, whereas my husband would never be called attractive, because his features lacked classical proportions. Despite their mismatched pulchritude and a vast difference in their ages (though not as large as the difference between my own two and twenty, which was less than half of Edward's midforties), many thought that he and she made a good match.

But Blanche's heart harbored no real love for Edward. Indeed, the Ingram family was only fortune-hunting. To expose their avarice, my husband caused a rumor that his income was only a third of its real value. In a blink, the Ingrams had dismissed him as a suitor.

When they discovered that they had been tricked, and when Edward proceeded to marry a governess—me—both Blanche and her mother thought themselves very ill-used. They responded by blackening my name to all and sundry. Mrs. Carter fell prey to their disappointment. I learned as much the last time I traveled through Millcote on my way to London to visit Adèle, but I chose not to share the news with my husband. What was the point? Why upset Edward further? He and I both valued Mr. Carter's opinion. If Mrs. Carter thought me unsuitable, that didn't matter a fig to me.

But her wrath did make this an uncomfortable situation, to say the least.

While my husband now enjoyed a leisurely cigar in the Carters' garden, Lucy and I were deposited abruptly by Mrs. Carter in her drawing room and left to our own devices. Through the walls of the house, we could overhear Mrs. Carter scolding her husband. Fortunately, Amelia had taken Adèle and Ned outside for a breath of fresh air, or they, too, would have been treated to hearing Mrs. Carter chastise her husband about my low character.

"Goodness," whispered Lucy. "No wonder the good doctor travels to London on a monthly basis. The poor man has reason to want to escape! But what on earth has kindled this attack against you?"

"The Honorable Blanche Ingram and her mother, the Baroness Ingram of Ingram Park," I said quietly.

"Ah. So even Mrs. Carter has heard Lady Ingram blame you for robbing her eldest daughter of Edward Rochester. Or more correctly, for robbing her of the Rochester fortune. As if Blanche isn't enjoying still being on the marriage market," Lucy said softly, "despite growing longer in the tooth every day. Rejecting suitors left and right. Honestly, Blanche takes it as sport, and her mother indulges her and plays along. It has been nearly ten years since she was presented at court. While all her contemporaries are happily married and raising heirs, she still appears at Almack's, flirting and fawning over men with titles."

"What is Almack's?"

"A social club. Admission is highly coveted. It is the most likely place that an unmarried woman would meet a suitor after she has made her debut."

"And you have seen Blanche Ingram there?"

"On occasion, as it is a grand place to see and be seen. Blanche and I are little more than nodding acquaintances, but Lady Ingram is sister-in-law to my dear friend Olivia Grainger. I would have introduced you to Lady Grainger the last time you were in London, but she was in Bath, taking the waters."

"Well, whatever shortcomings the Honorable Blanche Ingram owns, Mrs. Carter must think she hung the moon," I said.

"Yes." This came on the wings of a sigh from my friend.

The bell for supper rang, and we assembled around the Carters' table. Had Edward been able to see the derogatory glances Mrs. Carter cast my way, he would have been outraged by the woman's behavior. As it was, I pinched Lucy's leg black and blue in an effort to prevent her from leaping across the table and jabbing our hostess with a fork. Poor Mr. Carter struggled all evening, sending conciliatory glances first to me and then to his wife, gestures that she rejected with a sniff of disapproval.

I went to bed that night at the coaching inn grateful for the cover of darkness so that I could relax the pleasant but insipid expression that had frozen on my face. With Edward's sturdy back as my shelter, and his steady breathing as my lullaby, I finally drifted off to sleep.

The trip to London proved exhausting. Ned could not understand why he needed to stay confined to such a small space for the duration of three days. Passengers came and went, many with muddy boots and one whose head lice were determined to abandon their happy home and come throw their lot in with us. I smashed a dozen or more as they crawled up my arm.

The coach itself must have been missing its springs, a lack that exaggerated every bump and hole along the North Road. Our driver seemed to aim the conveyance toward any protrusion or rock in our path. He must have thought it sport to see how bone rattling a ride his passengers could endure.

The swaying of our carriage preyed upon poor Amelia's stomach, causing the girl to retch miserably until she finally fell into a swoon. Lucy tried to soothe the girl, while Edward, Adèle, and I struggled to keep Ned off the floor of the coach. His toys were of little interest, but the straw under our feet fascinated him. I shuddered each time he offered me a handful of dry stalks encrusted with muck, mud, and offal.

By the end of our journey, my jaw muscles ached from clenching, and my arms hurt from wrestling with Ned. Needless to say, my lower portions were sore and bruised from the constant jostling of our seats. How I envied those with more padding on their bones!

At last we arrived in London, bedraggled, cross, and buginfested. Williams, Lucy's coachman, met us at the carriage inn and quickly transported us to #24 Grosvenor Square, where Lucy's brother, Bruce Douglas, graciously overlooked our disheveled and dirty state and welcomed us to his sister's house.

Lance Corporal Bruce Douglas reminded me of the Greek god Helios. With his sun-burnished skin, strands of gold in his hair, and the glint of steadiness in his eyes, he was a specimen any artist would adore painting. All that kept him from being pretty was a fight-battered nose and a feathery mustache. A keen gambler, a bon vivant who loved to carouse, he worked as an inquiry agent, tracking down thieves and solving problems beyond the purview of the constabulary. Like his older sister, Mr. Douglas offered constant surprises, because they were both more complex, more loyal, more erudite in obscure knowledge than one might first suppose upon meeting them.

Fortunately, Higgins, the butler, and Polly, Lucy's lady's maid, represent the best of their professions. They adore their mistress and did not recoil from our miserable state. Instead, both took one look, assessed our woebegone condition, and began preparations for our benefit. I longed to submit to their tender care, but first I accompanied Lucy to her drawing room where she locked the King's letter in her strongbox. In short order, all of us were bathed, deloused, and sent to bed for some much-needed rest.

While we adults were catching up on our sleep, Ned and Adèle discovered that Bruce Douglas was a doting "uncle" who knew exactly how to entertain bored children, and that Higgins was a pushover for the Young Master and French poppet, or so I heard the next morning at the dining room table. Over a buffet breakfast, Lucy, her brother, my husband, and I discussed what we might see and do in the city. As I sat in comfort and nibbled at toast while drinking Lucy's favorite blend of black tea with bergamot, it occurred to me that perhaps a pampered life in London was exactly what my family needed.

Chapter 6

Despite the familiar irregular features and hazel eyes, the woman in the mirror scarce resembled me. My reflection wore a blue silk bandeau in her hair, which supported a gathering of white ostrich plumes and blond court lappets. A white satin slip with an embroidered border of blue flowers peeked out from under a blue petticoat festooned with miniature blue rosettes and clusters of seed pearls. Over the dress, she wore a robe train of gros de Naples in a darker shade of blue, ornamented with miniature blue rosettes. In addition, that strange mannequin staring back at me wore white satin gloves that stretched from the fingertips past the elbows. And around her neck was a strand of diamonds that caught the candlelight and broke it into rainbows with a million splendid colors.

Jane Eyre, governess, would never dress in such a flamboyant manner.

Mrs. Edward Rochester, wife of the country squire, might.

Surely one might fight for a middle ground!

I lifted my blue and silver wrap to decorously cover my décolletage and shoulders.

"No, no, no!" Lucy scolded as she readjusted the drape around my upper arms so that more of my skin was uncovered. "This shawl should softly embrace you, not bundle you up as if you were a parcel. Besides you want the Rochester diamonds to show. Their sparkle matches that of your eyes."

Lucy peeped over my shoulder and into the cheval mirror at our reflections. Our twin ostrich feather headdresses mingled in a flurry of downy white fluff. Behind us, I saw the sumptuous gold and white decor of Lucy's guest room. Rags, Lucy's beloved little white dog, stood watching us from the bed, his tail wagging like a king's standard flaps in the breeze.

"But I feel too exposed. This can't be proper."

"It's not only proper but required. The King sets the rules for court dress, and court dress is de rigueur at the theater. At least George IV has decreed that we won't be wearing hoops under our skirts. But the décolletage, bare arms, and ostrich plumes are still expected." Lucy admired her handiwork, since it had been her instructions that the mantua-maker followed when creating my lavish gown. "You look a picture, and I can't wait to introduce you. Shall I call you my sister?"

"I would be honored."

Any observer who compared Lucy's blond curls to my smooth wings of dark hair would quickly dispute the notion that we shared a similar provenance. However, if outward appearances were cast aside, one might soon discover that Lucy and I harbored the sort of affection for each other that would rival that of any two siblings.

"Polly? I daresay we won't be back until very, very late. I'll be sorry to wake you, but of course we'll need your help."

"Yes, ma'am." Polly quivered with happy expectation rather than inconvenience.

Lucy treated her abigail with much more familiarity than most treated their lady's maids, but rather than making the young woman impertinent, Polly seemed to revel in helping her mistress dress for august social events.

I cast a longing glance at my old brown muslin dress—a gown so plain that in it I could pass for a woman of modest means, the woman I once was. Polly noticed and placed the dress over her arm.

"I'll clean this for you and mend the tear, Mrs. Rochester."

A tear. Even that felt symbolic to me of my conflicted state of mind.

"I promise you," said Lucy, turning me so our eyes met, "this evening will be a revelation. A distraction. A reminder of what the larger world has to offer both of you. Even now."

"Lucy, I appreciate all you have done," I said taking her hand, "but I would feel much more comfortable in simpler attire. We are going to the opera house to watch the performance onstage. Why should anyone care what I am wearing?"

"You have so much to learn." Lucy shook her head. "A vast portion of tonight's entertainment will be in watching the audience. Everyone who is anyone in London will be attending tonight to see Corri-Paltoni's triumphant return to the London stage. They will use the evening to catch up on the latest gossip. The actors and singers will need to strain to be heard over the chatter and commotion!"

I touched my shawl and watched the silver threads glisten most alluringly. Lucy had given it to me as a wedding gift, and thus I treasured it. "Are we to be the object of such attention because your box is so prominent?"

"That is but one reason. For another, the entire routine of social calls is excruciatingly boring, so the appearance of any new personage infuses much-needed excitement to the mix. You wouldn't want to cheat the others of the spectacle, would you? As a newcomer to the social scene, tomorrow you will be the subject du jour!"

"I have no desire to be the subject du jour. I am attending the opera because my husband is eager to revive his memories of hearing Corri-Paltoni on the Continent, not because I wish to make a spectacle of myself!"

"Aye, there's the rub. You cannot do one without the other."

Polly draped our trains over our forearms so we would not trip over them, and I caught the scent of lily-of-the-valley perfume as Lucy moved me toward the doorway.

I admit I dragged my feet a little, scuffing my lovely silk slippers. "Won't the other patrons have more important subjects to discuss? Such as the quality of Corri-Paltoni's voice?"

"Bah! What does society know of musical talent? Not much, I assure you. But to see a new face in a fifth-level box, that is a subject they can explore with great amusement. Think of this as a grand lark, and you are perfectly prepared for your part."

I hardly thought so.

In fact, I felt a bit ill.

Chapter 7

Solemn male voices echoed off the marble floors in the entry hall of the Braytons' residence, where my husband and Mr. Douglas conferred in hushed tones. Lucy's brother looked wonderful in his impeccable eveningwear, but he was nothing compared to my husband. A rogue lock of hair fell over Edward's brow, and white hairs had recently joined the dark ones in his sideburns. I thought these signs of maturity a most appealing addition to his natural charms.

The men were discussing the trial of Caroline of Brunswick, King George IV's wife. Caroline insisted on being named Queen Consort, as was her right, but the King wanted her barred from his coronation, two months hence. To prove his wife unfit, he had collected salacious evidence of her adultery. The proceedings moved along slowly, even as George IV planned a coronation more elaborate than any ever held. But the previous autumn, Caroline had been found not guilty— and the crowds in the street went wild with joy. Whatever flaws Caroline had, they paled in comparison to the King's profligate behavior, his out-of-control spending, and his blatant disregard for the common man.

The men's low voices were overshadowed by giggles coming from Adèle and our son, Ned, nestled in the arms of his nursemaid Amelia.

Lucy's rapping of her fan on the walnut banister alerted all to our arrival. With her other hand, she stayed my progress, so that she and I stood paused at the top of the stairs, allowing the small assemblage below best opportunity to inspect our grandeur while Rags preceded us down the stairs, barking all the way.

"*Très belle! C'est magnifique!*" Adèle Varens, Edward's ward and my former pupil, clapped with excitement and turned a pirouette of pure joy. "*Chère Madame, tu es fantastique!*"

She rattled off a steady stream of French sentences that left her quite breathless, including the hurried comment that "the house wren has turned into a peacock!"

I did not correct her by pointing out that the peacock is the male of that species, and the female peahen is dull by comparison, but I did tuck the comment away for her future edification. Once one has served as a teacher, the urge to correct mistakes is a pressing desire, not because the teacher believes in her natural superiority, but because inaccuracy is the breeding ground of ignorance.

As Adèle hopped from one foot to the other, Ned caught the festive spirit and erupted with hoots of baby laughter.

Edward addressed his ward in her native language and suggested that she show the sort of restraint that the English admire in a young woman of breeding. But this chastisement was accomplished with warm affection in his voice, and although she bit her lip, Adèle's face did not sacrifice its effervescent expression of happiness.

"What visions of loveliness!" Mr. Douglas announced as Lucy and I made our way down the stairs. "Mrs. Rochester, the blue of your gown reminds me of spring bluebells in the forest, but the white of your ostrich feathers is more like freshly fallen snow."

Mr. Douglas has a kind heart. His description was solely for Edward's benefit. My husband squinted at Lucy and me, struggling to see us for himself. My heart plummeted at this additional evidence of continued deterioration in his vision. Lucy's method of decorating, which tended to excess, meant there were no clear pathways in her house, which further complicated Edward's attempts at self-sufficiency. Only hours earlier, he had tripped over an ornate needlepointed footstool and taken such a fall that I feared for his safety.

As I'd helped him to his feet, he'd admitted he could see less and less each day. "I had hoped to hide it from you, darling Jane."

I'd guided him toward a wingback chair, capturing the offending footstool and pulling it near him.

"Sit here, sir," I had said, before taking my place on the low stool. I sat with my head against his knees so that he could stroke my hair. Silently, I wondered to myself what would become of my husband when he could no longer navigate his way through the world without assistance.

"Mr. Rochester," I had then said quietly, "I thought we had agreed: There are to be no secrets between us."

"Ah, as if I could keep it a secret! You suspected as much, darling girl. There was no reason to alarm you further by confirming it." He'd sounded jaunty. As a postscript, he'd added, "At this rate I shall be blind as a tree stump in a month or two."

"No, no, my darling," I'd assured him, winding my arms around his calves. Privacy was a luxury in Lucy's busy home. "I am confident that Mr. Lerner can help you. As for your care after the fact, I think your idea of hiring him to work for us and among our tenants is a good one. Whatever obstacles your vision poses, your insight is still good. Once you meet this

Mr. Lerner, if you think highly of the man, I say we should engage him. We need another doctor in the county, and as squire it's your duty to take care of your tenants."

"How do you feel about the fact that he is a Jew?"

"Our Lord Christ worshiped in temple. The Jews are God's Chosen People. I am not sure what the farmers will say, but if he comes with Mr. Carter's approval, I think they'll give him a fair shot, don't you?"

"I hope so. I certainly hope so," Edward had said. His large hand caressed my face. "It has never been my wont to pray for myself, as that always seemed so arrogant coming from one who had received more than his fair share of life's bounty. However, in odd moments, my mouth forms the words, 'Please, God,' and I am stunned by the ferocity of my desire to regain at least a portion of my sight. Yet who am I to ask for more than what I already have? What sort of ingrate am I?"

"No ingrate, sir. Only a human being."

A little later, I'd told Lucy about Edward's diminishing vision. "Perhaps it is prudent to alert your staff to the matter. I do not wish—nor do I expect—for you to change your household to accommodate him. However, they can keep a sharp watch on trivial matters that could anticipate a crisis."

"Like a cigar ash rolling onto a tapestry chair?"

"Oh dear! Has that happened?"

"Yes, but it was quickly extinguished. You do not need to worry—my servants have already come to me individually to say they are being watchful."

My heart ached with relief and thankfulness. "How can I let them know their efforts are appreciated?"

"You've already shared with them your greatest treasures, Ned and Adèle. The sound of children's voices in this house is as welcome as the sound of eventide bells in the local church. Believe me, if the servants are half as thrilled with Evans when he arrives, this place will hum with happiness."

Now as I watched how tenderly Lucy's brother shepherded

my husband toward the front door, I reflected again on how fortunate we were to have such stalwart friends!

After saying good-bye to Adèle and giving Ned a kiss, I took my husband's arm. Higgins grabbed Rags or he would have gladly accompanied us out the door. Mr. Douglas nudged Edward toward the carriage by shadowing his other side. To the casual observer, nothing would appear amiss.

Keeping up his end of this ruse, my husband initiated gay banter with Lucy about the merits of a castrato's voice versus that of a soprano's. I noted how sincerely cheerful he sounded. Yes, my husband was painfully aware of his infirmities, but I hoped that diversions such as this would go a long way toward making him happier.

As Lucy, Edward, and I took our seats in the carriage, Mr. Douglas leaned out the quarter light to remind Williams that our destination was the Italian Opera Theatre in Haymarket.

"Haymarket?" Edward mused.

"You'd scarcely recognize the place," said Mr. Douglas. "Totally redesigned. One of the architects is a fellow named Nash. A great favorite with our new King."

"And like our sovereign, another man who revels in excess," sighed Lucy. "This monstrous building can seat two thousand and five hundred souls."

I could not imagine so many people in one place at one time!

Williams urged the twin bays forward. Peering through the curtains and enjoying the passing scenery, I caught myself before pointing out a trifling landmark to my husband. There was no need to make Edward more aware of his plight. Seeking to ease the awkwardness of the moment, I said, "By the way, Mr. Rochester, you are looking very dashing with your top hat and morning coat. You are turned out quite nicely, too, Mr. Douglas."

"I am sure we will both be as drab as dirt next to His Majesty. What a dandy he is!" Mr. Douglas laughed.

"What? Are you suggesting our sovereign will be in attendance?" My heart crowded my throat. This was a turn of events I had not foreseen.

"It is possible," said Lucy. "Perhaps even likely. But he is often surrounded by a large crowd of those currying his favor, especially because invitations to the coronation are so highly coveted. Those on the periphery of his circle seek to improve their chances at attending. We'll probably get our best look at him as he processes into his box."

"The letter?" That was all I needed to say; everyone in the carriage knew of its existence.

"Is still locked away," Lucy assured me, "and I have spoken of it to no one."

"Are you worried, my dear little Jane?" asked my husband gently.

"Don't be," said Mr. Douglas before I had the chance to answer. The role of protector came easily to him, and since he meant his rebuke kindly, I took it as such.

"Our King has been exceedingly fond of writing to his paramours. With the coronation approaching, his couriers are busily scouring the countryside and buying up his errant love notes. Your letter is but one of many." Mr. Douglas smiled at me in a reassuring way.

"But will he be here tonight? The King?" I could not decide whether the shiver that swept through me was the result of being thrilled or dismayed. After all, who would have guessed that I, an orphan girl shuttled off to a charity school, would have risen so high? Never did I dream that I might glimpse the sovereign of our realm, arguably the most powerful man in the world. No matter how dissolute or disappointing, this was our liege, and he was still our ruler.

I did hope for a good look at him.

"One can never tell in advance if he'll be in attendance, but he does enjoy performances," said Mr. Douglas. "Rather fancies himself an amateur thespian, or so I've heard. If he is here tonight, he might be escorting the Marchioness Conyngham, his latest mistress. He does fall for them with alarming regularity."

"Yes, he's had one woman after another and is rumored to have fathered many illegitimate children," said Lucy, "but there's a fundamental discontent driving his actions. The only woman he has truly loved is a person he can't keep by his side, Maria Fitzherbert, the woman he married without his father's permission. Furthermore, dear Brother, I am sure Jane's letter is unique, since in it the King acknowledges that he married Maria and that Minney Seymour was their own child, and therefore, an heir to the throne, albeit an illegitimate one. His affection for Minney is well-known. She is the one who nick-named him 'Prinny' because as a child she could not manage the title 'Prince.' Thus they became 'Minney and Prinny' to all." This last bit Lucy directed to me.

"Why would he dote on this particular girl when he has other illegitimate children?" I asked.

"He loves Minney because he loves her mother," said Lucy. "Isn't that one of the reasons parents long for children? To see their love for another person incarnate? Maria is not the most beautiful woman the King has wooed. She is six years his elder and had been twice widowed when he married her in 1785. Worse, she's not only a commoner but a Roman Catholic! Her nose is too long and her chin too prominent, though her eyes are huge and her complexion flawless. But she has such a gentle and loving nature that everyone who meets her is captivated."

"You speak as though you know Mrs. Fitzherbert personally," I said.

Lucy inclined her head. "We have been friends for many years. I respect and admire her. Minney is a darling, only a few years older than you."

"This is still confusing," I admitted. "If Minney is Maria Fitzherbert's daughter, why is Seymour her family name?"

"Officially, Minney was born to Lady Horatia and Vice-Admiral Lord Hugh Seymour. But that was all a sham, a way of protecting Maria from idle gossip. Moreover, as a ruse it almost went too far. When the Seymours died, one after another of illness, Minney was safe at home with Maria. But knowing the child was favored by His Majesty, Lady Horatia's sister tried to gain custody. Can you imagine? For that I do give him credit. Our King fought the one battle of his life in persuading the House of Lords that Maria should be able to keep the girl and raise her as her own."

"The man presents a total contradiction." I voiced my innermost thoughts as our carriage arrived at the theater and joined the others in the queue.

"What about Caroline of Brunswick? Will she be here?" wondered Edward. "I confess I am curious about her. Surely she cannot be as uncouth as she's made out to be."

"Her personal habits are appalling, her lack of modesty is an affront to all women, and her behavior is unbecoming," said Lucy. "Do you know that she has appeared in public with her breasts exposed? That she has told visitors quite plainly that she enjoys intimate relations and then she has gone on to invite her guests to join her in partaking of such?"

I felt a blush rise to my cheeks.

"Yet, Sister, the common folk love her," said Mr. Douglas. "They identify with her plight. She, like them, has been wrongly used by our King."

"When you compare them—the wife he chose for himself versus the wife his father forced him to marry—it is easy to see why the King prefers Maria," said Lucy.

"True, and yet the King must distance himself from Mrs. Fitzherbert. Especially now when he has not yet been consecrated as our sovereign."

"The coronation." Edward nodded. "That is the key. He must be presented to and acclaimed by the people, before he receives our homage. Perhaps he believes that once the ceremony is over, when he has been anointed, crowned, and blessed, the populace will have no choice but to accept him despite all his peccadilloes."

I had so much to learn. My sheltered upbringing offered me no insight into royal politics. Yes, I had studied our national heritage, but I learned it as a schoolgirl does, repeating what was told to me. None of my teachers would have ever dreamed to challenge the divine right of the King, and all its attendant privileges. Yet on a fundamental level, I had always believed that all of us were equal in the sight of our Lord. If we were, every one of us, endowed equally with his love, then it stood to reason that a monarch would be every bit as flawed and confused as the rest of us.

Perhaps even more so.

Chapter 8

A sedan chair passed us with its top propped open so that the rider's ostrich feathers could protrude skyward. Its curtains obscured the passenger, but Lucy glanced over and said, "Dowager Lady Sefton, one of the patronesses who presides over Almack's. I recognize the emblem on the doors and the chairmen's livery. They'll take her right to the front door—see if they don't!"

As we moved along in the queue, I watched passengers step out of the broughams and curricles ahead of us. All of the women wore white ostrich feather headdresses similar to mine, which went a long way toward making me feel less foolish. Reluctantly, I admitted to myself that observing the parade of conveyances and the arriving patrons was highly amusing. I had never seen such an array of finery in my life. As persons climbed out of their conveyances and walked toward the entrance, their jewels sparkled merrily in the light from the torchères.

At long last it was our turn to disembark. Bouncing down from his perch, Williams raced to set out the steps for us.

When we alighted, Mr. Douglas and I bracketed Edward to help him move forward with assurance. Under the cover of my blue shawl, I took my husband's arm. To help Edward navigate the steps, Mr. Douglas said casually, "Thank goodness there are only four steps up to the first level. We'll turn left once we make it inside." With the movement of the crowd shielding us, no one noticed how we guided Edward into the building.

Once inside the vast theater, the seating rippled out from the stage in a semicircle—and the exuberant level of activity stunned me. While Lucy nodded to this person and that, we slowly made our way forward. Patrons leaped over scarred wooden benches to speak to one another or to hail vendors hawking foodstuffs and offering beer. Others cried out as hot wax dripped down on them from the immense candelabras that dangled from the ceiling. The smell of yeast, sweat, and candle wax nearly caused me to gag.

Williams shuffled along behind us, carrying a picnic basket that Cook had packed. It must have been heavy because he huffed and puffed as we climbed the five flights of stairs to Lucy's box. At each level the boxes became more exclusive and the number of patrons moving upward along with us grew fewer. Upon arrival at the highest level, four levels above the pit area, it was plain to see why these lofty spots were so highly coveted. Their size and the views from these boxes were clearly superior to their neighbors.

An engineering marvel, the Braytons' box was cantilevered over the main floor, bringing us intimately close to the stage. The larger portion of the box was a rectangular dining area framed by a set of lush burgundy velvet curtains with gold fringe. If desired, Lucy and her guests could retire to her table and chairs in privacy by closing the drapes. However, the portion of the box facing the stage was flanked on the left and right by cutaway walls, sloping from ceiling to floor in a concave shape, allowing a panoramic view of all the boxes on either side.

Williams set down the picnic basket, bowed, and retreated to a seat in the back. The contents of the basket were glorious. Lucy had instructed Cook to prepare a variety of refreshments for our consumption: fricassee of chicken, sliced ham, veal, asparagus in aspic, carrots in honey glaze, fresh bread, butter, a selection of cheeses, fruit dipped in chocolate, and several bottles of chilled wine.

"Piffle!" Lucy laughed when I expressed my astonishment at this repast. "Bruce and I come to the opera often. This is what I always bring, although I admit it's a bit more fulsome than usual tonight because I hoped to please the two of you."

Her brother assisted her in removing her wrap and hung it over one of the gilded chairs. "Don't let my sister's casual manner fool you. Lucy is the consummate hostess. Her parties are much praised. Invitations from her are highly sought-after by the ton. When she entertains, the whole town rehashes the event endlessly. In short, although she is marvelously flexible and can acquit herself well in any circumstance, Lucy is very much a shining beacon of style on which the beau monde trains their quizzing glasses with great interest. To add to her accomplishment and natural manner, she had to learn this comportment on her own. Our parents did not entertain."

Lucy frowned slightly. "Let's eat, shall we?" She gave a brisk clap of her hands. The satin muffled the sound, but it was sharp enough to signal an announcement. "There is claret to accompany the meat, Tokay for taking with the pudding, and of course port and red wine. Williams will serve us."

Once Edward and I both had our plates filled, I described to him our surroundings. The crush of people below us astonished me. Nor did the noise abate when the first act, a quartet of singers, came out to entertain. If anything, the crowd simply increased its volume to hear one another over the noise onstage.

Men climbed over one another, over the seating, and over any obstacle to greet women or to chat, and women in all varieties of dress milled about on the first floor, some selling refreshments, others whispering in men's ears. A general distasteful odor of unwashed bodies floated our way. Staring down from our lofty vantage point, the sea of humanity below mimicked a fantastical bouquet of flowers where blushing faces played the part of blossoms. Ordinary visages were framed by colorful headdresses and *chapeaux bras*, the fashionable three-cornered flat silk hats.

The scene in the upper boxes was more uniform. In accordance with the King's decree, all of us women wore ostrich plumes in our hair, and our gowns were all similar styles in sumptuous shades of lavender, blue, aqua, or mauve. The men had even less variation, since all wore dark tailcoats with frothy white cravats that peeped out above their white waistcoats, partnered with black knee breeches and silk stockings, as well as thin slippers. Except for varying colors, trim, and gems, all of our costumes were nearly interchangeable. Lucy had been right to insist that I dress according to her instructions. In my simple silk gown, I would have looked woefully out of place.

Suddenly the tone of the chatter changed. The musicians in the pit raised their instruments and looked to the maestro in his long black swallowtail coat, who craned his neck to see over the crowd. That proved nearly impossible because the vast throng of people had gotten to their feet and jostled for position.

"The King is coming," Lucy said quietly, smoothing her skirt. "Rossini is one of his favorites," she said to me. "After Waterloo, the composer visited London, and the Regent convinced Gioachino Rossini to play a duet with him on the cello."

"As I recall hearing," Edward said, "His Majesty could not keep pace with Signore Rossini, but the artist generously suggested that 'few in Your Royal Highness's position could play so well,' thus earning the composer a lifetime of goodwill."

"There are two sorts of persons that Prinny never forgets: his friends and his enemies." Lucy's face remained impassive, but her eyes darkened to that deepest blue that signaled a sea change in her emotions, and I felt her tremble beside me. I recognized there was more to Lucy Brayton than I knew; more than her usual cheerful behavior belied.

"I have heard that there have been numerous attempts on his life." Edward spoke in a low tone.

"It is true," said Mr. Douglas. "There are many who would hope to see one of his brothers on the throne, especially since the death of Princess Charlotte three years ago left Prinny without an heir."

Meanwhile, the royal procession had struggled its way to the fifth level. A young page strode down the hall, calling out, "All stand for His Majesty, the King!"

We rose from our seats and turned toward the opening in the plush velvet curtains. After the page came three pairs of red-uniformed footmen. The gold braids on their shoulders and chests swayed and caught the light as they cleared the way, moving spectators aside. Behind the footmen came two equerries dressed in equally elaborate and stunning costumes.

The courtiers parted. "The King will be next," Lucy whispered as she sank into a deep curtsy. I did, too, and the men bowed low. From under my lashes, I glimpsed an enormous man so encrusted in medals, ribbons, jewels, and finery that he dazzled the eye as he clanked his way along, with his sword rattling at his side. On his head was an oversized and much-powdered wig of fluffy white curls, which sat almost comically askew. I rose slowly in time to see that he was accompanied by an equally immense and overly decorated woman.

"The Marchioness Conyngham." Lucy pitched her voice low. "Lady Elizabeth Conyngham."

"That was our King?" The words came as a gasp. The Prince of Wales had once been called the most beautiful man in our nation—or so everyone had said, praising his finely shaped calves, merry eyes, and pouting lips. But the man who waddled past us, leaning heavily on his cane, was grotesque in the extreme. Even from the back, I could see how his richly embroidered vest strained mightily to restrain his superfluous flesh. Nothing could disguise his bloated appearance, not even the elegance of his apparel. The perfume that lingered in the air was overmuch, cloying with its rich effusion of huile antique and jasmine.

Behind the King and his mistress came men and women of the court, many dressed in elaborate uniforms of His Majesty's own design. Their purpose was to cater to every whim of the King and his lady. One face in the crowd caught my attention: Phineas Waverly, a Bow Street Runner whose acquaintance I had made some months previously when he'd been investigating the death of Adèle's schoolmate.

"Look!" Mr. Douglas pointed his chin in the direction of the King's party. "It's Mr. Waverly. I'd heard he'd been assigned to guard George IV. Most agree that he's the best of the Bow Street men. I wonder how he likes his new posting."

Knowing full well Waverly's disdain for pretention, I would guess it made him uncomfortable. Very uncomfortable indeed.

Chapter 9

Soon after, once the King's party had ensconced themselves in the royal box, the conductor waved his baton. A two-measure drumroll heralded the anthem, "God Save the King." The voices of our quartet joined in. Despite our sovereign's less than admirable behavior and dissolute character, he was still the lord of our realm, and we owed him our fealty. None of us had any questions in that regard.

The crowd settled down, and a man stepped onto the stage and introduced the opera. The overture began, the curtain rose. The magic of the music, costumes, and set transported us to the Byzantine Empire, with its dazzling onion-shaped domes and sumptuous silken fabrics. Soon, I forgot how awkward I felt in my low-cut gown and elbow-length gloves. Indeed, the outside world melted away.

When the first act ended, I could not move, so engrossed was I still in the story of two families and their struggle against an enemy army. Edward's hand sought mine, and a quick squeeze brought me back to the present.

"Is it not glorious, Jane?"

"Oh, sir! I never imagined it could be thus! I am quite breathless with the grandeur of it all. I rather wish that Adèle could have come. She would have been over the moon with joy."

"True, but we would have been pestered unmercifully to give her opera lessons." His voice sounded stern, but I knew he indulged the French child in the exact manner that any loving father would his own blood.

"That might be worth considering. Singing lessons would keep her occupied and happy." I tucked that idea away even as I spoke, because a nod of his head assured me the thinking was sound.

To take advantage of the intermission, our party filed out of Lucy's box, taking care to bracket Edward. Soon we were swept up in the society crowd, a veritable sea of foamy white ostrich feathers. Other patrons milled around us, nodding and speaking to one another. All were patrons from the fifth level, so they presumably occupied the same social strata.

Lucy had insisted that I wear the Rochester diamonds. In this company, they were most appropriate and seemed almost modest compared to the preposterously large pearls and ropes of gold worn by others. In practiced hands, painted brisé fans like the ones that Lucy and I carried spoke a language all their own, sending encouraging or rejecting messages to the gentlemen. Lucy spoke to various acquaintances and made quick introductions, all the while scanning the audience for her friend Lady Grainger. I kept to one side watching the ongoing conversations and silently committing this evening to memory.

Suddenly, I saw Lucy perk up with excitement. "Lady Grainger! At last!"

Lady Grainger was a spindly woman in a dove gray dress that matched her intelligent eyes and slate gray hair. She looked to be in her early sixties, and either time or carelessness contributed to a tired appearance, a bit of threadbare elegance that spoke of better days. The women exchanged kisses on the cheek, although Lady Grainger was so much shorter than Lucy that my friend nearly stooped to deliver hers. Mr. Douglas crowded closer and bent to kiss the woman's hand.

"Mr. Douglas, so good to see you! Darling Lucy, you are back! Have you heard more about Evans? Oh, I am so excited for you. Which reminds me, I spoke to Claymore the other day. My solicitor. I'll have to tell you—"

The woman stopped when she noticed us standing behind my friend.

Lucy gestured toward Edward and me. "May I present to you my husband's dear friend Squire Edward Rochester and his bride? They are the Rochesters of Thornfield Hall in Yorkshire. I was recently their houseguest and now they are mine."

I curtsied and my husband bowed low.

"Of course! Lucy has spoken so warmly of the both of you. Mr. Rochester, you are Edmund Rowland Rochester's son, are you not? Rowland was your older brother?" I felt a frisson of alarm, knowing how Edward's relationship with his father and brother represented a painful portion of his life, a time rife with misunderstandings and disappointments.

"Come closer, please." Lady Grainger raised her quizzing glass to get a good look at my husband and, in response, Edward almost stepped on her foot, but the faux pas amused her. In that small window of time, I decided I liked the woman very much indeed.

"I am the same, ma'am. Although not so nimble as others in my family." As always, I found Edward captivating, but at this juncture, I was most impressed by my husband's bravado. He did not act like a man who was nearly blind. On the contrary, he maintained that dignity and stature so integral to his personality. I marveled at his effort, and I regretted what it must cost him to play his part so well.

"My late husband, Bertram, Lord Grainger, knew your father quite well. I remember Thornfield Hall, especially the huge battlements. What a pity that it has burned to the ground! A grave loss, both to the Rochester family and to the surrounds. We have a country home not far from Millcote. That is the village closest to your estate, is it not?"

"Indeed it is," said Edward. He and Lady Grainger launched into a discussion of how the county had grown, while I studied the swirling mass of patrons moving around us. Again I noted how, as Lucy had assured me, my sumptuous costume actually afforded me the opportunity to blend in. Despite my discomfort, I felt thankful for her tutelage.

I indulged my desire to surreptitiously glance at the King and his lady, standing in the center of a crowd of sycophants who were eagerly vying for his attention. But my voyeurism came to an abrupt halt when Lady Grainger turned toward the crowd and, with a wave of her fingers, beckoned to others. "I believe you must be well acquainted with my sister-in-law, the Baroness Ingram of Ingram Park, and her daughters, my nieces, the Honorable Blanche and Miss Mary? They are my houseguests."

Immediately, my hands turned cold as stones in a frozen creek even as my face flamed hot with remembered anger. When I served as Adèle's tutor, the Ingrams had made much sport of governesses, declaring that they found all of us to be "incubi." At the time, I was rather pleased with myself that even in my fury at this disparagement, I had not burst out with the correction that "incubi" are male demons, and that therefore the term they were wanting was "succubi."

"Silvana?" Lady Grainger called to her sister-in-law, Dowager Lady Ingram, and gestured for the woman and her daughters to join us. The three women turned our way. I stiffened my resolve; there was no way to avoid an encounter with them now.

But I had no desire to exchange polite commentary with the Ingram tribe. Blanche, Mary, and their mother all shared the same faults: Their minds were not original, their hearts were barren as weathered rocks, and cold calculation reigned where tenderness should have mounted the throne. Had Blanche been blessed with a loving temperament, or the ability to think for herself, or even a modicum of compassion, my whole being might have suffered the pangs of jealousy, for she was a very handsome woman and, supposedly, one of the best riders in the county, a person who regularly distinguished herself in the hunt.

In the event, I wrestled with my feelings and forced myself to stay right where I was as the trio advanced on us.

After all, I had as much right to be here as they.

All three of the Ingram women combined robust stature with haughty bearing, which, added to the imperious shape of their noses, would clearly indicate to any amateur who studied physiognomy their excessive self-regard. This evening, however, Blanche's typically dark complexion was unusually pale, and plum-colored circles under her eyes suggested her constitution had been compromised. Dowager Lady Ingram lowered her crimson and ebony fan to stare coldly at Lucy, and as she did those multiple chins of hers set to wagging. When the Dowager spoke, she did so with an air of condescension. "Yes, Mrs. Brayton, I recall our meeting, and I have seen you at Almack's. You are friends with Mrs. Fitzherbert, aren't you?"

Lucy nodded. "Among others."

"I believe you also know Mrs. Brayton's brother, Mr. Bruce Douglas," continued Lady Grainger.

"Charmed." Mr. Douglas faced the Ingrams and bowed deeply, planting a courtly kiss on each of their hands. Blanche and her mother basked in the glow of his approval, though Mary, the lifeless and dull one of the trio, merely stared at her feet without bothering to change her vacant expression. "It's not often I am privileged to meet three lovely women who share a surname." He spoke with utter sincerity, but I detected the glint of amusement in his eyes.

"Mr. Douglas, you are too kind." Blanche fluttered her eyelashes at him and stepped a little too close. Mr. Douglas managed to inch back by pretending to help Lucy square her shawl over her shoulders.

The Dowager turned to urge her younger daughter forward, but Mary only stared off into the distance as though she would rather be anywhere else but here.

I knew exactly how she felt.

However, I am no coward. I am Edward Rochester's wife, and I would meet their disapprobation with head held high, for I had no reason to fear any of them. After all, in the skirmish Blanche and I had fought for Edward's affections, I had been acclaimed the victor.

"Lady Ingram? Honorable Blanche? Miss Mary? May I present to you my dear friends? Mr. Edward Rochester and his bride?" Lucy emphasized that last word, and with a flourish she stepped aside slightly to reveal my husband and me.

"Yes, of course we know Squire Rochester. He is our neighbor," said Dowager Lady Ingram.

Under the cover of my full skirt, Edward's right hand reached for mine and grasped it tightly. His voice was brittle as a piece of shale when he said, "And my wife. I believe you've met her as well." With that he tugged me slightly forward so I was standing right in front of the Ingrams. I could feel the Ingram daughters' eyes boring into me, examining my apparel with interest. Once again, I was filled with appreciation for Lucy's oversight of my appearance. I knew that in every way, I looked my part as the wife of a member of the landed gentry.

As was proper, I waited for the Dowager Lady Ingram to acknowledge my presence.

Very slowly, the Dowager turned her head away from Edward. She adjusted her gaze so as to pinion me with her fierce and hard eyes. Long seconds ticked by. At long last, she slowly and deliberately turned away, so that she was looking past me when she said, "Lovely weather we're having, aren't we, Mr. Rochester? Who else is here that we know?"

Chapter 10

No one spoke. No one moved.

I considered my options, and in the end, despite Lady Ingram's rudeness, I decided not to respond in kind. Letting her dictate my behavior would be tantamount to giving her the power to control me. Instead, I began the expected curtsy toward her. But even as I shifted my weight Edward grabbed my arm and hissed, "Don't you dare!" in a tone so low that none heard him but me. To my amazement, he followed this with a sound something like a low growl. I glanced up at him to see the anger that had contorted his features.

The fullness of his rage startled me. Reflexively, I turned toward Lucy for an explanation, but she stood unnaturally still, her face drained of all expression. I heard Mr. Douglas's quick intake of breath, and the Dowager Lady Grainger gasped loudly, sparing no effort to hide her shock. Meanwhile, Blanche's eyes narrowed and her lips curved into a smirk. Her sister Mary simply seemed to withdraw.

Such a meeting had been bound to happen eventually. I had imagined it many times over, and now I could put my fears to rest, as the reality was no worse than I had conjured it. Up to that point, our evening had been enchanting, so I decided I would carry on. I would not give the Ingrams the satisfaction of taking away my happiness.

Only . . . Edward, Lucy, Mr. Douglas, and Lady Grainger seemed more affected than I. They stood still as garden statues.

At long last, Lady Ingram angled herself away from us and began speaking to Lady Grainger in low, urgent notes. The Ingram daughters circled their mother and aunt, listening in.

"That was a cut sublime. I have heard of such treatment but never have I seen such a public rebuke, such a mortal blow." Lucy's voice trembled as she whispered in my ear.

"A mortal blow? I do not bleed. I am still standing." I laughed, thinking back to punishments I'd endured growing up. "I feel no pain. Actually, I prefer not to be recognized by the Dowager Lady Ingram. She and her daughters impress me not one whit!"

"You don't understand, Jane. You're too innocent to realize." My husband's voice was so gruff, so annoyed, that I lost my grip on my fan and it fell from my hand.

Mr. Douglas bent to retrieve it. As he handed the fan back to me, he spoke very quietly. "Trust me. You have no idea what you just endured. The Dowager Lady has not only damaged you, but she has also dealt Lucy a horrible blow. In brief, because my sister sponsored you, this is a stinging rebuke to her as well. You have both been insulted."

This sobered me. While I could laugh off the slight and return to our country home, Lucy could not. She would live and die here in London, unless she chose to follow her husband Augie again to India.

"Oh, Lucy, I would never have knowingly caused you pain." I reached out to her.

She took my hand and squeezed it but said nothing. I could see the shimmer of tears in her eyes.

Her misery caused me to feel quite undone. Usually Lucy was magnificent in a crisis, which provided yet another reason that her response surprised me. How could it be that the Dowager Lady had caused her such distress?

"Lucy, darling, have a care. It will blow over . . . soon," said her brother gently.

"No it won't. We're in for a long, ugly siege," she said as she brushed a tear off her cheek.

"Ah! Good evening!" A familiar voice interrupted the tense atmosphere and set us all in motion, as though we were clocks that had been badly in need of winding.

Phineas Waverly bowed first to me and then to the rest of our party, his battered face showing little emotion. As usual, he carried a black baton under his arm. I knew from having seen it before that at one end it bore a royal emblem in gold, a symbol of the Bow Street Runners' responsibility to the Crown. Mr. Waverly spoke loudly, almost as if making an announcement. "It is a particularly pleasant surprise to see you here, Mrs. Rochester. Quite timely, too. His Majesty heard you are in town and expressed an interest in meeting you."

"Meeting her? Whatever for?" His greeting had caught Lady Ingram's attention, and she moved closer to inspect the newcomer. "Why would the King take notice of a common governess?"

The spark of that insult set the dry timber blazing.

"How dare you!" Edward snarled, but Mr. Douglas grabbed him by the arm and bent to his ear to say, "Stop! Collect your wits! Can't you see? This is exactly what she wants. All eyes are on you!"

He was quite correct, as a small clutch of onlookers had gathered to watch the drama unfold.

Mr. Waverly turned toward the Dowager, studying her from behind wire-framed glasses. A certain set of his shoulders, an intensity about his mouth told me that he had caught

Lady Ingram's aspersion toward me—and he was not pleased. Not at all.

"Allow me to introduce Mr. Phineas Waverly," Mr. Douglas said, with some gravity. "He is the senior officer at Bow Street, currently assigned to guard His Majesty."

"Which is why my visit must be brief." Mr. Waverly abruptly turned his back on the Ingrams. He wore a cutaway coat and a gray waistcoat that had seen much use, but his boots were shined to a glasslike finish. Although he was not as tall as Edward or Mr. Douglas, he carried himself in a manner that precluded any dismissal of his authority. He pointedly did not bow to the Ingrams or to Lady Grainger, and I noticed the Dowager's lips curling downward in distaste. However, he did turn back toward her as he said, "Ma'am, I must dispute your conjecture. I have reason enough to know that there is nothing common about Mrs. Rochester. Nothing! In every way, she is exceptional, and His Majesty wishes to applaud her meritorious conduct as should every citizen. Thanks to her singular bravery, a killer was brought to justice."

"Is that so?" Lady Grainger lifted her quizzing glass to study Waverly.

"Edward Rochester's wife involved with a murderer? How unseemly! Of course, what can one expect? She not only reaches above her station to marry a squire, but also dips below it to mingle with low criminals," Lady Ingram cackled.

"Silvana!" Lady Grainger hissed at her sister-in-law. "I had warned you!"

"How dare you? If you were a man, I would call you out!" Edward snarled.

But before my husband could continue, Mr. Waverly avenged me. The Bow Street Runner turned on the Dowager Lady and said, in the manner of a general announcement, "Mrs. Rochester did the Crown a great service. She posed as a teacher to catch a killer, a fiend who suffocated a child to death."

There was a collective gasp from the gathered patrons of the upper circle who'd all been openly eavesdropping.

"Mrs. Rochester's bravery is unquestionable, as is her character. The King wishes to thank her personally." Waverly turned to me. "Mrs. Rochester," he said, "would you be so kind as to wait right here? I shall divert the King on his way back to the royal box. When I told him that I had seen you in the crowd, he expressly asked that I present you to him so that he might show you his gratitude."

"This is an unheard of honor!" Lucy whispered in my ear.

"What do we do?" I asked, having never had the occasion to study royal protocol.

"Curtsy, wait for him to lead the way in conversation and in actions, do not attempt to touch him, and never turn your back on him. If you must leave his presence, after securing permission, you continue to face him and back away. The usual procedure would have been for Mr. Waverly to lead us to the sovereign, where you would stand in line to see His Majesty, and might eventually be presented. Or he might send around a note inviting you to be presented at court. But for the King to come to you? This is a high honor, indeed."

One glance at Edward and Mr. Douglas told me she was not exaggerating. Both men looked stunned, but that quickly dissipated as they stood a little straighter and adjusted their waistcoats.

Suddenly, the sting of Lady Ingram's insult mattered not at all. A new emotion roiled within me: pride. I swallowed hard, as my mind raced. All eyes were on me, and I was not sure how to react. Should I allow myself to look pleased? Should I wear an expression of calm? Should I simply remind myself that I was deserving, because I had, indeed, helped solve a crime of passion? Each of these emotions fought for dominance.

A heat rose in my face. I reminded myself that Mr. Waverly was a man skilled in serving his own purposes, and the glint in his eye when he spoke had suggested that through his actions he planned to vanquish the Dowager Lady Ingram. As the son of a cobbler, he knew all too well the disparity between those with titles and the working class. On that point, he and I were firm allies.

Perhaps this was little more than a game to him. Perhaps the King wasn't really behind this introduction at all.

Meanwhile, the Ingrams stood dumbfounded, their mouths hanging open with shock.

Chapter 11

Following Lucy's lead, I spread my fan wide enough to obscure the smile on my face as Mr. Waverly left to collect the King. Mr. Douglas was seized with a fit of coughing, a thin disguise for his own amusement but a genteel response regardless, but Edward's coiled tension did not subside. I could tell he was still angry. Seething, actually. Lady Grainger filled the time by asking Lucy about Evans and his expected arrival. The Dowager Ingram and her daughters talked among themselves in low tones, but they did not dare leave. I believe they still held hope that I would be mightily embarrassed.

We stood, waiting, and watching as the bobbing postures of those around us signaled the King's approach. Although Mr. Waverly usually moved at a fast pace, he slowed his natural stride in order to escort the King to our location. As George IV and his consort arrived, all of us displayed our obeisance, the men with low bows and the women with deep, slow curtsies—although the Dowager had difficulty getting up and down. Lady Conyngham and the Dowager Lady Grainger seemed to have at least a nodding acquaintance with each other, but Mr. Waverly now took charge of the encounter.

"Your Majesty, and Marchioness Conyngham, may I present to you these dear friends of the Crown? This is Mr. and Mrs. Edward Rochester, Esquire, along with Lance Corporal Bruce Douglas, whom I'm sure you will remember for serving you bravely in Calcutta."

One by one, we kissed the hand of our sovereign. Again, I was struck by the way that corpulence had distorted those features of his once acclaimed for their rare beauty. His eyes were rheumy, his complexion marred by blotches, and his false teeth sat poorly in his mouth. As I had observed earlier, the Marchioness was every bit as corpulent as her companion. Peering out from the pillows of flesh on her face, her eyes glittered with an acquisitional nature that caused me to shrink back involuntarily in self-protection. The hairs rose up on the back of my neck.

One glance past Lady Conyngham told me that the Ingrams were still shocked by this unexpected turn of events. The Dowager's body trembled with suppressed emotion, and her ostrich feathers danced as a result of her quaking. However, her sister-in-law, Lady Grainger, harbored a secret smile, as though she thought this occurrence quite fitting.

"What a pleasure to meet one of my own kind," sighed the King, directing his greeting to Mr. Douglas. "Oh, how I miss my days of soldiering! Such glorious times we had on the battlefield."

None of us dared look one another in the eye.

It was common knowledge that our King had never been in combat. His father had expressly forbade it, but that didn't stop George IV from claiming that he had served as a warrior. Prinny's so-called military service was one of his grand illusions, a manufactured résumé he persisted in buffing to a high shine. His fantasies were played out in his affection for designing uniforms and in wearing that curious assortment of medals and awards on his chest. They clanked and clanged, but signified nothing.

"You also remember Lance Corporal Douglas's sister, Mrs. Captain Augustus Brayton, of course. Her husband serves you at a posting in Bombay."

"Too right. One of my best men! Quite the horseman, isn't he? Many times we've ridden side by side into the fray, swords drawn, steeds charging. Have you heard from the Captain lately?"

Lucy responded in a manner wholly inconsistent with her usual self, a voice very flat and colorless. "Yes, Your Royal Highness. Thank you for asking. My husband has recovered from yet another attack of the sleeping sickness. His sixth, and each is a little worse than the one before. I shall be sure to write him and say you inquired about his health. It will mean so much to him to know that he's been remembered by you."

"Of course I remember him. How could I forget? Those days in Brighton . . ."

With a wild expression in her eyes, Lucy stiffened but said nothing. The King's eyes moved past her and searched the crowd that gathered around us. His fleshy lips puckered as he mulled over his response. "Indeed, please tell him I send my regards. Remind him that I care deeply for all who serve in the colonies."

"Of course, Your Majesty. He will be happy to know that he pleases you."

"Pray excuse me, ma'am." The King paused, pulled a linen handkerchief from his pocket, mopped his eyes, and said, "But I find myself quite overcome with emotion when I think of the sacrifices we fighting men make so that our country can live in peace!" With this, he dabbed as if catching tears, although I could detect no moisture. Yet he certainly sounded sincere as he took Lucy's hand in his. "Tell Captain Brayton that . . . I have not forgotten him. Promise me you will do that."

This was a message. What it really meant, I could not tell.

"So I will, Sire. Might I add to that a note of comfort? Could I give him hope that he might come home soon?"

"Oh, would that I could! But I am so terribly busy, and the weight of the nation demands so much from me, that I have decided such decisions are best left to my generals." The King fanned himself with his handkerchief. The Marchioness set a hand on his forearm, possessively.

"Sire, really, you care too much for all of us," Lady Conyngham said. "It preys on your health."

Lucy did not move.

"Of course, you miss your husband," said the Marchioness with a dismissive nod. "What we women are forced to endure! So often the men we love are overburdened by the cares of their posts. I am quite undone when I think of how our dear sovereign handles so many, many intrusions on his time."

"Always thinking of me, my dearest Lady Elizabeth, aren't you?" The King lifted the Marchioness's hand to his lips and kissed it wetly. "No one could please me more."

Mr. Waverly cleared his throat and gestured toward me. "Your Highness, Mrs. Rochester is the brave woman I was telling you about."

"You are the one who bested the murderer?" The King looked me over carefully. "You are not much bigger than a wren! And yet, you acquitted yourself admirably. Waverly has told me all about your mission. You have avenged someone very dear to me. A girl who reminded me of my own Princess Charlotte."

Now, his eyes really did fill with tears. "Ah, Princess Charlotte! How I grieve for her! They told me she was doing well, she and her son both, so I went to sleep happy in the knowledge that the kingdom had an heir, a healthy boy—and that I was a grandfather! What a loss!" He broke into a sob. His handkerchief could scarcely keep up with his weeping.

Whatever qualms I might have about the King's morals,

whatever distaste I felt at his gluttony, I could not ignore these raw emotions on display. Here stood a man still devastated by the loss of his daughter and grandchild four years earlier. But somehow the Regent had weathered the storm and righted himself.

"I want you to join me in my box, Mrs. Rochester. Your friends are welcome to join us, too," said the King.

This was not an invitation. It was a command.

The tension fled Lucy's face and relief took its place. Edward's posture slowly uncoiled, and the tight muscle along Mr. Douglas's jaw slackened. The King's issuance had a deleterious effect on the Ingrams, one that they could not hide, despite their valiant attempts to do so. A quick intake of breath by the Dowager Ingram signaled she was taken aback, while Blanche's eyes narrowed and her lips pinched together tightly. Only Mary seemed unmoved, while Lady Grainger again fought a tiny smile that she immediately snuffed out.

The King offered me his arm, and I took it, recognizing that he would be dependent upon me to support a portion of his great weight. As I struggled, he stumped along on his jeweled cane, and in this awkward manner, we hobbled our way to his box. By turns I felt giddy with excitement, worried with the responsibility for his person, and struck with wonder at the many ups and downs this evening had provided. Whereas I had been sure that the opera would be the most magnificent portion of the event, I now revised my opinion. Someday, I would tell Ned, and Ned's children, about how I had been invited by the King himself to his box. That I had touched him, something so rare as to be unheard of.

Mr. Waverly asked a footman to bring over a couple of chairs from Lucy's box. The Marchioness decided how she wanted these arranged. Of course, we could do nothing until His Majesty sank down onto his oversized armchair. While waiting, Lucy, Mr. Douglas, Edward, and I stood at attention like a row of toy soldiers.

"Come sit by me," the King said to me, patting the chair to his left. After I took my seat, he leaned in toward me, his false teeth gleaming in the candlelight. Speaking so softly that only I could hear, he said, "I believe you have something of mine. Something very, very valuable."

Chapter 12

"Did you read my letters to Pansy Biltmore?"

Up close, I observed that King George IV's eyes were blurry, and his expensive chypre perfume could not disguise the fumes of his excessive drinking. Although his gaze was imperious, his wig threatened to slip off his head. Various food stains marred his lace ascot. Soiled and tired, he struck me as unspeakably sad. His unkempt appearance seemed totally at odds with his position. While he leaned toward me, the Marchioness busied herself piling choice tidbits onto a plate for him.

"Letters to Pansy Biltmore," I repeated, hoping to buy time. I had not expected for him to know these were in my possession. But it should not have surprised me. After all, his minions had been charged with rounding up his love letters.

"I sent Waverly to retrieve them after her daughter died. He was told that you are the one who packed up poor Selina's things. Waverly says you are a bright little minx. He believes they are in your possession. Is that right?"

"Only one." I could not bring myself to lie. "The others I

burned. My intention had been to destroy them all, but my activities were interrupted."

"As I recall, ah, one of their number illuminates a rather damaging aspect of my private life. Of course, one might postulate that a king has no private life. There is that argument. It could be made honestly."

I said nothing. That seemed the wisest course. From the corner of my eyes, I noticed patrons in other boxes pointing at us, taking note of our conversation and the private nature of our talk. The Marchioness passed him the plate, but her attention seemed directed elsewhere, to the procurement of more claret.

"Do you still possess the letter to which I am referring?" the King inquired.

"I do," I said, and my stomach twisted into a hard lump. In my excitement at meeting George IV and in the aftermath of the Ingrams' insult, my worries about the letter had slipped my mind. Now I chided myself. How could I have been so foolish? Of course the King did not truly want to talk to me to commend me for my bravery. He wanted a chance to regain that which he'd given away: His deepest secret. A record of his marriage to Maria Fitzherbert.

"And what do you plan to do with it?"

"I have no plans for it." My mouth was so dry, my lips caught on my teeth.

He raised an eyebrow at me. "There are those who would give a great deal to possess that letter. Those who long to have power over me."

"Yes. So I have heard." *Why*, I wondered, *did he not demand that I return it?*

"Waverly thinks highly of you." He drummed his thumb against his chair, allowing the huge ring he wore to clack rhythmically.

"The feeling is mutual."

"He says you can be trusted, and I have taken note of the

fact that you have asked us for nothing. Although you could have. Others have."

I pondered this. I have never been fond of obfuscation. Plain speaking cuts to the core of the matter, establishes trust, and assures all parties that nothing is amiss. I watched the Marchioness fill another goblet of wine for the King.

"Why should I? There is nothing that I need. If the occasion should develop, I would come to you as any one of your subjects approaches her sovereign. Empty-handed and with a hopeful heart."

For the first time, he showed his humanity. His face nearly crumpled with relief, and I daresay with vulnerability. No longer did I gaze upon a king; I felt I stared into the soul of a man. I saw his heartache, his failures, and his frailty. Out of respect, I looked away and down, so that my eyes met those of nearly everyone in the theater. Patrons on the first floor and in all the upper tiers were gazing at me curiously.

This was exactly the sort of inspection I had ardently hoped to avoid!

"Sire—" I was interrupted when the vast theater curtains began their slow parting, and the orchestra commenced the opening strains of the second act.

Our private conversation was clearly ended. The Marchioness plucked at the King's sleeve. Taking advantage of the distraction, I looked over at Mr. Waverly. His gaze was steady, bequeathing me a certain comfort. He was a man to trust, and as I watched him, he raised his chin slightly and mouthed the word, "Later."

Over the course of the evening, the King drank quantities of claret that would have staggered a horse. Lady Elizabeth matched his tippling glass for glass. Nor did they lack for foodstuffs. I had thought Lucy's basket a bounty, but the King's box was a constant parade of servers bringing a variety of cheeses, sliced meats, sweet breads, cakes, and other dainties. Lady Elizabeth titrated a few drops from an amber-colored bottle into the King's glass of claret. "For your pain, Sire. I know how you suffer!"

"Oh, my angel," he said with slurred speech. "My treasure. Everything you do pleases me so. Dear, dear, Elizabeth. You care so deeply for me!"

The liquid was laudanum; the label said as much.

I caught Lucy's eye, and she did not speak, but I knew exactly what she was thinking: How can he be drinking so much wine and taking laudanum and yet function?

Paying attention to the stage challenged me, as I believe it also taxed the concentration of others in my party. We were all alert to the possibility that at any moment our King might well topple over and gasp his last. Yet the man continued as though unaffected. Indeed, for the most part, the King chattered nonstop through the performance, whispering to and kissing Lady Elizabeth as the two of them held hands. I did my utmost to forget myself by attending to the heroic story of Tancredi. However, I would only just shut out the King's antics when His Majesty would tap me on the shoulder to pontificate on some arcane point regarding the performance. His knowledge of history and setting astonished me, but I would have much preferred to have heard his asides later rather than in the midst of the singing. All in all, my sovereign managed to ruin the performance for me. When we stood for the final round of applause, I prayed that the chance had come to pick up my wrap, say our good-byes, and leave.

However, that proved impossible, because the King decided to stay for the pantomimes that followed. Since he wasn't going anywhere, none of us could leave, either. One glance at the faces of Lucy, Edward, and Mr. Douglas let me know that they were as tired as I. The King could not have missed our exhaustion, as he yawned in tandem with Edward, but he settled his overfed self into his overstuffed chair and proceeded to drink more wine. At this point, we were more like captives than guests. A self-satisfied glimmer in his eyes told me that he reveled in this petty power. Lucy later told me stories about levees where people were nearly dead on their feet, hoping for our ruler to end the festivities—but the night went on and on until the next day. "He seems to enjoy knowing that others are discomforted," she explained.

I wished with all my heart that I had never come to his attention.

Much of the crowd took their leave. The luster had worn off the evening, and our surroundings had lost their appeal. Soot clung to every surface as the tabletop candles burned down to stubs. Globs of wax had melted and fallen from the candles in the chandeliers overhead. So much beer had been spilled on the main floor that a sharp yeasty fragrance thickened the air.

Oh, how I wished for the sweet, fresh scents of the heather fields surrounding Ferndean!

Chapter 13

"I still don't understand why Lucy evidenced such distress," I told my husband when we were alone in our room and snug in our bed with the eiderdown coverlet pulled over us. After looking in on Ned and Adèle, I had been more than ready to retire. "Lady Ingram greeted Lucy without warmth but respectfully. The slight she dealt me is my burden and mine alone."

Edward sighed and rubbed his forehead. "My dear innocent wife. The customs of the social set hold no allegiance with rationality. Conflate the Dowager's dismissal with a stain, one that creeps outward and taints its surrounds. So, too, did her rejection of you ripple outward to include Lucy."

"And what of it? Lucy has friends, alliances, and those who admire her. Her brother told us of her prowess as a society hostess."

Edward moved closer to kiss my forehead, my nose, and my lips. The crisply ironed pillow slips cracked beneath him. "The Dowager's slur was so outrageous, so public, that tongues will wag all over London."

"But the King invited us to sit with him. Doesn't that count for anything?"

"How can I explain this? Let me think. All right. When you were a schoolgirl, did you ever have peers who acted properly in front of the teacher but quite differently behind her back? It is thus. The ton must revere the King if they wish to benefit from his favor, but beyond the peerages he can confer, beyond the alliances such as marriages to minor royals and positions in his household, he means very little to them. The fact that he was attentive to you incites their curiosity. His approval caught their attention. But their world is a shadowy place. Each one in it rises up at the expense of his friend. They would rather have reason to look down their noses at you—and Lucy—than to admire you. Society will happily assume that Lucy deserved Lady Ingram's disapproval, and they will shun her. Worse yet, they will shun Evans when he arrives."

"Ah!" My breath quickened as the understanding dawned. Lucy's concern was for Evans. All the child needed from her was her love and her protection, but she truly believed that her greatest gift would be launching him as a part of the ten thousand.

"If he is accepted, his illegitimacy won't matter. Doors will open for him. He will be offered a berth at the best schools. Friends of the better sort will be his. Oh, Jane, I know that you and I recognize the insubstantial nature of these benefits. We both prefer to look deep into a person's heart rather than judge them by their exterior or their background. But make no mistake, such advantages have value."

I pondered this. "And now because of me," I said, "Evans might be shunned."

But Edward had already fallen fast asleep.

I untangled myself from my husband's arms, slipped out from the many layers of covers, and went to sit on the window seat, where I could gaze out on the silhouette of London after dark. Here and there a gaslight or candle lit a window. The night watchman walked up and down the streets, swinging his lantern. This bustling hub was the Queen of the Universe, and as such, she never slept. Not entirely. At any time of night, one could hear the muffled clatter of horse hooves, the hoots of laughter, and faint strains of music. The ton sampled all of life's pleasures, living with enormous gusto, determined to wring the most out of every encounter. As I closed my eyes, and rested my head on my forearms, I imagined people talking. About me. About Lucy. About Evans.

Lucy had befriended me, sponsored me, presented me to society, and injured her position because of me, in one fell swoop.

I felt wretched.

Chapter 14

The next morning while Lucy slept late and the children played with Rags upstairs in the nursery, Edward, Mr. Douglas, and I took seats at the mahogany dining room table. Although Lucy's brother typically stayed at his club, owing to our late evening, he had slept in one of the guest rooms. From the sideboard came the scent of bacon rashers, ham, fried onions and tomatoes, and egg dishes of all sorts. Foreshadowed by the redolent sharpness of bergamot, Sadie, the maid of all work, came in carrying a heavy tea tray. All of us did our best to enjoy a leisurely breakfast and confined our conversation to an evaluation of Corri-Paltoni's voice. Edward thought her timbre and expressiveness quite fine. Mr. Douglas thought her range remarkable.

"This should prove an interesting morning," my husband remarked, "as I shall be interviewing Mr. Lerner. Here's hoping that he's a suitable candidate for the job. Not every young doctor would want a posting with so much territory to cover. But if he strikes me as competent, and since I know he has Carter's imprimatur, I shall be happy to offer him lodging as part of our agreement."

"I suggested to your husband that we meet the young man at Boodle's, my club," said Mr. Douglas. "There are private rooms where we can speak candidly."

"I asked Bruce to join me because my vision is so murky that I fear I am bereft of the ability to make the sort of observations that are necessary for judging a man's character," Edward said.

A lump formed in my throat. I knew this admission cost my darling husband dearly. My heart ached for him, and I found myself in the loathsome position of playacting at exaggerated cheerfulness to compensate.

"Of course. I rather enjoy interrogations. They are one of my specialities." Mischief dripped from Mr. Douglas's every word, and we all laughed at his sardonic manner.

"Jane, what do you have planned?"

"I was hoping to spend time with Ned. After the press of bodies last night, I believe a walk in the park is warranted," I said as I bit into a piece of toast slathered with raspberry jam. "But I credit your idea highly. Better for this new doctor to pass muster with you and Mr. Douglas than either of you alone."

When we could avoid the subject no longer, Mr. Douglas turned to me. "Mrs. Rochester, can you tell me, what was the King whispering to you?"

"He wondered what I had done with his love letters. I explained that I had burned all of them. All but the most telling one. Curiously, he did not ask for it. I guess it is not that important to him." I shrugged, and added, "So it remains locked away. Perhaps forever."

"Perhaps he did not ask for it because he recognized it to be safer with you than in the palace," Mr. Douglas said, as he stroked his mustache thoughtfully.

"How could that be?"

"You saw the state the man was in last night," he continued. "I've heard it said he's more often in his cups than sober these days."

"I saw the Marchioness dose the King liberally with laudanum," I noted.

"I wondered," said Edward. "The man's speech became more slurred and incoherent as the night wore on. What do you know of the woman, Douglas?"

Mr. Douglas poured us all another cup of tea and settled back in his chair, crossing his legs as a prelude to a long discourse. "She is not from an aristocratic family. Her father was a wealthy banker, and her fortune was her face and figure. She married Henry Conyngham—Viscount Conyngham—an Irish peer, but she has had many, many admirers, including the Tsarevitch of Russia. Early on, however, she set her cap for the Prince of Wales. Perhaps I am being cruel, but it seems clear that she saw a dalliance with him as the most reliable way to benefit her family of two daughters and three sons. The courtiers surrounding the Regent have always been an avaricious and ambitious lot. The Marchioness seeks only to advance her family. There is talk that her second son, Francis Nathaniel, will be named Master of the Robes and First Groom of the Chamber.

"As you can surmise," concluded Mr. Douglas, "having an incriminating document in the safekeeping of an honest woman might well be the wisest course of action for the King."

"Speaking of wise courses of action, I have been thinking." Edward directed his comments toward Mr. Douglas. "I am heartily sorry for your sister's distress, and I believe it to be my fault. I should have made my peace with the Ingrams long ago."

"Lucy does not blame you. I had the chance to speak to her before she went to bed, and I know she doesn't."

"Be that as it may, I plan to visit them at Lady Grainger's home and try to mend our fences. If only I had gone to them at the time and apologized for misleading Blanche about my fortune—"

"You might have married her?" I admit to the mischief in my question.

"Never!"

Chapter 15

It was close to noon when the men left to talk to the doctor about securing his employment. Polly arrived soon after to help me with my hair.

"How is Mrs. Brayton?" I asked.

"Still sleeping," said the abigail. "Rags was whining at her door, so I let him in and set him up on the bed so he could have a cuddle."

Against Polly's better judgment, I had donned my simple brown muslin and my country bonnet. The familiarity and simplicity did my heart good, for it reminded me that there was a world beyond the sprawl of this harsh city. "For a walk in the park with my son, this is perfect," I had answered her protestations. "Ned can do no harm to this old dress, and I shall feel quite comfortable leaving Amelia behind. At Ferndean, he and I often take rambles together."

She sighed, and I guessed what she was thinking: That was Ferndean and this was London. But all she said was, "I believe Mr. Higgins has a surprise for you, ma'am. You'll see it when you're ready for your walk. Amelia's changing Master Ned's pinafore. Adèle is still in her room, having a grand time with some old ribbons that belong to Mrs. Brayton."

She was right. Adèle was in her room, happily weaving the scraps of fabric through her hair. Polly had also located several of Lucy's older court dresses, and the little French girl was in her element, trying on the finery and parading in front of the long cheval mirror in order to view the results.

"*Veux-tu venir avec nous au Hyde Park?*" I asked.

"*Non*, I have no wish to go to the park." She pouted, so I let her be.

I was on my way downstairs when I heard Ned giggling. Looking into the entryway, I discovered that my little boy was sitting in an adorable child cart, a neat, scaled-down version of a pony cart, with tall sides and robust wheels. The tongue, which would normally have been yoked to small horses, extended far enough to provide excellent leverage so that the entire contraption could easily be rolled along the pavements.

Playing the part of both horse and driver, Lucy's butler Higgins towed the cart first one way and then the other. Each short journey brought gales of laughter from Ned's rosy lips.

"Where did this come from?" I reached for Ned but he scooted down into his seat, gripping the sides of the wagon firmly. Along with his father's black eyes, my son had inherited Edward's fierce determination.

"I commissioned a coach builder to construct one for Master Evans. Since the child has yet to arrive, I sent word that we needed a second such contraption, so each boy could have his own."

The cart was a marvel of design, complete with a padded frame so my son could sit without assistance. The wheels rolled easily, and the bright red paint gave it a jaunty air.

I thanked Higgins profusely for his thoughtfulness.

The sky was clear; a walk would be perfect. At my direction, Higgins carried the cart and my son down the front stairs and set both on the walkway. My son regarded the butler solemnly and gestured to him, clearly indicating that he expected the butler to accompany us.

"No. Not this time, Young Master. You go with your mum, you hear? Tell those squirrels 'hul-lo' for me." The butler straightened and adjusted his waistcoat. With a perfectly bland face, he said, "Master Ned has taken quite a fancy to watching a pair of squirrels down the street who like to chase each other."

A red blush started at Higgins's collar and spread up his neck as he bowed to me and headed back into the house, leaving me to stare in wonder at the closing door. So my son had softened the butler's heart!

I would have to share this bit of news with Lucy. She would agree that there was magic inherent in a child's smallest gesture. Here I'd thought that Higgins would be impervious to any sort of emotion. But I'd been wrong. The man's austere exterior had been breached without effort by one little boy. Cook had supplied me with a bag of bread crumbs when she'd heard of our plans. The whole household had fallen in love with my boy, a situation that could only augur good tidings for Evans's arrival.

Ned's interests—not to mention his impact on others—had come as a bit of a revelation to me, who'd never spent much time with children so young. I found some people were charmed, others irked by Ned's constant motion. My son's impulse, it seemed, was to launch himself unreservedly at the world around him, with his eyes open and his hands grabbing, in a relentless attempt to experience every morsel that came his way.

With effort, I managed to roll the cart along the pavement to Hyde Park, passing a dozen large houses as we went. Along the way we passed several nannies out airing their charges. Their nods confirmed they took me as one of their own. I am sure to most matrons of my standing, my approach to child-rearing was anathema, but our life in Ferndean had afforded me the luxury of spending time alone with my son. The habit of our companionship had thus been established, and rather than avoid it, I found it to be one of my life's great joys.

Ned's head swiveled on his chubby neck, taking in his surroundings, gazing at the fine houses with their colorful window boxes. Our progress was interrupted frequently because everything seemed to inspire my son's delight. As I pointed out squirrels, he hooted with laughter. Even the pigeons brought a smile to his lips.

I reflected that coming to London had not been a bad idea after all . . . as long as we could avoid outings with the social set in the future.

No footpaths like this wove their way around Ferndean. The landscape there suffered from a sort of benign neglect, and many of the lanes there had become overgrown. I vowed to speak to Edward about creating an outdoor space at home where the child cart could travel. Meanwhile, I promised myself to schedule an outing like this with Ned every few days.

We'd chosen a grand time for an adventure. The park was full of pleasure seekers from every walk of life enjoying the brilliant sunshine. Couples strolled, arm in arm, up and down the footpaths. I tugged the cart to a spot by an empty bench, where Ned and I could enjoy the scent of flowers nodding at the sun.

I showed Ned how to toss the breadcrumbs to the birds. Of course, the pigeons needed no encouragement to come visit us. Once the message spread among them that we were offering sustenance, a flock engulfed our bench, their iridescent neckties of silver, blue, amethyst, and green shimmering like the glow of precious stones. But then the approaching loud voices of an arguing couple scattered the birds, causing them to fly off in a whirlwind of grays, tans, and white.

"I know you care for me—and I do not want to wait any longer. I can prove what a good wife I shall be!" A fashionable woman walked alongside a shabbily dressed man and tugged on his arm most insistently. Her voice and form suggested youth, though her face was obscured by her fashionable bonnet decked out with ribbons of every color. The man's face, however, was quite clear to me, and his expression was one of extreme discomfort. Especially because he realized that I had overheard her protestations. His eyes caught mine, and I turned away to attend to Ned rather than share my impressions of his overwrought friend.

"Please! You do yourself a disservice in this public place." He kept the lady at arm's length with one hand, while in the other he carried a worn leather satchel that flapped open, exposing papers that threatened to spill on the ground. "I beg you to listen, miss. Although I hold you in the highest regard, we have no future together. I have done nothing to give you any other impression."

"But you have! You are so kind to me. I see your affection in your eyes! And we are ideally suited. We have the same interests, and—"

"I regret that you might have misinterpreted my professional concern for a greater devotion."

"We are meant to be together! I saw it in a dream." The young woman's voice became ever more strident and her gestures more animated. I felt embarrassed on her behalf—to my way of thinking, she had already exceeded the bounds of good taste. Clearly the young man did not return her affections. Why could she not see that?

"I really must go." The man seemed quite desperate. "I am expected—"

"Hail a hackney for both of us! Mama won't notice I'm gone. Come, it'll be easier from the street—" and she grabbed at his arm.

But instead of following her as she tried to lead him, he loosened her hands from his sleeve. That was when he noticed his precarious satchel and started shoving the papers down deeper so they would not fall out. Even as he worked furiously to restrain them, he kept dodging her entreaties. "Please! You cannot keep following me around like this! I do not know how you came to your conclusions, and I regret any action on my part that might have encouraged you, but—"

At first, his actions struck me as ungallant, but the longer I watched them from under my old straw bonnet, the more I sensed that he was desperate. The woman was clearly refusing to listen. I lifted my head and did a quick survey. The quarrel had drawn attention: strollers turning to watch, nannies stopping prams to listen in, and couples casting glances this direction.

The woman launched herself at the man, grabbing at the collar of his jacket. "I feel your love for me with every beat of my heart! From the first moment you stepped into our parlor, I knew!"

"You are mistaken. There is no future for us. I have tried to speak kindly to you, and I abhor the fact that I might hurt your sensibilities, but you must listen to me! There is nothing between us. There never was." He worked at her fingers to disentangle them.

"I know you care for me!" She changed her grip and took hold of one of his cuffs.

"No! I love another!" With a mighty effort, he pulled away, and with a loud rip, the fabric of his sleeve came loose. The surprise of this caught them both off-balance. Several of his papers had worked their way toward freedom again, and a couple flew out of his satchel. As he bent to retrieve them, she stepped in close, getting her face near to his.

"Who is she?"

From a near crouch, he looked up at her, pausing as he chased his papers. "Her name is Miriam Goldstein. I hope to marry her."

Somewhere deep inside me, an alarm bell chimed. Some instinct told me the woman was marshalling her energies, but to what purpose I could not guess. I lifted Ned and pulled him close to me, shielding his face with my hands.

"Miriam?" she screamed, then slapped the man hard across the face. Her blow was so well timed and her aim was so true that he sprawled flat on his back. He stayed there for but the blink of an eye, before scrambling to his feet and running off.

The young woman's back was still to me, but I watched as her shoulders shook. She commenced to crying, her bonnet bobbing under the weight of her emotions.

I settled Ned in the child cart and watched the woman as she cried. My heart went out to her, while my mind suggested she would be better off somewhere more private.

In the meantime, Ned had caught a pigeon feather in his pudgy hands and was examining it with studied earnestness. From deep in the pocket of my old brown muslin, I dug out my own handkerchief and walked toward the crying girl. Perhaps a kind gesture would remind the woman of how public her display really was. With one eye on my son, I extended my arm to offer up the folded square of linen. "Miss?"

When she did not respond, I tapped her on the shoulder. "Miss?"

"Don't touch me!" With a fury, the young woman turned on me. I was shocked to recognize the mild, nearly catatonic Mary Ingram. But the recognition was one-sided. Taking in my simple brown muslin and my worn straw bonnet, Mary said, "Get away from me, you beggar woman!"

Chapter 16

At second glance, she realized who I was. "Oh! It's you. Nothing is beneath you, is it? Now you spy on people?"

To such an assertion, there could be no suitable response, so I said nothing.

With a flounce of her head, she turned on her heel and stomped away.

Mary was never considered terribly bright, or so Mrs. Fairfax had told me. So it shouldn't have come as a surprise that she had not recognized me at first. And now I regretted that she had yet another reason to dislike me: I had been a witness to her rejection.

Determined not to let our outing be spoiled by the odd encounter, I played various simple games with my son. I dropped leaves and he giggled and tried to snatch them midair. After a bit, that bored him, so I offered up a handful of acorns and a sprig of wild mint, so that he might recognize the joy of natural fragrances. When he grew uninterested in that, I again played the part of draft horse, pulling his child cart back toward Lucy's house. Along the way, I mulled over the scene I'd witnessed and decided that the Ingram women suffered from a general need for self-restraint. Furthermore, they walked this earth blind to anyone who did not offer them some immediate personal gratification of their wishes.

It is my belief that those who divide the world into "those who have something to offer me" and "those who do not" will often find themselves at the mercy of others, because they are likely to be wrong as often as they are right.

In short order, Ned and I returned to #24 Grosvenor Square.

"Hello, Higgins. Is my husband home?"

"No, ma'am," Higgins greeted me with his usual neutrality, but his eyes sparkled as he helped me with the child cart. "If you'd like, I'll take Young Master up to his nursemaid. She's been expecting him, and Polly is waiting to help you freshen up. Mrs. Brayton wants your company."

Each time I stepped out of doors, a fine rain of coal silt settled on my garments. I had read somewhere that the quick-growing population of the city burned a staggering amount of coal each day, and this accounted for London's murky veil of smoke and fog. Whilst under the canopy of trees in the park, it was bearable, but a traveler on main streets was subjected to the worst of the dark residue that combined with the copious horse droppings and running streams of human waste to make a stink such as I had never endured in my life. Fortunately, Polly was always at the ready to brush the soot off my dress and shake the dust from my bonnet.

But when I arrived in my room, I could see that the lady's maid had other plans today. My claret silk dress was hung up and neatly pressed.

The abigail answered my curious look by saying, "You're to go on calls with Mrs. Brayton. Morning calls."

"But it's three in the afternoon!"

Polly giggled without any malice. "I know! Morning calls start at three. Ain't it funny?"

Polly started unbuttoning my brown muslin. "Mrs. Brayton's been pacing the floor, waiting for you. You're to go to Lady Grainger's house straightaway."

I understood that Lady Grainger was dear to Lucy, but a visit to her home would surely mean another encounter with one or more of the Ingrams. That was an experience I would prefer to avoid.

Polly began to lift my brown muslin over my head.

"Stop," I said. "Please stop. I would rather stay here. In fact, I'll go and tell Lucy—"

"Oh no, Mrs. Rochester. Mrs. Brayton insisted that you was to go with her to Lady Grainger's house."

"But we saw the woman only last night!"

"Aye." Polly lifted the muslin off me and carefully lowered the silk over my head. Since I am not tall, it was easy for her to do. "She sent word asking that the both of you visit first thing. See, Lady Grainger thinks the world of Mrs. Brayton. Considers her like a daughter, almost. I heard there was some nastiness last night, and, well, I can imagine that Lady Grainger don't want that to fester. Wants to pinch out that candle right fast. If anyone can put things to right, her ladyship can. A cunning old bird, she is, if you don't mind me saying."

I dampened down my dismay that news of last night's snub had already reached down into the servants' quarters.

"And she can do that?" I wondered. "I mean, is it really possible that Lady Grainger can force her family to bend to her will?"

"I hope so. I dearly do." Polly's fingers flew along the buttons of my dress. I watched her in the mirror and noted the concentration on her face. "Mrs. Brayton cried herself to sleep last night. Oh, she'll put on a good face for you, 'cause she's like that, but she told me what that nasty cow, Dowager Ingram, said. How she snubbed you. This has to be nipped in the bud, quick-like. Before all of London sniffs it in the wind."

Seeing my downcast expression, Polly paused and her hands rested gently on my shoulders. "No one blames you, Mrs. Rochester. No one. Lady Grainger's maid, Dorsey, she's told me how those Ingram women have caused all sorts of mischief among Lady Grainger's staff, even accusing her cook of thievery—and saying the butler has been overly familiar. Can you imagine? That younger girl, she's been helping herself to Lady Grainger's garden, hacking away, taking whatever flowers strike her fancy, while the Dowager and that older one keep serving milk to Lady Grainger's dog so it's always getting sick on the floor. Don't matter that Lady Grainger asks her not to. She don't care one bit. Have you ever heard the like?"

Polly bustled around, smoothing the bedclothes and tidying my meager wardrobe.

"I am truly sorry to hear the Ingrams have caused such distress. Especially among Lady Grainger's staff," I said as I put on my nice pearl ear fobs.

Because of my former position as governess—which occupied an intermediate social position between the gentry and the household servants—I understood the delicate web of relationships common to the belowstairs staff. At their best, servants covered for one another's failings, putting the needs of their masters first. At their worst, staff would blame and snipe, in vain attempts to curry favor with their employers. Any accusation of one cast a shadow over all, as suspicion ran riot, debilitating and serious as an outbreak of milk fever.

"But what does Lady Grainger say when her staff is treated so poorly?" I slipped on my kid gloves while Polly busied herself tucking sprigs of lavender into the bureau with my chemises.

"She ain't happy, but the Ingrams are family. The mother and her girls come to London all the time. There's a boy, too, but he stays back at Ingram Park, I've heard. Oh, but their father, Lord Ingram, was a crafty one. On his deathbed, he made Lady Grainger promise to take care of his sister and her three children. Deathbed promises are stronger than iron chains."

"Ah yes, I know."

My mother had exacted a similar promise from her brother. Then on his own deathbed, my Uncle Reed made the same request of his wife, but alas, Aunt Reed seethed over the obligation. Caught between her word and her virulent hatred for me, she had ultimately been the one who shuffled me off to Lowood, a bleak, poorly run school.

Yet, against all odds, I had survived and completed my education, allowing me to work as a governess. This remembrance brought a fresh appreciation for Polly's status. Despite my family's respectable status, had it not been for Lowood, I, too, might have gone into service.

Polly straightened and rubbed her lower back. "The missus told me that the Dowager delivered a cut sublime to you. Blimey, it must have been an awful shock."

I shrugged. "It might have been if I cared about society. As it stands, my concern is for Lucy. It grieves me to know she was hurt by the slight. I wish I knew how to remedy the situation."

"Well, Lady Grainger, she's one to reckon with. If anyone can make those nasty Ingram women act right to Mrs. Brayton, Lady Grainger can."

"At least she can try," I said, as I adjusted my nice bonnet.

Polly's smile was as weak as watered-down tea. "Aye, she can certainly do that."

Chapter 17

Lucy was waiting for me in the entry hall. When I arrived, she put Rags on the floor and turned to me with open arms. In her embrace, I felt the strength of our friendship.

"I am so sorry," I started.

"Hush." She put a finger to my lips. Although the red rims of her eyes affirmed that she'd spent time crying, her lovely dress of rose pink with white stripes did wonders to revive the cheerful bloom in her cheeks. "You have done nothing to warrant this. Ever since I learned about Evans, I have suffered from a vehemence of emotion that has overruled my sensibility. Last night, the slight you endured hit me hard. I felt helpless. But I know better. In the cool light of day, I have decided that this will not do—and Olivia Grainger supports me in this. While you were at the park with Ned, she and I exchanged a volley of notes. A street urchin made a nice fistful of coins today."

"Good for him," I said sincerely.

"Yes, and I think he brought me luck. I have news about Evans. His nanny Mrs. Wallander writes that she has received the funds I sent for their travel. Her daughter's fever has finally broken, and the girl seems to be on the mend. Mrs. Wallander and Evans will be leaving Brussels this week. Can you believe it, Jane? Given the time it took for the letter to reach me, he could be here any day!"

"I am so glad for you," I said, and although I am not as inclined to physical gestures as Lucy, I could not help myself— I hugged her. Hard. I knew Lucy had always wanted a child and that Evans was the answer to her prayers. As we separated, I added, "Have no fear. You will be a splendid mother. I know you will. So . . . we go to challenge the Ingrams?"

"No," she said with a sweet smile. "We go to face them. Olivia had specifically counseled all of the Ingrams in advance that we would be attending the opera. The women had given Olivia their word to receive us politely. Naturally, she was furious with her sister-in-law and nieces' behavior. My friend has told them in no unclear terms that they will treat both of us with civility."

I still had no desire to mingle with them, but I understood that such a meeting would be important to Lucy, so I took her hand and we moved forward.

Once inside her carriage, I said, "Tell me more about your friend Lady Grainger."

"As you will see, we are near neighbors, but that is not why or how we met. It happened when we were both in want of a dog. Her Mags is a sister to my little Rags. By happenstance, we arrived at the same time to look at the litter, and as a matter of course, it was easy to strike up a conversation." Lucy drummed her fingers on the coach seat as she talked.

"And her interests?"

"She is a keen gardener. Not that she digs in the soil, but she stands over Benjamin, her young manservant, and directs him. Lady Grainger's garden runs along the side of Bayswater, the length of that hedge." To illustrate her point, Lucy parted the carriage curtains and pointed to a massive wall of boxwood bushes. "Lord Grainger installed that lych-gate at the back. I believe he thought it would provide easy access for wheelbarrows full of flowers. Soiled flowers."

My face admitted my confusion until she clarified, "Women of low virtue."

I absorbed this and reflected on how sad it was that for many families marriage is but a business transaction, a barter devoid of love.

"Perhaps if Olivia had given her husband a child, he might have felt more kindly toward her. Instead, he was happy for the wealth she brought him and the home she made. Otherwise, she was of little consequence to him."

I knew that Lucy regretted not being able to give her husband a child. Was that why she and Augie lived apart? Had he thought of her as a disappointment? I hoped not, for her sake.

As the carriage pulled up to Lady Grainger's front door, I closed my eyes and used the fragrances as a guide to imagine the riot of colors: the crimson red of roses, the light purple of lavender, the delicate pink of snapdragons.

"You and Olivia will find much common ground. She is well read and compassionate, an original thinker without prejudices. Her life revolves around her garden and Mags, who means the world to her. With no children of her own, she dotes on Mags. She's a very, very spoiled pup."

"And then there is you," I said.

Lucy's smile lit up her eyes. "Yes, I daresay I am closer to her heart than her Ingram nieces. She has told me as much."

"Little wonder at that," I murmured.

"Well said." Lucy reached over and gave my fingers a squeeze, the warmth of her hands radiating through our kid gloves. "And the curtain rises."

Chapter 18

Stanton, the Dowager Lady Grainger's butler, a tall man with a widow's peak and a Romanesque profile, met us at the door and escorted us upstairs to the drawing room. There the Ingrams sat in a row, like rooks on a fence, and every bit as cheerful. Our hostess wore a mobcap and a dark blue at-home dress that had seen better days. It occurred to me that Lady Grainger cared little for the trappings of society. Like Lucy, she did what she needs must to blend in and move among those of the ton, but she did not allow society to dictate to her. Nor did it provide the yardstick by which she measured others.

The Ingrams were dressed in the latest fashion, or so I judged their gowns to be, based on the fashion magazines Lucy and I had combed over when deciding what I should wear to the opera. Lady Ingram and her daughter Blanche were dressed in very similar "morning" dresses, both of an appealing shade of medium blue.

Although Lady Grainger seemed to ignore her wardrobe, her domestic touches told me that her home mattered to her a great deal. I took special note of our surroundings, a harmoniously appointed sitting room done in deep maroon with gold touches. The walnut étagère, low table, chairs, and occasional tables gleamed. On every surface sat lush ferns, each perfectly suited to its pot, with fresh shades of green that contrasted nicely with the stately dark furniture. In glazed pots along an east-facing window, exotic orchids burst into saucer-sized blossoms. The effect enchanted me. I had never seen an interior that combined the salutatory benefits of the natural world with that of the restrained dimensions of the man-made. Lucy's home was lovely, but Lady Grainger's revived my weary soul, making me realize she and I were really very much alike in our tastes.

Everyone stood to greet us. Lucy and Lady Grainger exchanged hugs and cheek kisses before presiding over my reintroduction to the Ingrams, who gave me the barest nods of acknowledgment but otherwise played their parts. This change of heart could have been attributed to the King's accolades or Lady Grainger's admonishment. I did not know which, nor did I care. Instead, I rejoiced that now Lucy would be free to continue her life as she had before—and that Evans would not suffer because his new mama had taken me for a friend.

Thus having achieved a sort of détente, we took our seats in a circular pattern while our hostess called her dog to her side. Into the room raced a small bundle of white fur, all wriggles and waggles. Mags licked her mistress, excited as she was lifted onto the woman's lap. Taking into account the coloration, size, and personality, I could make no distinction between this dog and Lucy's Rags. I watched Lady Grainger stroke the pup's head methodically.

"Welcome to my home, Mrs. Rochester. Your husband visited earlier," said Lady Grainger. "Squire Rochester was on the way to the club with Mr. Douglas when he stopped in to apologize to Blanche and her mother."

"Did he indeed?" I said, thinking that perhaps the new acceptance I was enjoying could be the result of my husband's having made amends.

"Or more correctly, he tried to. I believe Blanche and Silvana will now owe *him* an apology. Certainly Blanche does." She cast a pointed look in the direction of the mother and daughter, who squirmed in their seats uncomfortably.

"Yes, Aunt," said Blanche, in a tone of resignation.

"You see," said Lady Grainger, "Blanche is a bit under the weather. She hasn't been feeling well lately, so her temper must be excused. Isn't that right, Blanche?"

"Yes, Aunt."

"But you are better?" asked Lucy in a kind voice. "I hope?"

"Somewhat," said Blanche. She enjoyed the attention, and she knew she needed to be polite, but she found it taxing to put aside her sense of injury. It had become familiar to her, and she relished it.

"And how are you, Miss Mary?" asked Lucy, politely.

"Fine." Mary had changed her dress from her walk in the park.

"Your nose is a bit pink, dear," said her aunt. "Are you coming down with a chill? I warned you not to walk outside without a wrap."

"I am fine," she repeated, sending a quick glance my way.

I decided to hold my tongue. I couldn't blame her for not wishing to discuss the scene I'd witnessed earlier.

"How is Rags?" Lady Grainger asked Lucy, after she rang the bell for tea.

"Mischievous as always. He is enjoying our young visitor, the Rochesters' son, Ned. No matter how fast his nursemaid acts, the boy always leaves a trail of crumbs for Rags. Speaking of sons, dearest Olivia, I've had wonderful news just this morning I wanted to share with you."

Lucy summarized the letter that had recently arrived from Evans's nanny.

"Evans?" Lady Ingram arched an eyebrow. "Is that the name of your husband's bastard?"

Chapter 19

"Silvana! You promised!" Lady Grainger shook a finger at her sister-in-law, but the scolding was interrupted by a loud rapping at the front door. We paused as we heard it open.

Stanton fairly bounded up the stairs, carrying in his hand a silver plate, bearing a thick ivory card. The Lady Grainger picked it up and started searching for her quizzing glass. Stanton came to her rescue. "The Marchioness Conyngham wants to know if you are at home, Lady Grainger."

"Oh!" Blanche's hand flew to her mouth and her eyes grew large. Although Lady Ingram said nothing, she lifted her chin higher and assumed a more pleasant look on her face. Even Mary seemed to rouse from her stupor, turning toward her mother to gauge the older woman's reaction. Only Lucy's slight frown told me that rather than being thrilled, she found this visit worrisome.

"Please tell her I am." Our hostess shifted her slender form nervously, causing Mags a little inconvenience. "What an honor . . ."

I reviewed what I'd seen and heard about the Marchioness

and her designs. Was this merely a social call or was something more sinister in play? I wondered about her objective, but just as quickly, I chided myself for being too dramatic. Of course the Marchioness might simply have been moved to visit Lady Grainger after seeing her at the opera last night. That was not terribly remarkable.

Or was it?

We took to our feet and waited respectfully while the heavy woman clumped her way up the stairs. When she arrived, I was further surprised to see that Marchioness Conyngham was escorted by none other than Phineas Waverly, his tipstaff again tucked under one arm.

Clearly accustomed to being the center of attention, Lady Elizabeth Conyngham leaned on her ebony cane patiently while we curtsied to her. Lady Grainger introduced us one by one.

"You may go, Waverly." Lady Conyngham dismissed the Bow Street Runner with a flutter of her fingers, causing the numerous rings on her hands to glitter.

"I shall wait for you by the carriage, ma'am. If you need me . . ."

As Mr. Waverly turned to leave, his eyes sought mine and clearly bade me to follow. With an almost imperceptible raised finger, I signaled that I understood, although we both knew it might take me a while to join him.

"Oh, my dear young friends!" The Marchioness Conyngham opened her arms.

At first I did not realize that she was signaling a planned embrace of Lucy and me. Not wishing to embarrass ourselves, or her, we submitted to her affection. She gathered us to her copious self, where it was impossible to avoid the pungent scent of ambergris and patchouli. Amidst the cover of the Marchioness's many ruffles and furbelows, Lucy's eyes went wide and met mine. The situation was highly uncomfortable, but regrettably unavoidable.

At last, the august visitor released us and studied us as though Lucy and I were both long-lost friends of the highest order. "Dear Mrs. Brayton, you look lovely as always. And dear, dear Mrs. Rochester! What a pleasure to be in your company again!"

This shocked me. I had not reckoned on her taking note of my name. I had assumed last night was an aberration, a one-off event, and it would never happen again. But here I was, and the King's lover acted as if I was dear to her in every way. I worked hard not to let my feelings show on my face.

What, I wondered, *is the cause for this?* I had only just met the woman. *Why is she making such a fuss over me?*

Behind the woman's back, Blanche and her mother watched this pantomime. I detected a sense of defeat, an acceptance of my newly improved status. With the wiles of a skilled hostess, Lady Grainger launched a tedious discussion of the weather. To the relief of us all, the Marchioness chimed right in.

"Oh my!" I said with a start, as I lifted a hand to the side of my head and slipped one of my earrings into my palm. "I do believe I dropped one of my ear fobs. Ladies, please excuse me while I search for it."

"I can ring for Dorsey, my abigail." Lady Grainger smiled at me kindly. The atmosphere in her drawing room had changed from one of discord to acceptance, and inwardly I thanked our hostess for seeing to this turn of events. Although Marchioness Conyngham's fulsome greeting had much to do with the shift, none of this would have happened without Lady Grainger's interference. The tired lines around her mouth suggested there had been much haggling behind the scenes to bring us to this happy juncture.

"Thank you kindly, ma'am. No need. I believe I can recollect exactly where it might have happened. I shan't be but a minute." With that, I took off to find Mr. Waverly.

I found him leaning one shoulder against Lady Conyngham's lavish purple and gold carriage. A troubled frown creased his forehead, and one hand was jammed deep into his pocket, while the other twirled his black baton in a spinning circle.

"Mrs. Rochester! Thank goodness you came!" He withdrew his pocket handkerchief and wiped his brow. Waverly is not a man given to nerves. In fact, his character would best be labeled steady or resolute. Yet, a tremor in his fingers gave me pause, as did the uneven timbre of his voice. "I must ask: Do you still have the letters we once discussed?"

"Why?" I hesitated to answer him.

"I must know. This is important. Do not toy with me, Mrs. Rochester. I think a great deal of you, but my job is to protect our King, and right now, you stand in the way of that." He bit off each word as he spoke it.

"Yes. I have the one," I told him. "The others I burned."

"Did the King ask you about its disposition?"

I wondered what Waverly knew, what the King had said, and why Waverly seemed to suffer from his nerves. After all, if the King was happy to have me hold on to his letter, why should it bother the Bow Street Runner? "Yes, but he did not ask for it to be returned."

Mr. Waverly responded by running a shaky hand through his hair. "Just as I expected. This grows worse and worse. Who else is aware of its existence?"

"Lucy knows of it. Edward does. Mr. Douglas knows because his sister shares everything with him, and I trust him implicitly."

"Lady Conyngham knows about the letter, too. She likely listened in while you conversed with the King, and I suspect she queried him afterward." He groaned. "You saw the copious spirits and laudanum she dispenses to him. The man was never good at holding his tongue, but under the influence of such agents, he is helpless, and puts himself—and our nation—at great risk."

"But why does that cause you to worry? He called her his

treasure. Why would she want to hurt him? Isn't it to her advantage to keep him on the throne?"

"My good Mrs. Rochester, while deception is foreign to your character, others wear it as a cloak to hide their true intentions. I cannot discuss this with you further. Not now. But you must listen to me carefully: Promise to keep the letter safe. Give me your word! You cannot imagine the problems it might cause—nor can you guess at how eager Conyngham is to procure it."

"Whatever for?"

"In truth, I am not sure why she is so determined, either, since it might threaten her blissful position as the King's 'dear friend.' But that's neither here nor there. She is wholly dedicated to its retrieval. I suspect that's why she came to visit today, to judge your mettle. To calculate how best to persuade you. I asked to accompany her because I suspected her motives. I told the magistrate I should be assigned to her, and he agreed when he heard my reasoning. Swear to me that you will keep the letter hidden."

His urgency served to increase my fears. "I promise. But if the letter is so important, why did the King not demand that I return it to him so he could destroy it himself?"

"Because he is never alone. Ever. She has surrounded him with spies. Granted, he sent couriers to buy the other love letters, but those were not so explicit. Embarrassing, yes, but not dangerous. Those he did destroy. But this letter is different. Vastly so. If he were to gain possession of it, a courier would surely snatch it away and deliver it to the King's enemies. The spies around the King are well-paid, well-placed, and although it appears that they serve His Majesty, in actuality, they work for others. And as you have seen, our King is weak. He is often in a confused state, his health is poor, and I regret to say this, but he applies all his alert moments to planning his coronation."

"So the most powerful man in the world is really also the weakest," I said.

"Yes. That sums it up nicely. He would rather put you at risk than take on that risk himself. So you must promise me that you will be careful. Do not travel anywhere alone. Never go to the park again with only your son! Do you understand me?"

A cold breeze lifted the hem of my skirt and set my teeth to chattering. I rubbed my arms and wondered, *How did he know where I'd been? And that Ned and I had been alone?*

I longed to ask him, but the longer I was away, the harder it would be to explain my absence. So I had to make do with nodding vigorously and returning to the drawing room, where I took my place in the circle between Lady Conyngham and Lady Grainger.

Chapter 20

The Marchioness was holding forth. It was not a conversation, because a conversation requires give-and-take. This was a soliloquy, and the Marchioness was center stage, commandeering the visit. In short order, she nattered on about problems with the Irish, the deplorable conduct of Queen Caroline, and new fashions from Paris, "Women there are wetting their muslins and letting them dry on their bodies. *Très* revealing!" She paused to catch her breath.

"Ah, the refreshments have come! Thank you, Lillian." Lady Grainger smiled as a bovine-faced maid set down a silver tea service and the accoutrements for our enjoyment. On the maid's heels came the butler Stanton carrying a three-tiered serving plate piled high with scones and crumpets. Lady Grainger had been juggling Mags but finally gave in and put the excitable dog on the floor. The pup ran from chair to chair, waving his tail merrily. Mags sniffed at the pastries with hope-filled eyes, but Stanton gave the pup a warning look that withered the dog's bright interest.

"What a wonderful evening we had at the opera last night.

Signora Corri-Paltoni did a splendid job, don't you think?" said Lady Grainger.

"His Majesty enjoyed *Tancredi* immensely, especially since it was written by his good friend Rossini," said the Marchioness as she heaped several spoonfuls of sugar into her tea. "Musical ability is the hallmark of a cultured individual, is it not? The King himself plays cello admirably. All of my children took instruction in voice and piano."

"Speaking of children," said Lady Grainger as she poured a cup for her sister-in-law, "Mrs. Brayton was just telling us her good news as you joined us, Lady Conyngham. Please, Lucy, do repeat it for the Marchioness. I am so pleased for you!"

Lucy again explained about the letter she had received from Evans's nanny. She ended by saying, "The boy is due to arrive any day now."

"My dear, dear girl. I know how much Olivia thinks of you, and I know that your own mother has long since passed, so I must speak to you from my mother's heart." The Dowager Lady Ingram set down her cup and tilted her head while considering Lucy carefully. "And I tell you in all honesty that I would rather die in this chair than have one of my daughters saddled with an illegitimate child by her husband!"

A long silence followed. The Dowager's framing had been so clever that no one could accuse her of cruelty. But the result was as she had intended. Lucy's mouth quivered and her eyes blinked rapidly.

"Actually," I said, because I could not let this go unanswered, "I respectfully disagree with you, Lady Ingram, in the strongest terms possible. To my way of thinking, there is no such thing as an illegitimate child. A liaison might be unrecognized by the church and the state, but the child of such a relationship is not responsible for the method of his arrival. Every child is a blessing from God. How could any of God's gifts be illegitimate? We are all precious in his sight."

"Well said!" Lady Conyngham nodded at me, her effervescent

response changing the mood entirely. "Exactly right, Mrs. Rochester. I agree with you wholeheartedly, and I, for one, am excited to meet this young fellow. I know the King will be, too. He has a special fondness for children. In fact, we have had many conversations about how to involve them in his coronation ceremony. We are thinking they might scatter rose petals along the carpet before the King processes."

I sighed with relief as the subject changed to discussion of the upcoming coronation details. The Ingrams perked up considerably at this topic.

"Of course, His Majesty has requested that I help him make a list of those who will be invited," said the Marchioness. "Actually, there are many lists. One is for those to be honored by the King for their service. Another for those who will be participants in the ceremony. Yet another for those invited to view the ceremony at Westminster Abbey. And of course, we also create a list of those who would be invited to the fete afterward."

"I am sure there is no difficulty in finding room on your list for beautiful young ladies from well-bred families. Families with a history of service to our Crown," said Lady Ingram coyly. "Such as our own."

"Alas! It is my sad duty to cull names from the list. I think it so important that the King be surrounded by youth, since they represent the future of the realm." A sly smile played on Lady Conyngham's lips. I remembered what Lucy had said about Blanche Ingram's spinsterhood lasting far too long. The game that she and her mother had played was about to catch up with them. And Lady Conyngham had handily reminded them of that, although she'd done it so deftly that I couldn't help but marvel.

Blanche's face turned first dark red and then white as chalk.

Her mother responded with a grimace. If she had expected reassurance from the Marchioness, she'd been sorely disappointed. Instead, the Marchioness had reminded the Dowager that her daughter was eight and twenty, well past the age when most girls marry.

The knowledge must have hurt. As we watched, Lady Ingram shifted her weight in her chair restlessly, wincing as she did.

"Mama? Is your neuralgia bothering you?" Blanche asked.

"I shall fetch the rose hips." Mary spoke for the first time in our long visit. "The ones that Mr. Lerner left for you."

My ears perked up at the sound of the familiar name. Although on reflection, it wasn't surprising, at all. Mr. Lerner had come highly recommended by our own Mr. Carter, who also served the Ingrams at their Yorkshire estate, so it stood to reason that he might also have recommended the man to care for the Ingrams while they were here in town.

"Go on, Mary. Why didn't you remember them sooner? I am sure that more than an hour has gone by—you know how often I should have them!" Lady Ingram waved her younger daughter away with a flicking motion of her hand, as if batting away an annoying insect.

Mary bolted from her seat and ran out of the drawing room as an uncomfortable silence followed.

"Lucy, pour another cup of tea for me, please?" asked Lady Grainger. "Ladies, please help yourselves to the pastries. Cook is an excellent baker."

When Lucy lifted the pot to pour, Blanche snatched her cup away. "Thank you, but I've had enough tea. I much prefer coffee. All the best people are buying theirs from Fortnum and Mason. In fact, I recently purchased a bag with hazelnut flavoring. Marchioness Conyngham, would you like some?"

Although the effort was not subtle, it did the trick. The Marchioness considered the offer and then said, "Thank you, but I prefer tea."

"Oh, you'll at least want to catch the scent of it!" Blanche hopped up, disappeared, and came back directly, carrying a small tray. On it she had placed a bright blue tin and an unusual sort of glass vessel.

"Where is your sister?" said Lady Ingram to her older daughter.

"She had her head stuck in a cupboard, still searching for those rose hips. I can't imagine how she could have misplaced them. No matter, Mother, I'll serve you coffee instead. I'm sure it will help."

Blanche lifted the lid of the tin and a robust fragrance wafted our way. "Ah! The fragrance is so rich!"

She passed the open tin to Lady Grainger, who handed it quickly to me. Even though I had not been invited to do so, I smelled the contents and found them enjoyable. I passed it on to Lucy. My friend breathed deeply over the tin and then handed it to the Marchioness Conyngham.

"His Majesty and I adore Fortnum's," said the Marchioness, smiling with approval as she handed the tin back to Blanche. "Their picnic baskets are divine!"

Blanche used a teaspoon to scrape along the bottom of the tin. She managed a few spoonfuls of a finely ground meal. These helpings were carefully poured into a cloth bag and placed into the glass vessel, which I could now see was actually two glass globes set on top of each other. Last of all, she added hot water onto the grounds and clapped the lid down securely.

Lady Ingram rustled about in her chair, moving this way and that, wincing as she did. "That girl. Why is Mary taking so long? Oh, my legs. The pain is nearly intolerable."

"Mama, I wager this coffee will do you more good than those silly rose hips. Come, let us share this pot. Mrs. Brayton, please hand this to my mother."

"My flower, my loving Blanche," said the Dowager Lady, beaming at her child. "I have been blessed with a wonderful daughter, a paragon of young womanhood. Of course, my family line can be traced back a hundred years, and good breeding always shows, doesn't it? One can tell."

Lucy and I exchanged quick glances under our lashes. A smile played on her lips, but I didn't dare stare at my friend for long lest we both display our amusement. If the events of the night before were an example of "good breeding," then their stock needed an infusion of genteel blood. But to quell my desire to laugh at her ironic assertion, I added sugar to my tea, as did the Marchioness while Lady Grainger took hers plain with cream.

For a few minutes, we were each content to enjoy our hot beverages.

"Ah, this is delicious. So invigorating," said Lady Ingram, first sipping and then resting the cup on the arm of her chair. "Blanche, you always take such good care of me . . . Oh!"

Lady Ingram released her hold on the handle of her coffee. The cup dropped to the carpet and bounced twice before rolling under her chair. And then before our astonished eyes, the Dowager Baroness Ingram fell face-first onto the floor.

Chapter 21

Blanche screamed but stayed glued to her seat, while Lucy went immediately to the fallen woman's aid. I joined her on the carpet. Together we rolled the Dowager onto her side. Lucy patted the woman's face to rouse her. "Lady Ingram? Ma'am? Can you hear me?"

Lady Grainger yanked hard on the bellpull. "Stanton?" she yelled. "Stanton! Come quickly!"

Blanche cried out, "Mama? Mama!"

"Come on," said Lucy as she slapped the woman a little harder. In the melee, Mags darted out from under Lady Grainger's chair and lapped up the spilled coffee.

"No, no!" said our hostess, grabbing at her dog's collar. She dragged the pup back to its spot under her chair, and tossed her napkin over the spot.

"Olivia, do you have smelling salts?" Lucy asked.

But Lady Grainger was distracted by Stanton's appearance at the door. "Get a doctor! Hurry!"

The Marchioness dug around in her reticule and retrieved a small frosted bottle with gold trim. "Here," she said as she handed it to Lucy. Once uncapped, the noxious fumes caused all of us to gag. All of us save Lady Ingram. Through watering eyes I watched as Lucy waved the bottle under the woman's nose.

The Dowager did not respond. Not even to blink or sputter.

"There's nothing we can do," whispered Lucy in my ear, all the while waving the smelling salts under the woman's nose. "She's too far gone. Totally unresponsive. I'm simply stalling for time until the doctor arrives. Grab a napkin and fan her to keep everyone distracted."

I nodded and did as I was told but I couldn't help noticing that Lady Ingram's eyes were flat as shale tiles. The electricity that surrounds living creatures had quickly departed. Her mouth hung open and her eyes stared fixedly.

"Dear, dear," muttered Lady Conyngham, fanning herself furiously.

Meanwhile, Blanche seemed to have realized this was more than a swoon. She got on her knees, pushing Lucy and me to one side. "Mama? Speak to me! Is it your heart? Come on!" When that garnered no response, she turned and shoved me hard. "Go away. Don't touch her."

I did as she asked.

"Mary?" Blanche shouted. "Where is my sister? Mary!"

Miss Mary Ingram entered, carrying a small muslin bag. Her steps were quick but tremulous, as if she were walking on ice, and her face was white as an Easter lily. She peered around me, glancing down at the floor.

"Mama! Mama?" Mary lost her grip on the bag, sending orange and yellow rose hips bouncing along the carpet. Ignoring them, Mary ran to her mother's side and grabbed at her mother's hand. "Why, she's cold. How can this be? I only went to get the rose hips!"

"Yes, and you took your sweet time. She was in pain! Now see what you've done? Her heart couldn't take it!" Blanche said cruelly.

Mary moaned. In an instant, she started peppering her mother's face with kisses. "No, Mama! Don't leave me! No! Please, no!" she cried.

Blanche sank back on her heels, covering her face and sobbing into her hands. Her sister collapsed in a heap next to their mother.

The Marchioness sighed and shook her head.

"What's going on here? I heard shrieking." Mr. Waverly came to the door of the drawing room. One look told him all he needed to know. He squatted and pressed the fingers of one hand to the Dowager's neck, never relinquishing his grip on his baton. Then he leaned his ear to her mouth and listened. Finally, he glanced up at me and I knew what he was thinking.

"It's no use. She's dead."

Chapter 22

"She is in God's hands. My condolences," Waverly said, as his fingertips closed the Dowager Lady Ingram's blank eyes. We all stared at the prostrate form on the floor. Whatever her faults, Lady Silvana Ingram had doted on her children—well, on her daughter Blanche and her son, Lord Ingram, at least. Poor Mary was rather an afterthought, but even so, I remember the Lady's pride three years ago when they appeared at Thornfield Hall for a weekend party. No mother could have thought more of her children than she had.

And now she was dead. How curious it seemed that a woman so lively and opinionated could be rendered so still and silent so quickly. Death had crept among us like a thief and had stolen her spark of life.

My own mother died when I was so young, I scarcely remembered her. She was more of an impression than a person. However, as a mother myself now, I could feel the wrench of pain caused when I contemplated leaving Ned. My heart crowded my throat, and I pinched the spot between my eyes to hold back the tears.

In her last breath, did Lady Ingram realize she'd been denied the chance to say good-bye?

I shook my head to clear it. This was not the time or the place to give in to grief. There was too much to be done. The practicalities of death would keep us all busy, moving forward, until the reality of the loss could be admitted.

"I have sent a footman for Mr. Lerner," Stanton said, as he appeared in the doorway. The butler ran a shaking hand across his jacket. Habit, really, because his jacket rested perfectly on his broad shoulders. He stared at the woman on the floor but reserved his real attention for his mistress.

"On behalf of the staff, I share my deepest sympathies with you, Lady Grainger, and of course, the young ladies. I shall prepare the house for mourning."

"Thank you, Stanton." Lady Grainger's voice was raspy with emotion. She touched her handkerchief to her eyes. "But for right now, please wait here. We might need you."

"As you wish, ma'am." He lingered by the door, standing at attention, his eyes trained on the hallway to give us privacy.

"Could you bring us a sheet?" asked Waverly.

Stanton seemed startled. Obviously, he had not thought of that, and I could tell by the red spreading across his face that he was chagrined by his oversight. "Certainly. Immediately, sir."

The Ingram girls were crying softly now. Each had sunk deeply into a chair, turning away from each other. Lady Grainger glanced at Waverly, then at Stanton as he left, and looked puzzled, as if asking herself, *How could this have happened?*

"Waverly? I want to go home," said the Marchioness suddenly. Almost as an afterthought, she added, "I offer all of you my condolences. I shall leave now."

Waverly bowed deeply and his finger traced the tip of his black baton where the crest of the sovereign was embossed in gold. "Would that I could escort you, ma'am, but I can't. My duty is to the Crown. I cannot go until . . . until certain things are seen to. There will have to be a report filed and submitted to the magistrate. Since I'm here, it might be easier . . ." He glanced at the sobbing Ingrams ". . . if I get this done myself. A courtesy to the family."

The Marchioness sent him a sour look. "If you must. Are you sure? Well, then, carry on. At least until someone else can take over for you."

"As usual, ma'am, you have the King's best interests at heart," said Waverly without the slightest trace of irony. Pulling a crumpled notebook from a back pocket, he continued, "Can we start with the lady's full name?"

"Lady Silvana Ingram, wife of the late Baron Ingram of Ingram Park," said Lady Grainger. The words were written on a sigh.

Suddenly I felt very, very sorry for Lucy's friend. Here she'd arranged this visit as a courtesy to Lucy, an attempt to make peace, and look what had happened! The unexpected visit from Lady Conyngham should have been a triumph for her as well—certainly Lady Grainger had no reason to suspect the Marchioness's more sinister motives.

But now, this lovely place, this welcoming room, would forever bear the imprint of this tragic event.

In fits and starts, Lady Grainger answered Waverly's questions. She explained to the Bow Street Runner that her sister-in-law had long suffered from a bad heart. "Mr. Carter and then Mr. Lerner both treated her at home, back in Ingram Park. Of late, however, it was her neuralgia that had been bothering her. For that Mr. Lerner had prescribed rose hips and left a bag of them for her use. Mary had been dispatched to bring them back so that Silvana could steep them in with her tea."

"I did my best!" Mary said. "I tried to find them! But they had been moved!"

"Your staff," said Blanche in a petulant tone. "Incompetent. Every one of them."

"Blanche, please, not now." Lady Grainger sounded bone weary. "Girls, I share your sorrow. I, too, am heartbroken! But trying times expose one's character. So we must carry on, as your mother would have wanted, and be kind to one another."

Blanche pulled back slightly, as if she'd been slapped, but a sullen look came over her face.

"Mary, everyone knows you did your best. It's not your fault that your mother's heart was weak. She looked perfectly fine, except for the pain of course, before . . ." Lady Grainger stopped.

"A hackney has just arrived. I believe Mr. Lerner is here." Stanton held a white bundle. Together he and Mr. Waverly solemnly opened the sheet, unfurled it, and gently settled it over the remains of Lady Ingram.

Mary and Blanche began to sob even more loudly. Lady Grainger touched her eyes repeatedly with her linen handkerchief, but she missed a few tears, and they streamed down her face, dripping off her chin.

"What has happened? Who is hurt?" A young man carrying a tattered and overflowing satchel appeared in the doorway. He was stopped in his progress because Stanton and Mr. Waverly had retreated to the threshold, and they blocked his way. Once I had a good look at the newcomer, my hand flew to my mouth in surprise.

Mr. Lerner, the young doctor recommended to Edward by Mr. Carter, was the same man whom I'd witnessed arguing with Mary Ingram in Hyde Park just this morning.

I could also tell by his change of expression that he recognized me, although the confusion that came next suggested that he could not recall exactly why I looked familiar.

Despite the slap she'd dealt him earlier, Mary's eyes couldn't hide her adoration for the doctor. Now I put together how it happened. Mr. Lerner had called on Lady Ingram, leaving the rose hips for her pain, and Mary had followed him into Hyde

Park. He must've been on his way to Boodle's to meet with Edward and Mr. Douglas when Miss Mary had waylaid him.

"Mr. Lerner, I take it? I'm Phineas Waverly from Bow Street." The constable offered his hand for a shake. "I happened to be here in my capacity as escort for the Marchioness Conyngham, a dear friend of His Royal Highness. I'm afraid it's one of your patients, Lady Ingram. I believe this woman's weak heart got the best of her." And with that Mr. Waverly led the young man over to the body but continued with, "You know, of course, Lady Grainger? And the Ingram daughters? As I understand you have been here before?"

Mr. Lerner gave a brief nod.

I averted my eyes as Mr. Lerner knelt beside the still form on the carpet, but I still heard the sheet rustle as he folded it back. Out of the edge of my vision, I noticed that he moved swiftly, pressing his fingertips here and there. The whole procedure lent the Dowager a vulnerability she had not owned in life. Death robs us of our individuality. No modesty is accorded the spent carcass that was once a vibrant member of the human populace. With impersonal haste, the doctor checked for her heartbeat at her neck, held a mirror under her nose, and listened at her chest. Sinking back on his heels, he admitted defeat. "My deepest condolences," the doctor said to everyone and no one in particular. "Her heart was always irregular. I fear it finally beat its last."

Blanche continued her soft sobbing, but Mary wailed loudly. Mr. Lerner cast a glance at the younger sister but carefully kept his distance.

"I'll stay here until the undertaker arrives, but I suggest that all of you adjourn to another room." His manner was matter-of-fact but firm.

"Lady Grainger, would you kindly lead the way?" asked Mr. Waverly.

"Yes, yes, of course." After mopping her face, she slowly

stood up, gripping her chair for balance. The recent events had robbed her of her color, and she seemed a bit lost, as though she'd suddenly awakened in someone else's house. It took her a minute to gather her wits. Lucy and I rose to our feet. Lady Conyngham planted her cane and hoisted herself up. The Ingram girls uncurled from their spots and stood wearily but kept crying. We were all ready to leave when Lady Grainger looked around her feet. "The dog. My dog. Where is Mags?"

"She must be hiding under your chair. Probably frightened, poor dear," said Lucy. "Too much commotion."

"I'll fetch him, Lady Grainger." Stanton crossed the floor and knelt under Lady Grainger's chair. "Come on. Here, Mags." When she did not answer, he rummaged in his pocket for a treat. "Biscuit?"

But the dog did not obey.

"I can see her, but she's being stubborn. Ignoring me." Stanton reached under the chair skirt. He tugged at the dog and then stopped abruptly. "Oh my."

"What is it?" Lady Grainger gripped the chair arm and leaned over to watch the procedure. "Oh, Stanton, just grab her."

He sat back and shook his head. "Lady, I . . ." Very slowly the butler thrust both arms under Lady Grainger's chair. As he crawled backward, a mass of silky white fur followed in the same direction. But something was amiss. Something was not right.

The dog did not move.

Chapter 23

"Mags?" Lady Grainger peered down at the dog in her butler's arms. As the man lifted the dog toward the Lady, the pup's head rolled back on its neck. All of us watched in horror as its mouth fell open and a pink tongue dangled from one side.

"Mags," Lady Grainger said wonderingly, as though trying to understand. "What is wrong with Mags? Oh, oh!" she said, and she sank back into her chair.

Stanton stood up, holding the limp beast. The expression on the butler's face was one of horror. "She's . . . gone."

"This tears it," muttered Waverly as he stepped over the dead woman to examine the dog more closely.

"Please? May I . . . hold her?" Lady Grainger sounded childlike as she turned to her servant. No one spoke as Stanton gently transferred the pup to the woman's arms. Something broke loose inside of Lady Grainger; even the grief she'd felt for her sister-in-law did not compare to this. She moaned, a sound that came from deep in her heart.

"My dear, dear little Mags! My friend. How could you have left me?" Lady Grainger repeated. Lucy rushed to her friend's side and embraced Olivia Grainger with great strength. The lady turned to Lucy. "Something is wrong. First Silvana, and now Mags. What is happening? Do you know?"

One blow after another had been dealt Lady Grainger, and her mind was struggling to catch up. Her eyes were vacant, her face slack, and she moved like an automaton.

Lillian and another female servant had come to the door. They stood wide-eyed on the threshold, peeping around the doorsill to watch.

A quick glance at the Marchioness told me that she was surprised by this turn of events. I could almost see a sparkle in her eyes as she pondered what it might mean—and how she might use the situation to her advantage.

"Someone fetch me a glass of water," Mr. Lerner snapped at them. "She's had a shock."

The young man reached into his messy satchel, disturbing several sheets of paper. After a search, he withdrew a small brown bottle. When the water appeared, the doctor added a few drops of laudanum. With great care, he guided the glass to Lady Grainger's lips. "Drink this. Come on. Good. That's right."

Setting the glass down, the doctor spoke to Stanton. "We need to get her to her bedroom and see that she lies down. She needs to stay quiet. Once she's there, I can attend to her in privacy."

Waverly moved closer to our hostess, his presence offering aid.

"Ma'am?" said Stanton, and he held out his arm to his mistress. Still clutching the dog, Lady Grainger wobbled to her feet, but when it was obvious that she might collapse, Stanton and Waverly reached behind her, forming a sort of chair with their arms. Lady Grainger did not seem to notice that she was being carried. As the men moved her, she clutched the soft white curls even closer to her breast. Her lady's maid fell in behind them.

Mr. Lerner turned his attention to the rest of us. "Ladies? I suggest you remove yourselves to the library."

Lucy led the way. Blanche stopped in the middle of the hall, wrapping her arms around her waist and whimpering, "I feel light-headed. I think I'm going to . . ."

But Mr. Lerner caught her before her knees buckled.

Mary gave her sister a hard look before following them into the library.

I waited beside the Marchioness. She stared up at me snappishly. "Fetch Waverly. Tell him I have had enough. We must leave! Right now."

"Of course, Lady Conyngham," said Mr. Waverly as he returned to the drawing room. "But first I must make certain of your safety. Lady Ingram is dead. Miss Ingram nearly collapsed just now. Lady Grainger is incapacitated, and her dog is dead as well. Don't you see? I can't take you back to Carlton House until I know what is happening here. I can't risk it. Not for your sake or for our sovereign's."

She did not like it, but she could not argue with him. Leaning on Waverly's arm and grumbling in his ear, she stumped her way into the library. Once there, Lucy helped Mr. Waverly make the Marchioness comfortable, bringing her cushions and adjusting a footstool. Then he turned to me. "Mrs. Rochester? Will you accompany me to Lady Grainger's room? I think it improper for me to go alone."

I nodded. Of course, Waverly's explanation was nonsensical because Lady Grainger would be attended by her lady's maid, but he pronounced it with such seriousness that Lady Conyngham took him at his word. I suspected that as long as she felt herself to be cosseted, she would concur with him.

With due haste, I rose and followed the man down the hall.

The lady's maid responded to our quiet knock on the door. Lady Grainger rested under her covers with her eyes half closed. However, she had not relinquished her hold on Mags. In fact, the dog was wrapped in her arms, tightly, as a child holds a stuffed toy.

"What is your name?" Mr. Waverly asked the abigail.

"Dorsey, sir. Dorsey Evers." She kept her chin tucked down and her gaze on her feet.

Something caught Waverly's attention, and he craned his

neck to get a better look at her. It was the first time since arriving that I'd seen the abigail up close, and when I followed his gaze, I saw what intrigued him.

"Your face," he said. "What happened?"

Dorsey kept her eyes on the floor. "Lady Ingram struck me."

"Why? What incurred her wrath?"

"I canna please her, sir. I tried, but I canna do it. May she rest in peace."

"Yes, well." He shook his head. "Please assist me. I need to look at the dog. I don't need to take him."

"Her," corrected Dorsey.

"Her. And I don't want to alarm the Lady."

"I'll do my best." Dorsey joined him at the side of the bed. Speaking in soft tones to Lady Grainger, she soothed the nearly unconscious woman while Mr. Waverly bent close to the pup's mouth. I watched as he opened the animal's jaws, peered at the gums, and then put his own nose next to the dog's mouth and smelled it.

"That's all I needed. Thank you. You were very helpful." He gave a courteous half bow to the maid before using a jerk of his chin to beckon me into the hallway.

We walked to a spot at the opposite end, as far from the library as we could get, so we could talk privately. "What do you think happened, Mrs. Rochester?"

"Sir?"

"I know you to be observant and clear thinking. I ask that you share your opinion."

"First, Mr. Waverly, please tell me: Did the dog smell of coffee? I saw it lap at the liquid that ran out of Lady Ingram's cup, but Lady Grainger scolded the pup, so I don't know whether the dog managed to consume any of it or not."

"Its mouth did smell of coffee. So you can guess what I was after: Someone poisoned Lady Ingram."

Chapter 24

My mind reeled at this news. Poisoned? That would mean that someone in this house was a murderer. And try as I might, I could not conceive of such a thing. Lucy? Lady Conyngham? Mary? Blanche? Lady Grainger? No, no, no, no, and no. There had to be another explanation. "Couldn't it be that she simply reached the end of her days? That her heart gave out?"

"But the dog . . ." said Mr. Waverly.

"What do you know about poisons?" I asked. I had only recently learned about ratiocination, the art of solving a puzzle by applying logic, but Mr. Waverly had worked as an enforcer of the law for some time.

"Not much. Oh, we have the odd case here and there where a bloke foams at his mouth and thrashes about, but . . ."

I shook my head. "This was nothing like that. Lady Ingram simply rolled off of her chair. I was there the entire time. I saw nothing suspicious! We all ate from the same tray. Although, I suppose it's possible that both Lady Ingram and the dog ate the same biscuit or pastry."

In silent agreement, we went into the drawing room, where

the doctor was bent over the corpse, working to arrange Lady Ingram's arms over her chest. Willing myself to look away from Mr. Lerner's activities, I pointed out to Waverly where the older Ingram girl's coffee cup still sat on the side table. "See there, Mr. Waverly? There's only a bit left in the bottom of the cup. If there had been poison in this, Miss Ingram would have—should have—died, too. If the drink was poisoned, how can one explain that Miss Ingram is still alive?"

"Hmmm." Mr. Waverly had his thumbs tucked into his vest pockets and regarded me thoughtfully.

"Both Lady Ingram and Blanche Ingram drank coffee from the same pot. If the Dowager was poisoned, why did her daughter not suffer its ill effects as well?"

"Tell me exactly what happened here," said Waverly.

I revisited the afternoon's events leading up to this moment, ending my summation with, "As you can tell, those two events happened concurrently—Lady Ingram's demise and the dog's death as well."

"I take your point, but until I investigate further, I shall reserve judgment," he said. "Come, let us return to the others." Mr. Waverly took off for the library as I followed right behind.

The Ingram sisters each occupied a chair. They were both crying softly. Lucy had taken a spot at Lady Grainger's desk, where she stared out the window, as did Lady Conyngham from her seat deep in a tapestry-covered wingback chair.

"Miss Ingram, how are you feeling?" the Bow Street Runner asked solicitously, inclining his head toward Blanche. "I mean to say, how is your general health?"

"I've been a bit under the weather," she said, blotting her face. "And my head was spinning when I stood up." She paused and her eyes narrowed. "Why?"

He turned on his heel and left the room. Low voices told us he conferred with Mr. Lerner as they reentered the library together. The young doctor rummaged in his bag before withdrawing a small envelope. He rang for a servant, and when Lillian appeared, he requested a large carafe of water and enough glasses to serve all of us ladies.

"I shall need more water, please, and dry toast, too. Cook it as near to burned as possible," he said to Lillian. Walking from one person to another, the doctor dispensed what looked like small lumps of charcoal, such as can be found in the hearth after a fire.

"Swallow these, please, with a full glass of water. Drink another full glass as soon as you're able. I'll want you to each eat a slice of toast or two, and consume as many glasses of water as possible throughout the day."

Lady Conyngham stared at the black lumps in her hand. "Whatever for?"

"A precaution, ma'am," inserted Mr. Waverly.

"Precaution for what?" she demanded. "Enough. I want to go home. I am tired. The King will be very cross with you, Waverly, when he learns you did not obey me."

"I dearly wish I could, Lady. As it stands, I need to speak to all of you." He waited until the Ingram girls gave him their attention. "I regret to say this, but I have reason to suspect that Lady Ingram has been poisoned."

"What? Poisoned! Poisoned? What makes you think that? What?" Mary shrieked.

"What?" Lucy's jaw dropped.

"Are you saying that someone killed my mother?" Blanche glared at Mr. Waverly.

"It is possible. I can say no more than that."

Blanche sank down further in her chair. A sheen of perspiration covered her forehead. She grabbed the arms and gripped them tightly. She swayed a bit in her seat. "Then perhaps I was poisoned, too, because I feel horrid."

Mary turned to her sister. "Don't be ridiculous, Blanche. You've been feeling poorly all week. It's a game you play. Nothing more."

Blanche shook her head in violent disagreement. "But I have been ill lately! You know that!"

"Could it have been cumulative?" asked Waverly in a low voice to Mr. Lerner.

The young man pursed his lips speculatively, but said nothing.

"The girl is not alone in feeling unwell." The Marchioness wiped her forehead with a trembling hand. "Oh my. I am quite certain that I was the intended target. Waverly, you know how jealous people are of my friendship with His Majesty. That's all the more reason that you must take me home at once. I want to be away from here!"

"Yes, Lady Conyngham. I am nearly done here." Mr. Waverly bowed to her. "As soon as a constable arrives, we can go."

I reflected that the Marchioness had felt perfectly fine until she heard Waverly's analysis. Furthermore, given the vast quantity of sweets and tea she had eaten, there was no way that the poison had been in our food. If so, the Marchioness should have been the first stricken. No, I was certain it had come from the coffee. That alone would account for the deaths of Lady Ingram and the dog.

"And, Samuel, do you agree with him? That our mother was . . . poisoned?" In her unhappy state, Mary Ingram had called the young doctor by his first name, but no one else seemed to take note of this impropriety other than me.

"I think it possible," the young man admitted slowly, "but it is early days."

Waverly intervened. "Lady Conyngham, if you could narrate your visit, I might be able to send you on to Carlton House."

"Yes, of course," she said. "I am desperate to leave."

Then it dawned on me that this was not only a tragedy for the Ingram family, and a loss for Lady Grainger, but a huge blow to all concerned in the eyes of society. When word went out that someone had been poisoned at a gathering attended by Lady Conyngham and hosted by Lady Grainger, our hostess would be persona non grata in the ton. Of course, Lucy's reputation—and mine—would suffer apace, especially as the last known activities of the dead woman had been to publicly slight us. Here we'd hoped a visit would quiet problems—and now the situation was made worse! Much worse!

The Marchioness started talking, and I decided to concentrate on her words. "We had gathered for tea. Just us ladies. The Dowager Lady Ingram was drinking hers when she dropped the cup and fell to the floor."

Not exactly, I thought.

"After Lady Ingram died, Lady Grainger's poor little dog Mags was found under her chair. Dead," Lady Conyngham continued her dissertation.

"Ah, but what was the sequence of events?" Waverly pulled his briarwood pipe from his back pocket. He paused to pack the bowl but did not light it, preferring to chew on the stem. The rich scent of cherry tobacco filled the small, crowded library.

"We were drinking tea and eating when the Dowager's neuralgia flared up," said Lucy.

"What did each of you eat and who served it? Miss Ingram, could you start?"

Blanche lifted her chin. "I had a crumpet. Only a half. My digestion has been delicate of late."

"I ate a crumpet with bilberry jam and a scone with clotted cream," Mary said.

Lucy closed her eyes and thought. "A biscuit with candied ginger, a scone with a dab of clotted cream and strawberry jam, and a crumpet." She blushed. "I neglected to eat breakfast this morning."

"One crumpet," said Lady Conyngham.

To our credit, no one laughed at this blatant falsehood. By my recollection, the woman had eaten at least two crumpets, if not three, and two scones, plus a handful of biscuits.

I reported my own lone crumpet and the bilberry jam.

"And the beverages?" he asked. We explained we had all been drinking tea up until the time that Lady Ingram's pain had intensified. At that point, Mary left us to get the rose hips.

"What took you so long?" her sister chided.

The girl blushed. "I thought the rose hips were in Mama's room, but they weren't. I searched for them there before I looked in the kitchen."

"And where did you find them?" asked Waverly.

"Under a tea towel in the kitchen. I must have misplaced them."

Blanche agreed. "That wouldn't surprise me, Mary. Not one bit. You've been off woolgathering lately. Of course, it's also possible that one or more of Auntie's staff helped themselves to the rose hips. Servants do that, you know. Mother was particularly put out with the lady's maid. Perhaps she took the rose hips just for spite."

Waverly did not dignify this with a response. Tears streamed down Mary's face.

"In the meantime, Dowager Lady Ingram drank something else?" Waverly pressed Blanche.

"Coffee. I made it for my mother and myself. I have a tin that I bought at Fortnum and Mason," Blanche said. Her voice was rough from crying, and despite our history, I felt great sympathy for her. As bad as this was, the coming days would be worse. We don't lose people in one blow, but piece by piece over the days as we yearn for them and remember anew how they have moved on.

"How much did your mother drink?" asked Waverly.

"One cup only." Lucy picked up the thread. "When the Dowager Lady Ingram collapsed, she dropped her teacup, and it rolled along the carpet. That was when Mags lapped up some of the liquid, before Lady Grainger stopped her."

"Then what did the dog do?" the Bow Street Runner asked.

"She disappeared," Lucy said. "She crawled under Lady Grainger's chair."

Waverly chewed on his pipe stem thoughtfully. "I know this will be distressing, but if you could all think back—did any of you notice any change in Lady Ingram before she fell? Did she mention discomfort? Difficulty breathing? Heart palpitations?"

"None but her neuralgia," Blanche said. She set her face in a scowl. "I think you are mistaken about poison, sir. Our mother died from the stress placed on her heart, made worse by long-standing sciatica. If my sister had gotten her the rose hips promptly, as our dear Mama requested, the pain would not have overburdened her heart. She would be alive today."

Chapter 25

Shortly thereafter, Waverly dismissed us and left with the Marchioness. Once Lucy had looked in on the Dowager Lady Grainger, we left as well.

"How was she?" I asked when we were in the coach.

"Asleep. That dog was her whole world. I know it may seem silly, but Mags provided Olivia with all the love her husband denied her. The dog was always merry, always thrilled to see her mistress after she returned home, and entirely sensitive to her moods. While I am sorry for the Ingram girls, I do not know them well, but I know what devastation poor Mags's death will mean to Olivia. Especially on the heels of her sister-in-law's death."

"I am very sorry for her." I watched the line of stately houses go by. "How curious it is. Now Lady Ingram's snub is the least of our worries."

"Oh yes," said Lucy with a bitter laugh. "Is it really possible Lady Ingram was poisoned?"

"I've turned this over and over in my head, and there can

be no other explanation. Her demise came so suddenly, and with poor Mags gone at the same time, it has to be thus."

"But why didn't Blanche die as well if it was the coffee?" Lucy said. "Could it have been in the cream? I don't take it in my tea, do you?"

"No. I grew up without it, since they were too mean at Lowood to allow us the luxury. Does Lady Grainger add cream to her tea?"

"Yes, she does. So that can't be it, either. Could it have been the sugar?"

"Nearly all of us indulged in that. The Marchioness heaped piles of cubes in her tea. She would have collapsed first if the sugar was the culprit."

"But," reasoned Lucy, "I don't think that all poison acts upon the victim immediately. I recall Augie telling me about men in his company who supped with a temptress who slipped an herb into their tea. They came back to their barracks, seemingly in fine health, but two days later, they sickened and died."

"But then how do you explain Mags's death? I mean, the dog's demise gave away the game; otherwise, we would have surely concluded that Lady Ingram's heart gave out. That happens."

"With regularity," Lucy said. "But you are right. Someone somehow administered poison to Lady Ingram—or Mags would never have died immediately after lapping up the coffee!"

Chapter 26

Once back at #24 Grosvenor, Lucy sent word to Boodle's and asked that Bruce and Edward come back right away. Amelia heard our arrival and carried my darling down the stairs so I could kiss my son hello. "Isn't it a lovely afternoon, Mrs. Rochester? I believe the fresh air today did his appetite good. See? There's your mum."

Ned reached for me, and I held him tightly, brushing my chin against his silky hair and taking joy in the undisguised love that radiated from his face.

In front of others, Amelia called me "Mrs. Rochester" as was proper, but when talking about me to Ned, she slipped into the informal "Mum." In a more formal household, that would never do, but I was loath to criticize the girl. I had not chosen Amelia for her rigid propriety. No, I had selected her for her warm heart, her extensive experience with young siblings, and her unfailing cheerfulness. The loving way she kissed my son made up for any lack in her understanding of society's expectations.

Back upstairs, Polly helped me tidy up. "The young lady

is helping Cook in the kitchen," she said with a wry grin, referring to Adèle.

"Oh? Is she causing mischief?"

"Lands, no. Cook has had young 'uns of her own. She loves 'em. Last I saw, your girl was having a go at sprinkling sugar on top of biscuits."

"Did any of the sugar land on its target?"

Polly erupted with an unrestrained guffaw. "Some! Only some!"

Once refreshed, I sought my hostess. Lucy paced the length of her library, a walnut-paneled sanctuary filled with leather-bound volumes. The cracks along the spines and the uneven spacing on the floor-to-ceiling shelves told me these books were not decorations but old friends with whom Lucy conferred regularly. Against the northwest wall, under a magnificent painting, the "Shipwreck of the Minotaur," by Turner, sat a wonderful polished oak desk where Lucy wrote her letters. Whereas most ladies used a piece of furniture that was little more than a small table with one drawer, Lucy had procured a robust piece with a middle drawer that was flanked by three more drawers on each side.

"I have nothing here on poisons." Lucy sighed as she stared up at row after row of books on shelves approaching the ceiling. "At least, I think not. Will you help me look?"

But before we could drag over the wooden ladder, a brisk banging of the door knocker told us that her brother had arrived with my husband.

While Edward offered me a kiss on the cheek, Mr. Douglas asked, "Sister? What crisis demanded our immediate arrival? Edward and I were engaged in a rousing discussion of the inequities in our justice system. We'd almost won our argument, too, by persuading Lord Nottingham that to mete out the same hanging punishment for the theft of a ha'penny as well as for a murder was ludicrous!"

"Lady Ingram is dead."

Lucy's lack of preamble startled both the men.

"How did she die?" asked Edward, reaching behind him to be sure he was close to a chair before sitting down.

"It might be poison," I said.

"That's a right turnup for the books." Mr. Douglas sank into a burgundy leather wingback chair and moved it closer to the fireplace.

"Mr. Waverly was there as an escort to Lady Conyngham— she was also a caller—and a doctor was called in after the fact. Your young Mr. Lerner, in fact," I said.

"Indeed? Well, Lerner has certainly had a busy day," Edward mused. I bit my tongue and decided to wait and tell him in private about the spat I'd witnessed in the park between Mr. Lerner and Mary Ingram.

"Both men were convinced?" Mr. Douglas rubbed his hands together over the coals. "Poison can be hard to trace under the best of circumstances."

Lucy sighed. "Admittedly, their decision is not conclusive, but both harbor grave suspicions. Lady Grainger's dog also lapped up some of the same coffee as Lady Ingram drank— and also died."

"I'd say that's as clear an indication as any magistrate might need. No wonder Waverly has his suspicions," said Edward.

"Not that they'll act on them." Mr. Douglas stirred the coals on the hearth with a poker. "Unless they suspect the culprit is a member of staff. No society woman has been hanged in London for years. In fact, if Waverly assigns the crime on Lady Grainger or one of the young Ingram ladies, he'd find it very rough going, indeed. No, his station precludes any sort of a real investigation, since the Ingram women are daughters of a baron. I'd say that someone got away with murder." To emphasize his point, he brushed a bit of coal dust off his hands.

"I have sympathy for the Ingram girls, but I am also relieved," admitted Edward. "At least Lady Ingram won't be going around town blackening Jane's name and casting doubt on you, Lucy. Ladies, Bruce and I visited the Grainger home before you arrived, on our way to the interview with Mr. Lerner. I planned to offer my heartfelt apology to Miss Ingram for any slight she received at my instigation."

"I heard. Lady Grainger gave the impression Miss Ingram did not receive you kindly."

"No, not kindly at all. I stood there, hat in hand, as she plumbed the depths of her vocabulary to call me all sorts of names. When she paused to catch her breath, I suggested that I might also address her mother with an apology, and Lady Ingram joined us, but her response was little better."

"Ha!" Lucy smirked. "I can just imagine the justification for their behavior. Mother and daughter promised Olivia to treat us—Jane and me—in a polite manner, but neither Ingram agreed to speak politely to Edward."

"Oh, civility was not on the program, dear Sister," said Mr. Douglas. "Trust me. The Ingrams used the visit to their full advantage to excoriate Edward. Their words would have ripped the hide off a less sturdy fellow."

A wry smile twisted my husband's lips, giving me a glimpse of the young man he once was, a preview of our son at a later age. Edward continued, "Bruce was waiting for me in the entryway, and after Stanton walked me downstairs, I found my friend on the floor, clutching his sides with laughter. Stanton could scarcely control himself, and in short order, we all had to step outside lest our guffaws reach the still-fuming ladies."

He paused. "And now she is dead. The mother at least. If anyone here thinks I ought to say I'm sorry for this turn of events, he or she should think again. That woman has caused much mischief over the years, but I chose to overlook her troublemaking ways for the sake of harmony among neighbors. Furthermore, whatever the Dowager did not instigate, her daughter Blanche did. Without her mother's whispers urging her on, perhaps Blanche will marry and obey a husband with better sense than she."

"That might be hard," Mr. Douglas said. "The wags at Boodle's say that the Ingram family is nigh desperate for an infusion of funds."

Edward cleared his throat. "When the Baron Ingram died, he left an entailed estate. Young Lord Ingram stays at Ingram Park. I believe he's trying to be a good steward, but the debt the land carries is crushing, in part because so much was borrowed for Blanche's coming-out Season. And she has continued spending every Season since."

"Now that their mother is gone, when Lady Grainger dies, the three Ingram children will be her heirs. In the meantime, she has offered to help them along until the girls marry. Of course, no one expected that Blanche would still be single nearly ten years after her debut," Lucy mused.

"It's been so long that people have started to talk," said Mr. Douglas. "While at the club, Edward and I learned that the Ingrams had succeeded in ginning up a bit of sympathy with their outrageous actions last night. I believe that they snubbed Jane as a way of trying to claim a moral high ground, although they were also happy for the chance to punish Edward for deceiving them about his fortune. The gambit paid off, because onlookers wondered what Jane had done to deserve such a rebuke. Happily Edward and I set many of them straight."

"The interlude in the King's box did much to dispel their one-sided version of events." Edward held out his good hand, a signal to me to come nearer.

"But wasn't that risky?" I asked. "For the Ingrams, I mean. Certainly there are those who know Lucy as all of us do. They would reject any aspersions cast her way."

"Even so, you were an easy target, Mrs. Rochester," said Mr. Douglas. "You have no sponsors here in London except for ourselves. As the newcomer, you were vulnerable. Furthermore, they had the element of surprise. On the battlefield, I observed that a straightforward attack often so confused the enemy that they scattered, and as a result, the battle was lost to them. I believe that's exactly what they hoped to achieve last evening."

Edward chuckled. "That shows how little they know of you. Imagine! They thought they could force you to retreat, to run home and never show your face in public again!"

"I had no intention of going home until I was ready," I said.

Lucy stood and went to her desk. She pulled a stack of notes from under the box of blotting sand. "And I have here letters from Olivia Grainger confirming that the Ingrams promised her to be on their best behavior! Such perfidy! And subterfuge!"

Before I could reply, Higgins announced the arrival of Mr. Waverly, who burst into the room and said, "Mrs. Rochester, I desperately need to speak with you!

Chapter 27

"What problem with my wife so concerns you, Mr. Waverly?" Edward half rose from his chair.

"I prefer that she and I talk in private, Squire Rochester. This is a matter of grave importance," Waverly said, as he tugged at his waistcoat and stood a little straighter. I could see the beads of perspiration on the man's forehead.

"I have no secrets from my husband or my friends," I said. "Furthermore, if this matter to which you refer is so worrisome, then it stands to reason that my husband, and my hostess, might need to hear about it as well. As for Mr. Douglas, you know him to be a resourceful ally. Therefore, pray continue."

"How cool you are, Jane." Mr. Rochester covered my hand with his and gripped my fingers hard. "By the gods, I have always suspected you have the warrior heart of Boudicca herself, and here you prove it."

"There is no other course, dear husband. I am no coward. I will not turn tail and run like a scalded dog. So tell me, Mr. Waverly, what have you come to say?"

Adjusting his wire-rimmed glasses, Waverly took a breath

and said, "Could I trouble you for a drink, Mrs. Captain Brayton?"

"Certainly. I think we could all use something stronger than tea," Lucy replied. She poured us tumblers of whiskey. Waverly took his glass and upended it. "Thank you, ma'am. This whiskey is excellent. From the Auchentoshan distillery in Scotland, I take it?" She nodded. "Yes, so I thought. There's no taste of peat in it. Delicate and sweet."

I had never had whiskey before. I thought to decline it but instead chose to sip mine carefully, while Lucy poured Waverly another helping. Before meeting Lucy, I'd never had anything other than wine with a meal. But once in a while, stronger beverages with curative powers seemed necessary. This was definitely one of those times. All of our party seemed to study the amber liquid, searching for answers or fingerposts to direct our actions.

"You all know about the letter Jane holds? And that there are those eager to possess it?" We all nodded, and Waverly continued. "Although I profess to be offering protection to Lady Elizabeth, the Marchioness of Conyngham, in truth I train my attention on her because she's capable of much mischief. You've seen how she offers the King laudanum and spirits. He is incapable of keeping secrets from her. When the Marchioness is not watching the King like a hawk, her husband trains a falcon's eye on their prey. The magistrate is well aware that she accepts bribes and furthers only those who find a way to reward her. She needs leverage over the King. Recently, she proposed that he make her husband part of the Privy Council, and her son Master of the Robes and Groom of the First Chamber. Don't you see? His Majesty will never escape their influence. Her husband and son will be the most powerful men in the realm."

"Well!" said Mr. Douglas, giving the coals a poke that caused a storm of sparks to fly. "Sounds like Lady Conyngham will get exactly what she wants!"

But Waverly frowned. "Not exactly. The King is giving

her every indication that he refuses to follow through on her desires."

"So she wants Jane's letter to hold over his head? And she will go to any means to get it? Then I say, hand it over to Conyngham, my darling. Let the King take responsibility for what he has wrought. Let him buy or lie or fight his way out of this, and leave you alone," Edward said quietly. "We can go back to Ferndean. There are cottages, simple hovels, where we can live quietly until this blows over."

"I wish it were that simple," said Waverly. "In short, our King clutches a viper to his chest, which is the real reason I have been ordered to stick by her side." He put down his tumbler and studied it sadly. Lucy moved to fill it once more, but the Bow Street Runner waved her away. "When we returned today from Lady Grainger's house, the Marchioness told me she was tired and wanted to retire to her chambers to be alone. But I had a suspicion, and following suspicions is a part of my success. As Mr. Douglas will tell you, a man who faces danger learns to listen to his gut. Instead of walking away, I secreted myself outside her rooms. As I suspected, she never intended to rest. No, after five minutes, she came down the hallway. I followed her into St. James's Park. I had wondered why she had been so eager to quit Lady Grainger's house. Usually any sort of drama captures her interest. But very soon, I understood . . . she had been eager to leave because she had a meeting, an assignation. I saw her there in the shadows, talking to someone."

"Out with it, man," barked Edward. "Who was her contact? What did he want?"

"She was talking to the Duke of Cumberland."

"Oh!" Lucy raised her hand to her mouth. "The King's brother? What can they be in league over?"

"This meeting with the Duke of Cumberland is ominous." Mr. Douglas took the cut-glass decanter from his sister and poured himself another drink. "Waverly? You and I know what he's capable of. While the Duke of York, the King's other brother, adores Mrs. Fitzherbert, and has openly stated he considers her a dear friend, his brother Ernest Augustus, the Duke of Cumberland, is a staunch defender of the faith and violently anti-Catholic."

"That's right," said Waverly. "And Mrs. Fitzherbert is a member of the Catholic Church. Since the King becomes the head of the Anglican Church after his coronation, there is a timeline here. One that concerns me gravely."

"So the letter I have would not only destroy the King's right to ascend the throne . . ." I let my voice trail off.

Mr. Douglas picked up my thought and saw it to its natural conclusion. "It could also be used to rally crowds in the street. Protestant crowds. Crowds that already think Caroline was badly used. Masses who would be furious if they knew our King had married a Roman Catholic widow ten years before he married the Queen."

"While George IV has the Bow Street men and the palace guards to protect him, Maria is alone in the world," said Lucy. "What's more, she's due to return to London from Brighton any day now, as she usually does, with Minney, and she has no idea that they are in danger. And they certainly could be, if the Duke of Cumberland is plotting to expose his brother's bigamous marriage!"

"I believe he is," said Waverly. "While the Lady Conyngham relies on her wits, the Duke could easily stoop to violence to achieve his aims. At least, that is what I've been told—and I hear it from reliable sources. So I worry that if the Lady told him that Mrs. Rochester has a letter he could use . . ."

Without going further, his concerns became quite clear. I said, "I understood the situation to be turbulent, but I must confess that the full gravity escaped me."

"Please know, Mrs. Rochester, that I heartily wish the seriousness was lost on me as well. Instead, I find myself in the awkward position of safeguarding a blackguard from his own paramour."

At some point Lucy had rung for Higgins, but her action escaped my notice because I was too deep in thought. The memory of being alone—orphaned and without benefactors—had shaped my character in such a way that my sympathies were easily won by those who were friendless or without resources or who fought to survive against great odds. I knew what that was like, and I had vowed never to forget it. In fact, I prayed I never would, because it seemed to me that to forget was the first step along the road to foisting the same harm on other innocents.

"Cook is preparing sandwiches. They'll be up directly." Higgins noted the nearly empty decanter. "I shall be pleased to bring up more whiskey from the Captain's barrels."

Lucy thanked him, and a few minutes later, Sadie carried in a tray laden with egg and watercress sandwiches, slices of ham and mutton, thick wedges of cheese, and a warm loaf of bread. We helped ourselves to the foodstuffs, and I admit they revived my acuity.

"Where is the letter?" asked Waverly, as he helped himself to more ham.

"In a safe place," I said.

"How could the British Empire have come to this? You jest with us," said Edward to the Bow Street Runner. "At the very least, you indulge in exaggeration. Are you in fact here to fetch the letter?" he asked. "Is that why you really came, Waverly?"

Of late I'd noticed that Edward had grown more and more abrupt, which I determined was a natural consequence of his burgeoning sense of vulnerability. As his faulty vision caused the world around him to shrink, my husband became agitated. I couldn't blame him, but his moodiness worried me. Even so, I appreciated him asking Waverly the question that had preyed upon my mind.

"No, no, Mr. Rochester. Quite the contrary. I think your

wife is safer with the letter than without. No one would believe her if she said she destroyed it. It is too valuable! As long as she has it, or as long as people believe her to have possession of it, then she is a force to be reckoned with."

"Are you entirely confident that the contents are so inflammatory?" Edward asked. "Perhaps your impression of the message has overshadowed its real substance." He turned to me. "Jane, perhaps you should show it to Mr. Waverly and let him judge for himself."

I agreed—I felt I could trust Phineas Waverly and reassure him about the secure lodging of the papers. I looked at Lucy and nodded.

"Bruce? A little help, please." Following his sister's direction, Mr. Douglas lifted the Turner seascape from its spot on the wall. The painting had disguised a niche in the wall, a cubbyhole where a strongbox fit neatly. Bruce lifted out the metal receptacle and set it on the far end of the large polished oak desktop.

"Thank you, Brother. All I need is the key." Lucy leaned over to open a bottom drawer. We waited as she searched blindly with her hand. "There's a trick to opening the secret compartment where I keep the key," she explained. We heard a satisfying click and Lucy held up a silver key. After turning the lock in the strongbox door, she withdrew an oilcloth pouch and handed it to me.

Unwrapping the protective covering revealed the six pieces of thick ivory stationery, each embossed with the red imprint of the Crown. I read the message aloud to my friends:

My Darling Pansy,

I miss you more than I can say. My love for you threatens to burst my heart! Never have I met such a woman as you! What a treasure you are. Hearing that you are with child worries me. Will your husband treat you well? I hope so, because as you might

*guess it is beyond my power to intercede on your behalf at the
present time. Not when my own situation is so distressful!*

*As you might have heard, I am estranged from that loathsome
creature who pretends to be my wife. God knows that our marriage is naught but a sham. Had I not been wholly desperate with
my debtors pressing on me from every side, I would never have
consented to a public spectacle. But my father was quite out of his
mind, as you know, so I had no choice but to proceed and bow to
his wishes, for the good of our nation, by agreeing to an alliance
that would help me preserve my ascension to the throne—even if
it cost me my immortal soul. Such a humble servant I am to our
nation! But as I told you before, and as you well know, I had
already honestly sworn before God and in the presence of a priest
to love and honor another woman. A woman I met in my younger
days before my father met his end, a death that could not cede the
throne to me soon enough.*

*Together she and I have had a daughter, a darling girl, who is
the joy of my life. Although circumstances have forced that lady and
me to live apart, she and she alone is my true wife. So as you can see,
as much as I care for you, I am already bound to another. If that
were not true, I would certainly spend every resource at my disposal
to elevate you to the status you deserve, and to provide for you.*

On the last page, he had dropped down to the center and
scribbled a few last lines above his signature:

*Pity the poor head that wears the crown! No one can imagine
what dangers and pressures assail me on every side. The dreams
I have of my time on the battlefield! The terror I relive! Sometimes
I fear that I am every bit as mad as my father!*

George

"What an extraordinary document," said Mr. Douglas.
"His admission that he lied under oath when marrying

Caroline is almost as damning as the admission that he committed adultery while receiving the sacrament of holy matrimony."

"And at his coronation this man is to be named head of the Anglican Church!" said Lucy.

I had never seen a graver look than the one on Bruce Douglas's face as he said, "One of my friends, Bootle Wilbraham, is fond of saying that 'Radicalism has taken the shape of affection for the Queen.' Caroline's 'acquittal' was greeted by the firing of muskets and cannons in the street. A general roar of approval amidst cheering and hurrahs. The government realizes how close a call the monarchy endured because the Queen's lawyer, Henry Brougham, had managed to possess a will written by George IV when he was but a prince. In it, our King named Maria Fitzherbert his wife. It has since been destroyed, or so I presume, for the safety of the realm. The populace is already enraged at the King's extravagant spending while they suffer so much poverty and hunger. To know that he also has committed both adultery and bigamy, when he's soon to be named the head of the church, would further incense them! There are many who worry that just like our neighbor France, we are poised on the brink of a bloody revolution."

"And if Lady Conyngham has her way . . ." I started, but the specter was too frightening.

"And if the Duke of Cumberland gets his hands on this document . . ." Lucy said.

"Then rather than parading through Westminster Abbey with a crown on his head, King George IV might lead a march to a guillotine where he and his head part company," said Waverly.

Mr. Douglas spoke in a hoarse whisper, "While the rest of the aristocracy find themselves following in His Majesty's footsteps!"

Chapter 28

"Is it possible that Jane was the one who was supposed to die this afternoon? Could the poison have been meant for her so that Lady Conyngham might procure the letter?" Lucy asked. She was leaning her head on one fist and staring into the dying embers of her fire. "Is the Marchioness so vicious?"

Sounds from the nursery drifted down to us. Directly overhead, Adèle played a game with Rags. While Lucy had been visiting us, Williams had taught Rags to dance on two legs. My children benefited immensely as the French girl dressed the pup in gay ribbons and Ned watched the animal perform like a tame bear.

I was not afraid of dying. My old friend Helen Burns had shown me how to face the end of my physical life with courage. Ferndean had taught me that life was an endless cycle. But I did want to raise my children to adulthood, to give them a proper start in life, that beginning that they could return to over and over, if only in their minds. Did that letter really put me at risk? And worse, did it endanger the people I loved?

"Doubtful. It would be stupid to kill Mrs. Rochester before

knowing where the letter is," said Mr. Douglas. As an inquiry agent, he often put his mind to such conundrums, with good result.

"However, once I knew the Duke of Cumberland was involved, I did become fearful for Mrs. Rochester's well-being. There are many ways to pry information from an unwilling person. None of them are pleasant. In the event, your reasoning is sound, Mr. Douglas," said Waverly. "I predict that the Marchioness will demand the letter from Mrs. Rochester. It's possible she'll resort to threats, though I cannot tell you what shape those might take. I do fear for Mrs. Fitzherbert's life, as her removal would make all of this somewhat of a moot point. Without the lady to point to, the problem of the King's illegal marriage is greatly minimized."

While we had been talking, the shadows had shifted, moving the crossbeams of the mullions nearer my feet. The sun was completing another day's work and fading behind the trees. Slowly the room chilled and became uncomfortably cold. Mr. Douglas stirred the fire with the poker, but most of the coals had long since spent their heat.

For a while, none of us spoke. Silence is an empty vessel that cries out to be filled with words. But words can—and often do—betray us. Better to hold one's tongue and let others expose their weaknesses than to rush forward into the fray.

"Thank you for your hospitality, Mrs. Brayton. I bid you all good evening." Waverly got to his feet.

"You cannot go, Mr. Waverly, without telling us where your investigation stands in the matter of Lady Ingram's death," said Lucy.

He turned his empty hands palms upward. "You know everything that I know. At this juncture, I cannot even prove she ingested poison, but the doctor sent a message 'round to me last night. Seems he took the coffeepot back to his clinic. There was a slurry in the bottom, and he thinks he can use scientific methods to determine if there's poison in it."

"Then what?" Edward asked.

"Then we open an investigation into the murder of Lady Ingram," Waverly said.

After the Bow Street Runner left, Edward and Mr. Douglas smoked cigars in the drawing room, while Lucy and I went into the library. Borrowing paper from my hostess, I penned a quick letter to Mrs. Fairfax, requesting a report on John's condition. I knew that my letter would probably cross a letter of hers in the mail, but I still made the effort. When I was done, I sprinkled blotting sand on the note. After returning the sand to the box, I folded the note, added a wax seal, and set it on a silver tray so Higgins would post it.

By candlelight it was hard to see to our projects—my drawing and Lucy's sewing— so my friend lit several oil lamps that cast a cheerful illumination. I continued to fill in around the letters of Evans's name, adding flowers and insects, vines and leaves. On my lap was an illustrated guide to English gardens, one of the many beautiful books that Augie and Lucy had purchased from Hatchards Bookshop on Piccadilly. I hoped to have my gift done and framed before the boy's arrival, but the work took much time and patience, as it was easy to spoil by dragging my wrist across the damp ink.

Meanwhile, Lucy stitched smocking on a tiny shirt. At eight o'clock, Amelia brought the children down to say good night. After dispensing kisses and hugs, I sipped a cup of cocoa. Lucy held up her work for my inspection. "I hope it's not too small for Evans. Polly helped me shape it. We cut it slightly bigger than what might fit Ned. I would rather that he grow into it than have it not fit."

"I am sure it will be fine," I said, noticing how a tear dripped down her cheek and onto the blue muslin blouse. "What is it? Are you frightened, Lucy? Do you want me to remove the King's letter from your house?"

"I wasn't even thinking about that. I was thinking about

what happened today to the Ingram girls, and how sad it is that Evans has also lost his natural mother."

"Do you remember yours?" We'd never discussed this. She knew I'd been orphaned at an early age, but I knew very little about Lucy's youth.

"I'll never forget her; she died when I was thirteen and Bruce was eight. Of course, Evans isn't even nine months old, so he won't have vivid remembrances of his mother, but still . . . I wonder if he'll always sense his loss? I imagine he will. No one can replace your mother."

"But Lucy, he will have you and you'll be the world to him."

She waved away my comment, causing the wooden spool of thread to roll off her lap and across the floor. "Perhaps. I hope so. I shall certainly do my best, but I am frightened, Jane. What if I can't take his mother's place? Since Evans is not my natural child, what if I won't know how to care for him?"

Putting my pen aside, I sighed at her. "Look around you. Everywhere you go, you see people. All of them had mothers. Some did a splendid job. Others stumbled along the way. But even so, their children survived. You are applying your mind to matters of the heart, and the fit is poor. I know for certain—and I can say this because I've been in Evans's place—all a child wants is someone to love him! Someone to believe in his or her innately good nature. That is it, simple and straightforward."

Her face brightened. "You are right, so right. I guess I am being silly. Thank you for being such a good friend," Lucy said, giving me a brave smile. "That reminds me. Tomorrow, I shall try to locate a singing teacher for Adèle. Who knows? We might succeed in turning our dear little cuckoo into a nightingale!"

Chapter 29

After all the excitement of the day, I had entirely forgotten to ask Edward how the interview with Lerner had gone. By the time we were alone again, exhaustion claimed us, and we fell fast asleep in each other's arms. The next morning, after he had dressed and gone downstairs where Higgins would read the paper to him, Lucy stopped in to see me as Polly was braiding my hair. My hostess looked stunning in a morning gown of lavender and a mobcap over her curls. "Off to see the doctor this morning?"

"Yes." My voice broke as I thought of what lay ahead. How would Edward cope if the doctor pronounced his case hopeless?

"Dear friend," she said, putting a gentle hand on my shoulder. "All will be well. You'll see. I've heard that Mr. Parmenter, the oculist, is thought to be a genius. After your letter sharing Mr. Carter's recommendation, I asked around, and all whom I have contacted think Parmenter is brilliant. We must have faith, little sister. He'll have the answers for you."

"But what if they are not answers we want to hear?"

"Then you will stay the course. You and Edward have

already weathered the greatest storm, the one that kept you apart, and though it might now be rough sailing, you'll row together until you're on the shingle. Right?"

"Thank you," I said. "You are a good friend, Lucy."

"You are the same to me."

After breakfast, Edward and I kissed Ned and Adèle goodbye and set out for our appointment with Mr. Parmenter, the ocular specialist, and Mr. Lerner, his student.

"Mr. Carter assures me that this man is the best in his field." A muscle twitched in Edward's jaw.

So much hinged on this visit.

I intended to be cheerful for Edward's sake, but he had other plans. As Williams slapped the reins against the horses, my husband said, "This might go very badly, Jane. Have you thought about our lives and how they might change if the man says there's no hope?"

"There's always hope, sir. Yes, Mr. Parmenter is an expert, but he's not the only ocular specialist in all of Europe. If he suggests there's no . . . no way forward, we will seek another opinion."

"And another and another? When would it end, my darling? Now, listen carefully to me. If Parmenter says I'm going to be stone-blind, you must take over more of the day-to-day looking at accounts and ledgers. I have no doubt you are fully capable, but it will take you a reasonable amount of time to learn—"

"No," I interrupted. "We will work together. I will continue to read to you and let your input guide my efforts."

He sighed heavily. "Dearest Jane, I am trying to be realistic. You must be, too. Yes, of course you can share information with me, and yes, of course, I will respond, but in all honesty, there will come a point where you will understand the bookkeeping and take it over. I am telling you that I trust you implicitly. There's no need to feel you must check with me on every small decision. For you to do so would sap all your time and energy. Don't you understand what I'm saying? I married you for your mind and spirit. I am trying to make clear that I have no desire to hang over your shoulder or second-guess your decisions."

I understood entirely what he was doing: He was making me the head of our household.

He was giving up.

"We will work together," I said through gritted teeth. "Even if we have to hire a bookkeeper to make reports to both of us."

With a loud harrumph, my husband sat back into the carriage seat. "Ah! You are too stubborn for me to quarrel with, especially today. But at least hear me out. I am telling you that you have my total trust and faith. If at any time you need to make a decision because it is timely and prudent, you do not have to wait for my approval. I have complete faith in you and your judgment."

For once I was happy that he couldn't see, because I could brush away my tears in private. Every portion of me wanted to argue with his decision, but I doubted it would do us any good. Edward was trying to make my life easier. In some ways, it would. But it would serve to make me feel more isolated, more separated, and for him to feel cast aside.

"Tell me what you think of Mr. Lerner," I said, in a tone that was all too bright for the occasion.

"I liked him. So did Bruce. Good head on his shoulders. No nonsense. Smart. Determined. Very up-to-date. He meets regularly with his peers to swap ideas about treatment. I believe that Lerner is vigorous and could withstand the rigors of traveling from farm to farm. At least, Bruce seemed to think he could, judging by his looks. How was he in a crisis like you witnessed yesterday?"

"Kind but firm. He was in a tough spot but did as well as anyone could have given the circumstances. You see, sir, I observed him telling Mary Ingram that he had no designs upon her," I said.

"Say what? Are you suggesting he's a Lothario?" Edward smothered a laugh.

"Not at all. I think Mary is quite desperate for a husband. From what little I saw and heard—and you must understand that I was eavesdropping while Ned and I were on a park bench and they happened by—she has translated his professional interest into something more personal than it is."

"That could cause problems if I agree to bring him on."

"Not if he is married," I said. I wished that Edward could see the twinkle in my eyes.

"To Mary?"

"No!" I laughed. "He indicated that he cares for another, a woman named Miriam. Perhaps if he's given this position, he'll ask for her hand."

"And I have a wife named Cupid!" Edward slapped his knees and threw back his head as he roared with laughter. "Well done, Jane. I certainly would not want to stand in the way of a happy marriage. I shall tell the man the position is his if he wants it."

That deserved a kiss, so I gave him one.

Chapter 30

The address of the surgery confounded Williams. "It should be here, sir, but all I can see is a passage. It isn't wide at all. We're four streets south of Marylebone, just as we are supposed to be. But this should be the place."

"Perhaps if I can move in closer to the façade, I'll discover an entrance. Or where we've gone wrong," I said.

Williams helped me climb out of the carriage, and then while Edward was stepping out, I walked nearer to the brick-fronted buildings. As the driver had explained, between the two structures was a narrow passage that needed sweeping with a good broom. Beyond the clutter of dead leaves and old newspapers was a door once painted white and now streaked gray with an overlay of coal dust. Nailed to that singularly unwelcoming entrance was a small sign with the words "PAR-MENTER/3RD FLOOR."

It did not seem at all promising, particularly for a man meant to be a renowned oculist, but what other options did we have?

None.

I led Edward up the narrow stairs. At the top, a painted sign with one word, "OCULIST," swung from a set of rusty chains. An arrow pointed us down a hallway to the right. I knocked on the only door. In response there came the sound of footsteps across a wooden floor.

"Mr. Parmenter?" I asked when the door opened.

"Mr. and Mrs. Rochester, I presume? Mr. Carter wrote me about your case. Do come in. I believe you've already met Mr. Lerner? Good, good, good."

The man who greeted us had a face as round as a full moon, embraced by overgrown sideburns peppered in white and gray hair. I judged Mr. Parmenter to be in his forties or early fifties. The clothes he wore fit him badly, and his shirt cuffs were threadbare. But his eyes arrested my attention: They were gray as a wet cobblestone but soft as the feathers of a dove, and they seemed to take in every bit of me with great interest. Behind them, I could tell, was a quick-moving mind, with an agility that shone like a candle inside a glass jar.

The office's greeting area was Spartan, with three hard-backed chairs in a row like Grecian columns. Two very small and poorly done watercolor landscapes failed to brighten the dingy wall.

"My examination room is this way. Mind the threshold. Step up a bit, please." The specialist guided my husband with one hand on Edward's elbow. I followed along behind, blinking rapidly in the bright light. Here the walls had been recently painted with a coat of whitewash. Floor-to-ceiling cabinets with glass fronts displayed an astonishing array of implements, many resembling buttonhooks and crochet tools. On other shelves rested models of the human eye, animal skulls, textbooks with cracked covers, and clear glass jars in which unmoored eyes floated. I found the display both provocative and disgusting.

Mr. Parmenter led Edward to a simple cot, such as the ones used in our sickroom at Lowood. He encouraged his companion to step forward, saying, "Mrs. Rochester? May I present to you, Mr. Samuel Lerner. He's spoken to your husband already about working in your county."

"At your service, ma'am." As he bowed, Mr. Lerner's brow puckered with confusion.

"We've met, although we weren't introduced properly," I said. "We passed by each other in Hyde Park yesterday. And Mr. Lerner responded to a crisis yesterday when a patient of his passed away unexpectedly. I happened to be present when it occurred."

"Oh my," said Mr. Parmenter. "Oh my."

Mr. Lerner managed to control his mobile features, although a flicker of surprise slipped past. Like my husband, he had eyes of such a dark brown that they appeared to be black. His nose was rather large, but his high cheekbones and generous mouth offset it and balanced out his face, though in response to my reminder of our earlier meetings his face grew concerned.

"I sincerely hope you have not formulated a bad opinion of me, Mrs. Rochester. Given the circumstances of our encounters."

"Why should I?" I asked. I was curious as to how he would respond.

"Because my companion in the park was so . . . agitated. And because later, when I attended Lady Ingram, I was too late to help her." A look of worry creased his brow.

His desire to correct any wrongful attributions encouraged me to hold him in high regard.

"Mr. Lerner, I have heard nothing but praise for you. I will admit that I'm curious as to what you learned in your examination of the leftover coffee, however."

"Unfortunately, my tests aren't completed yet," said the doctor.

"At the risk of sounding rude, I'm afraid all his experiments will have to wait, Mrs. Rochester," said Mr. Parmenter. "I value Mr. Lerner's professional acumen highly, so I require his help as I examine your husband. Would you excuse us?"

"No!" Edward's abrupt command startled all of us. "Jane stays here. There is nothing you can do that my wife can't see or hear."

"But often women grow weak—"

"Not she. My wife is my helpmate and has the heart of a warrior. She stays or I walk out."

Chapter 31

"Then we shall proceed," said Mr. Parmenter. "Mrs. Rochester, please take a seat."

The ocular specialist took out a maple lap desk, a batch of papers, and a pen. "I have Mr. Carter's report on your injury, but I would like to see for myself what we are dealing with."

As Lerner guided Edward backward onto the edge of the cot, I noticed that my husband's jacket sat awkwardly on his person, and his hair, never neat or tidy, had fallen over his scarred brow.

A lump formed in my throat, and I fought the urge to burst into tears. How forlorn he looked! Edward's blindness caused him to be vulnerable in a manner totally at odds with his strong character. It was like seeing a fierce ox brought to its knees, with its head hanging low. All that held him upright was his pride, and that was slowly receding.

Mr. Parmenter showed Edward a variety of black-and-white images, some of which Edward could identify, but others he could not distinguish clearly. "Are you certain, Mr. Rochester, that your vision was perfect before the accident? Did it never give you trouble? Particularly at twilight and at sunrise?"

This stirred in me the memory of our first meeting, when Edward, on horseback, had not noticed me as he rode along the lane near Thornfield Hall at twilight. I said as much aloud.

"That is true, darling girl. I accused you of bewitching me, but perhaps even then, my eyes were failing. I recall another such mishap one morning as I walked to the barn. I misjudged a step and fell to my knees. I chalked it up to clumsiness, but now I wonder," Edward said.

Mr. Parmenter traced his fingertips along Edward's eyelid. "Mr. Lerner? See what you think. Touch his brow and lid. I wish to compare your impression with mine."

The young doctor did as instructed. When he finished, he turned to his mentor and said, "I believe there's pressure behind the eye. That could account for his symptoms, and it would match what I'm feeling with my fingertips."

"Just so, just so," said Mr. Parmenter.

"Is there anything you can do?" I couldn't keep quiet any longer.

Mr. Parmenter turned and looked at me, as if he'd forgotten I was there.

"As a matter of fact, there is. Lerner? Take Mrs. Rochester to the dispensary. I believe that new herb we just received from Asia is in order. You know the one?"

"Yes, sir," said the younger man. "Right this way, ma'am."

We walked together down a dim hallway to a small room, with a wall configured floor to ceiling with shelves. The lemon yellow morning light flowed through two windows, twinkling as it skipped across the faces of hundreds of glass jars labeled in hand-printed block letters, first declaring the common name, and secondly, in Latin, the genus and species.

Lerner followed the alphabet as he worked to locate the

medicinals. I thought this a good time to question him about his meeting with Mary Ingram. "Mr. Lerner, when I saw you in the park, you were quarreling with Miss Mary. She seems to think you have an understanding."

Supporting himself by resting the palms of his hands against the shelves, he closed his eyes and shook his head. "No. She is delusional. I accompanied Mr. Carter to the Ingram home. I served as his assistant in the care of her mother. Miss Mary took my ministrations as more than I intended." He opened his eyes and turned to face me. "I swear to you, Mrs. Rochester, I have never, ever led Miss Mary to believe that I have any interest in her! Her insistence otherwise is wholly unwarranted. I have tried numerous times to tell her that she's mistaken, but she refuses to listen. Why would I mislead her? To what advantage? There's no future in it. I tell you candidly, I do not find her in the least attractive! There, if that exposes me as a cur, so be it."

He paused to rearrange two jars and then turned back to me. "Mrs. Rochester, I always tell the truth, even when it is uncomfortable. Always. If I am offered the position by your husband, I would seek the hand of another young woman. Her name is Miss Miriam Goldstein, and she would be a wonderful asset to us all."

His gaze was clear and direct. His eyes were the exact color of the walnut table in Lucy's entry hall, and his curling hair crept down over the tops of his ears.

Lerner turned his attention back to the jars. I only recognized a few names: absinthe, cayenne pepper, camomile, hops, valerian, lavender, white willow bark, and mint.

"This is what Mr. Parmenter wants. *Cannabis ruderalis.* Commonly known as hemp. Grows throughout the Continent. A close cousin to hops. First discovered in China to have therapeutic benefits. Widely used now in India."

"Would I brew it in a tisane?"

"Does your husband smoke a pipe?"

"His preference is for cigars."

"This would be most potent if he used it instead of tobacco. It decreases intraocular pressure. The result should help improve his vision. I can come by later and show you both how best to use it."

My knees went weak with relief. "Really? An herb as simple as this can truly help?"

"Of course, there are no sure cures, but we've heard about the efficacy of this treatment in other patients, and I have every reason to think Mr. Rochester could improve. At least a little."

"How long might it take to see results?"

"That is uncertain. Could be as little as a week or ten days, or as long as several months. If I am chosen to fill the position in the county, I can track his progress and report back to Mr. Parmenter. He and I and Mr. Carter try to meet at least once a month to discuss . . . cases."

Once we were back in the examination area, Mr. Parmenter took the jar, ran a finger under the label, and nodded. "Yes, yes. My colleagues in the East have reported good results with this herb. I shall depend upon Mr. Lerner to help you learn how to use it to maximum effect, Mr. Rochester."

"Are you telling me that a simple plant could improve my vision?" Edward's voice was husky with emotion. I could read in his posture that he was holding back all his fears, trying hard to seem more casual than he truly felt.

"I am saying that used consistently, it could help," Mr. Parmenter handed the jar back to his subordinate. "Mr. Lerner? Measure out two weeks' worth of doses. We can revisit your condition in a fortnight, Mr. Rochester. While I cannot offer you promises, I can offer you hope."

"Thank you," managed Edward, speaking in such a way that I could tell he had been holding his breath.

I looked away from the men as I thrust my hand into my pocket to retrieve a handkerchief. I, too, wished to thank the doctor, but I could not bring myself to speak. Not yet.

Was it possible that my husband could see again? I cleared my throat, fighting the intense emotions. Oh, what an answer to our prayers!

Chapter 32

That afternoon, Mr. Lerner appeared at Lucy's front door. The young doctor had dropped by to show Edward and me how to administer the medicinal herbs via a pipe called a "lovat."

"You'll notice its bowl is small compared to some," said Lerner. "The size is important. By the way, you should not switch back and forth between these herbs and tobacco. Use this pipe solely for the delivery of your medicinal doses."

The doctor removed a small tin from his satchel. "Could I ask for a portion of honey from your kitchen? It protects the wood of the pipe from catching fire."

Sadie brought up the golden syrup directly, and I watched as the doctor smeared a thin coating of the bee's produce inside the bowl of the pipe. Mr. Lerner went on to explain how much of the herb to use, and how Edward should hold the smoke in his lungs as long as possible, before exhaling slowly.

A sweet, not unpleasant scent filled the library as the herbs caught fire.

"Thank you so much, Mr. Lerner," I said. "I suppose we

could have managed, but your oversight of the process is much appreciated."

The young man moved restlessly in the big tapestry chair, his large hands clasping and unclasping themselves, as though he longed to knead a sore limb. His eyes darted around the room, unable to find a spot worthy of their repose. His mouth slowly slid into a frown. "Yes, I was on my way back from Bow Street, and I thought it prudent to stop by . . . for several reasons. Earlier Mrs. Rochester asked me about the tests I was doing on the slurry of coffee from Lady Grainger's house. But I hadn't had the chance to complete my tests. Now I have."

This seemed a curious opening, but as to what, I could not tell, so I put away the leftover herbs and sat next to my husband. Edward finished the pipe and set it aside. I noticed that he seemed relaxed, and I wondered if this mood was caused by the herb or by the fact that at long last we had hope for improving his condition. "What did you find?"

"The dredges did contain some sort of poison. I informed Mr. Waverly of my findings, and when I did, he told me that he had received a letter last night from Miss Mary Ingram. In it, she accuses *me* of killing her mother."

I could not stop my sharp intake of breath. This was an astonishing and troubling turn of events.

"That makes no sense at all," said Edward. "If you had done, why would you admit the coffee was to blame? You had it within your power to claim that Lady Ingram died of natural causes."

"Yes, sir, that is true. But her letter arrived before I submitted my report to Mr. Waverly. In fact, I'm not even sure she knew I'd taken the coffee or that I planned to test it."

"From her actions in the park," I said, "it was clear that Miss Mary was overtaken with her affection for you, but even still, accuse you of murder? That is ridiculous, and cruel beyond words."

The young man nodded, his face wearing as forlorn of a

look as I have ever seen. "Yesterday afternoon, she sent me a letter by courier warning me that I should 'come to my senses' and proclaim my affection for her. 'Now or never' were her words. Again, she suggested that I had led her on!"

"From what I saw in Hyde Park," I said, "you made your lack of interest very clear. You also told her your affections lie with another."

Mr. Lerner fairly burst out of his seat with agitation. "I swear to you both, I was not involved with Miss Mary! Or her mother's death! I have done nothing but act according to my capacity as her mother's physician. Believe me, I have begun to rue the day I was called upon by Mr. Carter to assist him."

We were all silent, thinking our separate thoughts, when the young man settled back into his seat and hastened to add, "Of course, if I had not worked with Mr. Carter, I should never have come to your attention, Mr. Rochester. So I don't mean to sound ungrateful—and I am fully committed to being a doctor. Miss Mary has not shaken my belief in my calling."

Now he paused, "But under the circumstances I would understand if you no longer want to consider me for the position in your county."

Edward raised his hand to brush away the younger man's concerns. "No, Mr. Lerner, there is no need for you to withdraw your application. When making my decision, Miss Mary Ingram's accusation will not carry weight in my deliberations. Her finger pointing is illogical. You have no motive for murdering her mother. Furthermore, why would you take such pains to prove your own guilt? While I appreciate your recognition that I am in a difficult position if she continues to blame you, I am no coward. I will not pass over an outstanding applicant simply because Miss Mary is lovesick."

"What did Mr. Waverly say?" I asked. I could not imagine the Bow Street Runner giving the Ingram girl's accusation much credit. He was far too canny for that.

"At this juncture, he does not consider me a valid suspect," said Mr. Lerner. "However, there will be an investigation. It was ordered by the King even before I returned my verdict on the leftover coffee. Since the Marchioness was present at the time of Lady Ingram's death, our Majesty worries that his friend might be in danger."

"Naturally so, since attempts have been made on his life," said Edward, "and she is his close associate."

I shook my head, "But highly unlikely. None of us knew the Marchioness planned to visit—and poisoning takes planning."

Mr. Lerner kept his eyes on the carpet. I watched his throat move as he swallowed hard. "Mr. and Mrs. Rochester, while I heartily appreciate your support, if word gets out that I have been blamed, you really should consider distancing yourselves from me. In fact, after I leave here, I plan to visit Miriam to tell her the same."

"Why?" I asked.

"Because I am a Jew," he said quietly, "and when Jews are blamed for a crime, our entire community is often punished as well. If the investigation does point to me, the general unrest might well boil over. If I am seen as a lone predator, both of you—and Miriam—will be safer."

I had not considered how Mr. Lerner's religion would put him at exceptional risk. Or how it might spill over to involve us. But even as I tried to maintain my equilibrium, the coals of anger began to burn hot within me. What sort of woman would point a finger at the very man she had claimed to love? What drove Miss Mary to such extremes of perfidy?

A shudder swept through me. The King's interest in Lady Ingram's death could not bode well. It would be far too easy for Bow Street to find a scapegoat in order to make our sovereign happy.

Unable to sit still any longer, I got to my feet and walked to the window. Looking out at the bustling street, I calmed myself. *Surely Mr. Waverly won't allow a miscarriage of justice!*

No, that was not the type of man he was. I had faith in Mr. Waverly. I had seen him make hard choices, and he had always come down on the side of fairness.

"It seems to me," said Edward, "that Miss Mary Ingram has gone to extraordinary lengths to do you ill, young man."

I could not hold my tongue. "She is a woman scorned. You weren't there, Mr. Rochester, so you can't imagine how angry she was when she heard that he had affections for another woman. She even struck Mr. Lerner across the face."

Touching his face gingerly as he remembered the blow, Mr. Lerner gave me a sheepish smile. "It was certainly a stinging rebuke. I regret any disappointment I might have caused her, but I give you my word that I never, ever led her on. Why should I? Even if I found her otherwise suitable, we could never be wed. She's not of my faith! And frankly, her station is far above mine."

"But the news that you cared for another woman seemed to come as a surprise to Miss Mary," I said.

"I had no reason to share my personal life with her. Miss Mary did speak to me, as any patient might to her doctor, and told me how she longed to be married. The slow progress her sister has made to the altar is worrisome to her but I tried to reassure her. I can only guess Miss Mary took my attempt at consolation as confirmation that I found her attractive. I confess that I've never been very skilled at nonsensical chatter, or what passes for polite conversation, and I may have made a mess of things."

"So from this disappointment, she has manufactured a crime? A felony no less?" Edward shook his head in wonder. "The Ingrams grow ever more accomplished at punishing anyone who disappoints them. Well, let us hope that Waverly finds the real culprit, and that this storm blows over quickly. None of this makes me change my opinion of you, Lerner."

Even though he could not see me, I smiled at my husband. The world had not always dealt kindly with Edward

Rochester, but early in our friendship I had sensed that despite his travails, he had held fast to his innate sense of fair-dealing. Now I was overflowing with pride for how my husband treated this young doctor. But Mr. Lerner still harbored concerns. "This unsavory episode did make me aware of other problems that might lie ahead. Will the vicar of your parish take exception to me? If he does, your tenants might reject my services."

Edward inclined his head in the sort of contemplative gesture that caused my knees to go weak with love for him. When he spoke, it was with great kindness. "Since I support the parish, I doubt that there will be problems in that regard. I think if Carter introduces you around, you will be well accepted. I shall encourage him to make much of your fresh ideas."

The doctor's forehead creased in thought. "That is a benefit I bring to the work. I am fortunate to have many friends in the scientific community. These are men who eagerly seek the advancement of new ideas and methods."

"This honest discourse has convinced me," said Edward, congenially. "A man who cares more for others than himself would be a valuable addition to our county. My wife and I welcome you—and your young lady if she is agreeable—to our county. I hope you will come and serve my tenants with the sort of honesty and compassion you have exhibited here today. I want your introduction to be as seamless as possible, so I believe Carter should be with us when we talk of particulars."

"That's easily accomplished," said Mr. Lerner. "I am in receipt of a letter that states he'll be here in a day or so. He wanted an update on your case, and his wife had hoped to avail herself of many London shops."

"Capital," said Edward. "This should work out splendidly."

Chapter 33

"Pass the tomato and shallot aspic, won't you? Sister, your Cook does a wonderful job. The trout is perfectly boned. The crust on this bread is—" But Mr. Douglas's praise was interrupted by the doorbell. He, Lucy, Edward, and I paused while eating our suppers.

Higgins appeared carrying a silver tray. To all our surprise, he walked right past Lucy and thrust it at me! I took from it a card with a name embossed in gold: *Mrs. Tobias Biltmore.*

Mrs. Tobias Biltmore, aka Pansy Biltmore, aka the woman to whom the King had written the coveted love note currently in my possession.

"Whoever could it be? Imagine, the impertinence to come to my door at this time of night," said Lucy as she took the card from me so she could read it. "Oh."

A world in one little word: Oh.

Then, realizing that Edward could not read the script, she announced, "Mrs. Tobias Biltmore has come to call."

Mr. Douglas choked on his wine. "The one addressed in the King's love letter?"

"The same." I set down my cup. "I can imagine what she's here about, and waiting won't improve the situation. I'd best go see what Pansy Biltmore wants."

"How about if we give you five minutes and then I interrupt? I wouldn't want your dinner to get cold." A sparkle had returned to Lucy's eyes, and I was glad of it.

"A perfect plan." With that, I excused myself and walked to the drawing room, where Higgins had Mrs. Biltmore waiting. Pansy Biltmore was a big woman, with a voice that matched her size. I had seen her once at Alderton House, after the death of her daughter Selina, Adèle's schoolmate, but we hadn't been introduced. As I entered the drawing room, she stood and stared at me with an expression of puzzlement on her face. "You are . . . Mrs. Rochester? But . . . I mean . . . I was told you helped a constable capture my daughter's killer, and you are . . . small."

"Yes. I am." I stayed on my feet, hoping her visit would be a short one.

We stared at each other, as she took my measure. I did not have to take hers. I knew how Selina had been used to try to elevate the Biltmore family's status. Instead, the girl had provoked an enemy and been murdered in her bed.

I knew the family sincerely grieved for their child, but I also knew they had put her squarely in harm's way.

"I came for my letters," Mrs. Biltmore finally said.

"They have been burned. All save one."

She clutched her throat and could barely force out words. "Which one?"

"I think you can guess." I kept my eyes on Pansy Biltmore's face, where I saw myriad emotions pass.

"That letter is my property. You have no right to it."

I nodded. Fortunately, I had given this a great deal of thought and come to a conclusion. "You gave up possession when you handed them to your daughter. And she is dead." I bit my tongue before adding, "because of your avarice."

She paused to take in our surroundings before saying, "Did

you know that my husband was to be created a lord? Yes, he would have been Lord Ferris, but he died one week before the title was bestowed. An accident. His horse snapped a leg."

"I am sorry. Please accept my sympathy."

"Everything I dreamed of, and yet at what cost? I . . . I . . . would now gladly exchange the title for my husband—and my daughter!" Tears streamed down her face. "All I have left are my three sons and they revile me. C-Can you imagine? We need money badly, and they believe I can conjure up the sort of funds they desire! I came to London to plead for help. B-but the King tells me he's done all he can, all he will, for me. He says he has nothing to spare, and that he is too busy planning his coronation to do more." She buried her face in her hands and sobbed. "The Marchioness has promised me help. Money. My sons castigate me for having let the letters out of my grasp. None of them have the skills to manage our business. None have any interest in overseeing the tenants on our land. My husband left behind debts I knew nothing of. That letter is worth a great deal of money. To many people. It is also worth much in terms of . . . persuasion. Influence, if you will. The Marchioness assures me—"

"But you have no idea what she intends to do with the letter, do you?" This I said softly, because now I did feel sad for Pansy Biltmore. This feckless woman would be a small bump in the road, an easy mudhole for the Marchioness to drive a carriage over.

"The Marchioness assures me—"

"You trust her?" Lucy's voice cut through the sniffles of our guest as my friend stepped into the drawing room door. Mrs. Biltmore lifted her head from her hands and faced Lucy.

"Who are you?"

"This is Mrs. Captain Brayton, and you are a guest in her house," I said, as a gentle reminder.

"Wh-why would I not trust Lady Conyngham?" Mrs. Biltmore asked.

"Because she is hungry for power. Are you really so silly as to believe that once she gets her hands on this letter she'll be happy to assist you? Why would she be? Once she possesses this letter, she'll have no need of you." Lucy's tone was scolding, but she spoke the truth, and I was glad of it.

But Lucy's words had little effect on Pansy Biltmore, who turned back to me in supplication. "If you know that about her, you must realize you are my only hope, Mrs. Rochester. You will help me, won't you? Just give me my letter. There are many pages. I shall sell them to her one at a time."

Lucy and I exchanged glances. We both knew this would never work. Once Lady Conyngham learned that the woman had retrieved the letter, she would demand that Mrs. Biltmore hand it over to her immediately, in full. This stuttering, crying creature would never be able to resist the Marchioness. Particularly while her own sons put pressure on her.

"Ladies? A thousand pardons for the interruption." Mr. Douglas walked into the room and said, "We are waiting for you. Cook has created the most amazing charlotte russe. Will you be much longer?"

"We are almost finished here. Mrs. Biltmore was just leaving." Lucy tugged on the bellpull to call Higgins.

"Mrs. Rochester, I still hope for an answer," said Mrs. Biltmore.

"I shall consider it."

"I pray you do."

Lucy gave the visitor a cool stare. "Higgins will show you out."

Chapter 34

By the time I'd brushed out my hair that night, Edward was already snoring softly. Once again, the events of the day had tired us both—and robbed us of any privacy for sharing our thoughts.

The next morning, I visited Ned and found him fussy, so I held him while Amelia ran downstairs to get a little brandy to rub on his gums. "Teething, ma'am. Must hurt him like the very dickens," she said, cheerfully.

"*Pauvre bébé*," cooed Adèle, stroking his fuzzy head. She had taken very well to the role of big sister, lavishing much affection on her "little brother." This pleased me greatly. But having once been the child's governess, I thought she should also continue her lessons. Since French was her native language, Adèle needed practice reading in English. I assigned to her the story of St. Jerome from *A Child's Book of Martyrs*, saying that Adèle and I would discuss it later in the day, after Lucy and I made our calls. I suspected that our hostess would want to call on her friend, Lady Grainger, and see how the woman was doing. "And if you are good, I might have a surprise for you," I said. She loved wearing my new headpiece with ostrich feathers, and such an opportunity would make a fine reward for the child.

"Why don't you read to Ned?" I suggested. "Amelia? Please encourage Adèle to read to him, won't you?"

"Aye, ma'am." But then the nursemaid blushed. "I can't help her with the hard words though. I didn't get much schooling myself."

Edward and I both believed in the power of education. After we secured the employment of a doctor for our tenants, we needed to turn our attention to better schools.

But little of that could be done from London.

The hall clock chimed, announcing five minutes until breakfast. I kissed both children and left them in good hands. I was on my way to the dining room when Higgins intercepted me.

"A letter for you, ma'am." The butler held out a silver tray.

I thanked him and read it quickly. As I suspected, the highly efficient Mrs. Fairfax was reporting on John's condition. It seemed that Mrs. Pendragon was using a variety of herbs to control John's pain. A slight fever had ensued, but that had been quickly quelled. All in all, a good report, even though it was clear that progress would be slow. Edward would be pleased to hear this.

As for Ferndean, Mr. Farrell had finished his inspection and ordered supplies. The supporting beams had rotted through. He suspected he would find more of the same in the other parts of the manor, so Mrs. Fairfax had instructed him to do whatever was necessary to bring the hunting cottage back into repair. I agreed with her decision, and I would write to applaud her choices. But these efforts would take time—and when she noted that the weather had turned rainy and the lane nearly impassable due to mud, I understood her underlying concern. None of this would be done quickly.

No, Ferndean would remain uninhabitable until fall at the earliest.

I tucked the letter into my pocket and stared out at the trees lining Grosvenor Square, trees with leaves that had turned from delicate green to a hearty, deeper color in a few short days. I could see no help for it: We would have to stay in London through the summer. Really, it wouldn't be so bad. We could enjoy our time together.

Staying here in town would offer us a myriad of benefits. Not the least of which was Lucy's company—and a chance for our young families to establish close connections. Someday Adèle, Ned, and Evans would look back on this time and see it as the opportunity they had to build strong firmaments for friendship.

Time in London would give Edward's vision its best chance for improvement. He would take full advantage of Lerner's constant care and Parmenter's oversight. Such a stay would also accelerate the friendship I saw developing between Edward and Bruce Douglas. Though Edward had long known Mr. Douglas as his friend Augie's brother-in-law, the two men had never had much opportunity to interact. But this curious set of circumstances had given them good reason to spend time together—and I could hear in their voices how comfortable they were becoming with each other.

A stay here with Lucy would give me the chance to repay her friendship by supporting her as she took on a new role as mother. I had no doubt she would succeed splendidly, but I could not dismiss her worries. For someone who had waited a lifetime to be a mother, this was a dream come true. And when dreams come true, the fear of disappointment grows apace. I could help her through this. I could lend her my confidence until she could nurture her own.

As for myself, I would be resolute. I knew full well that I would never relish my time in London—the noise, the crowds, the rules of conduct, the dirt, and the lack of contact with nature combined to make city living incompatible with my soul—but I also knew that I could bear up under this. I simply needed to make a plan.

Walks in the park would give me the solitude I craved and put me in touch with the out-of-doors. Books from Hatchards would provide me an escape from the press of daily life among so many people. Working with my pen and watercolors would feed my creative self. And I would remember each day that my family was happy here.

Yes, I would be fine. Really, I would.

With that decided, I went and joined my husband for breakfast.

Our hostess had decided to sleep late. Bruce Douglas had arisen early and eaten at the club, so he sent 'round a note requesting Edward's company after we ate. Mr. Douglas had also suggested that the men drop into the Bow Street station and see how Mr. Waverly intended to proceed with his investigation.

"I think it wise to stay on top of this," said Edward, as he bit off a piece of blood sausage. "Mary Ingram's accusation of Mr. Lerner is but an early salvo, and more shots over the bow may follow. Tell me, darling girl, whom do you suspect is responsible for poisoning Lady Ingram?"

I'd been thinking about this, and I found no satisfactory answer. I took a piece of toast from Lucy's silver rack and formed my words carefully. "It is also possible that the poisoning was an accident. Perhaps something was spilled into the coffee whilst it was being stored. Anything could have happened before we arrived."

"But you don't suspect any one person from your gathering? Could Lady Grainger have grown weary of Lady Ingram? Ten years of paying for Blanche's finery would drive anyone to distraction. Perhaps she figured that if she killed her sister-in-law, Blanche would have no choice but to commit to a husband." Edward finished his sausage and started on his poached egg.

I couldn't imagine that. As I swirled the jam across my bread, I said, "If that were the case, Lady Grainger planned her crime rather poorly. You see, it was Blanche's coffee, and she only offered it to her mother because Mary was slow in finding the rose hips. No, I can't believe that Lady Grainger would poison her own sister-in-law—and if that had been her goal, I doubt she would have left so much to chance."

"Could either Blanche or Mary have done it?" Edward wondered.

"Why? Neither of them benefits from her mother's death. Blanche was her mother's darling, and Mary hoped to win her mother's affections. If this is a puzzle, how does poisoning Lady Ingram fit into the frame?"

"Then it must be a servant."

I concurred. "That's the only answer that makes sense. Polly is friendly with Lady Grainger's abigail, and she had heard how Lady Ingram and her daughters treated Lady Grainger's servants horribly—and from what I saw and heard they were at wits' end with the visitors. Furthermore, any servant in the house would have had access to the coffee tin . . ." I paused. "Except that dosing the coffee would have killed Blanche, not her mother. So why not simply target Lady Ingram?"

"Ah, but you of all people know full well how cruel Blanche Ingram could be," said Edward. "Maybe that was the intention—to kill Blanche—and the effort went astray. After all, it was a random act that caused her to share with her mother."

"Perhaps." I still wasn't convinced. "But why *didn't* Blanche suffer as well then? She drank the coffee along with her mother, and the only ill effect she took was a fainting spell, which I suspect to have been only manufactured drama."

"Well, at least Waverly is on the case," said Edward as he sipped his cup of tea. "But I can assure you that Blanche won't let this go. In fact, she's probably more determined than Mary to see someone hang for this. I had long ago concluded that Blanche has one aim in life, and one aim only, and that is to amass all the attention she can. Love does not enter into her calculations. Indeed, I doubt that she possesses what is commonly called 'a heart.' She's the sort of grasping harpy who milks any opportunity for unwarranted attention, as we know all too well because she's still causing trouble in the county about our marriage. She can use this tragedy to good advantage in drumming up sympathy for herself."

He paused. "Do you intend to return to the Grainger house today?"

"I am sure that Lucy will want to check on her friend. It's been two days now."

"Nevertheless, have a care, Jane, and be prudent. If Blanche Ingram was the target, another attempt on her life might be in the offing."

"At the very least, I'll avoid drinking the coffee."

"Good thinking, dear girl. Good thinking."

I leaned over and kissed my husband on the cheek. "Now let me read to you the letter that just came from Mrs. Fairfax . . ."

Chapter 35

As I had predicted, later that morning Lucy suggested that we visit Lady Grainger. We talked as she sat at her desk in the library, sorting through her mail. "I want to see how she is doing and console her regarding the loss of her dog. I can't help but worry over her. She's bound to be distraught over the death of her sister-in-law. I don't know about you, but that image of Lady Ingram sprawled on the carpet is one I won't soon forget. And yet, like Edward, I am relieved that she can no longer blacken my name or yours."

I told my friend about Mr. Lerner's visit and his report on the coffee.

"So it was murder!" Lucy's eyes flew open wide. "Well, that changes things somewhat! Tell me, who do you think is the culprit? I can't imagine Olivia doing something so dastardly."

"Nor can I," I replied, and I explained how Miss Mary had written a letter blaming Mr. Lerner. "Of course, that is nonsense. The logistics are impossible, and he would never have confirmed to Mr. Waverly that the coffee caused Lady Ingram's death if he were responsible. He's far too smart for that. No, Miss Mary was provoked because he spurned her affection."

"Oh my goodness," Lucy groaned. "Poor dear Olivia. Despite the fact that her late husband was a cad, she honored his wishes by taking his family as her own. Look what trouble it has brought her! If only Lady Ingram had insisted that Blanche marry *someone*."

"But Lucy." I tapped her on the shoulder. "I married for love. You did, too. Perhaps we are being too coldhearted."

Lucy sighed and looked at me. Her eyes were a soft blue as she thought this over. "I suppose. I knew from the moment I met Augie that we were meant for each other. Not every woman is so lucky. However, it seems to me that Blanche has merely made sport of men's affections. That is not the same as looking for the right person to marry."

"Whatever her motives were, her status certainly won't change for a while now. She can't marry until deep mourning is, can she? How long is that? Edward thought three months."

"No, six. Any fewer would be disrespectful. And it's not just marriage—she and Mary will have to sit out the coronation festivities and the rest of Season, too, as will their aunt. Not that Olivia would want to attend; she's much like you in that regard, a homebody who enjoys her solitude. That's another reason I want to visit her today: Lady Grainger will need help putting her house in order. Lady Ingram's body will be returned there for those wishing to pay their respects."

"I am happy to offer my assistance. I am sure there will be letters to write, and errands to run. Although the Ingram girls are unlikely to be happy to see us, Lady Grainger might feel differently."

Lucy slipped a piece of crust to Rags, who was lying in wait under the table. I had noticed that my hostess cuddled her pup even more than usual in the aftermath of Mags's death. "They will have to remember that it is Olivia's house, not theirs. I'm sure she'll have plenty for us to do, and we can spend all the time she needs, because Bruce has promised to take Edward to the bootmaker's shop. Your husband mentioned his jack-boot soles are worn thin."

"I cannot thank your brother enough. These are errands usually accomplished with Edward's manservant," I said, before telling Lucy about the letter from Mrs. Fairfax. "While John's absence is surely felt, I think spending time with your brother has gone a long way toward improving Edward's spirits."

"It is an ill wind that blows no good," said Lucy. "If poor old John hadn't fallen off your roof, I wouldn't be enjoying the pleasure of your company."

"I need to speak to you about that," I said, explaining about the repairs to Ferndean. "You have been so generous in open-ing your home to us, but I certainly don't want us to overstay our welcome. Edward and I could easily rent a house nearby."

"Oh no, you don't!" Lucy said with a stamp of her foot that reminded me of one of Adèle's temper tantrums. "No, no, no. You will not deprive me of the most enjoyable summer of my life. In fact, if necessary I shall bolt the door and throw away the key so you cannot leave me! This is the best present anyone could have ever devised." With that she threw her arms around my neck. "Besides," she whispered in my ear, "you'll want to be in London for the coronation."

I embraced her then stepped away. "Are you expecting an invitation?"

"Heavens, no. But I do want to hear all the gossip about it. It should prove terribly exciting. Furthermore, with such an event in the offing, the usual round of fetes, parties, and balls will be enlarged upon as those on the outskirts of the King's attention vie for spots on his guest list."

"And Lady Conyngham's attentions," I added.

"Ah yes. Have you given any more thought to Pansy Bilt-more's request? Before you answer, let me tell you that I'll gladly introduce you to Maria and her daughter as soon as they arrive from Brighton."

The mention of Brighton joggled my memory. "No, I haven't given Mrs. Biltmore's request a second thought. I've been too busy. But tell me, Lucy, when we were talking to the King at the opera, you asked him if you could send your husband a word of comfort. What was that about?"

"Augie is a keen card player." She sank back down into her chair and stared out the window. "He was involved with a group of players who were meeting regularly down in Brighton, when it was still called Brighthelmstone. This was before it became well-known as a resort because George IV, then the Prince of Wales, spent so much time there."

"Go on," I urged her.

"Prinny joined in these games often. As you might imagine, he's not very good. Not a keen thinker and not good at reading the faces of other players. Nor is he particularly honest. In fact, he's something of a card sharp."

"A card sharp? What on earth is that?"

Her smile was sorrowful. "A polite euphemism for a cheat."

I was surprised—most would probably let the sovereign win regardless—but it saddened me to think he would stoop so low.

"The long and short of it is that Augie caught the Prince of Wales hiding cards up his sleeve. Augie called him out on his cheating. Even worse, he did so in front of others." Lucy's hands clenched her skirt tightly, and she shook her head in dismay. "He and I have discussed the matter a thousand times since. I wish Augie had simply walked away. Done anything other than embarrass our future king."

Her emotions overcame her, and for a while, she couldn't talk. I poured her a glass of water and urged her to drink as she fought to regain control of herself. In a whisper, she continued, "But that's not Augie's way. He is devoted to what is right and fair. Two other men had lost their entire savings to the Regent that weekend. One hanged himself as a consequence. Augie's decision was courageous, even if the results were horrible. I doubt that he could have lived with himself if he'd kept quiet, so he spoke up, and the King punished him by sending him to India. Possibly forever."

The room felt suddenly stuffy, so I opened the window, pausing to inhale the crisp spring air. Lucy did not move. She sat still as a marble statue, and just as pale.

In the soft sunshine, tears glittered on her cheeks. Impetuously, I threw my arms around my friend. "Oh, Lucy. I am so sorry!"

Waving away my concern, she said, "Do not be. Augie's heart is bigger than his head sometimes, and I am a fortunate beneficiary of his kind nature. But I do wish, with all my heart, that he would have chosen another course of action. As for getting my husband back home, I keep pressing the King at every opportunity, as you saw. I remind myself that Our Majesty is highly susceptible to the opinions of others."

"Lady Conyngham?" I wondered.

"Possibly."

"Then I shall use the letter as leverage with her so that Augie can come home," I said.

"No!" Lucy shook her head violently. "As much as I love him and want him back, I cannot ask that of you."

"But Lucy!" I took her by the shoulders, "At least that ill-begotten missive would do some good."

"At what expense, Jane? Augie made his decision nearly three years ago. He was willing to live with it then—and still is. But Maria and Minney are blameless. Maria only married Prinny because he stabbed himself. Yes! He was bleeding when they brought her to his side, where he declared that he would die of love for her. In a moment of sympathy, she acquiesced rather than let our heir to the throne commit suicide. As I see it, she had little choice, but Augie did. He could have walked away. If you submit that letter to Lady Conyngham, you might condemn Maria and Minney to public humiliation. The crowds that were so angered by the King's treatment of Queen Caroline would rise up against a Roman Catholic woman and their unfaithful king. And then what? We would have riots in the streets? The very thing Augie struggles to quell in India!"

She was right, and I admired her for it.

Tears glittered in her eyes as she took my hands from her shoulders and squeezed my fingers. "There is more than one way for a person to do his duty. Augie is doing his, and I shall do mine . . . without him here at my side."

Chapter 36

We decided that a walk to Lady Grainger's would give us both some much-needed fresh air. The house was less than a mile distant, and we joined other ladies who walked in twosomes to show off their stylish promenade dresses. We worked our way around the outskirts of Hyde Park, ignoring the foppish young men who tipped their hats at us.

When we arrived, I noted that Lady Grainger's household had already begun preparations for a proper mourning. A large mourning wreath was suspended over the front door, and the door knocker was covered in black crape ribbon.

When Stanton answered Lucy's knock, he spoke in a whisper. "Good morning, ladies. Thank you so much for coming to see Lady Grainger. I know she'll appreciate it. Please come in."

"Good to see you, Stanton, as always," replied Lucy in a low voice. "If I may ask, where is Mags?" Lucy and I had discussed this on our way over. We agreed that the first order of business would be to see to the burial of the dog, especially since Lady Grainger had been so reluctant to let the animal go.

"I have the poor beast wrapped in a blanket in the gardening shed. Thought that once my lady was herself again, we would bury Mags in the garden."

"Very good. Thank you for thinking ahead," said Lucy as she removed her bonnet.

"As you know, I've been with the lady for years. This has hit her hard."

Lucy smiled at him. "You are a good man, Stanton."

"Dorsey will take you to her."

"Thank heavens you're here, Mrs. Brayton," said the lady's maid as she climbed the stairs with us. "Lady Grainger's been keeping herself busy, ordering mourning cards, sending word to family that's far away, directing us to hang the crape, and such, but she ain't herself. Keeps breaking down and crying. Upset about her sister-in-law, but"—and the abigail dropped her voice—"mainly just broken up over that dog of hers. She set great store by Mags. We all did. She was a great favorite of ours." Dorsey popped a hand over her mouth and dropped into a curtsy. "Begging your pardon, ma'am, for going on so."

"Hush, Dorsey. You know me better than that. I won't judge you harshly for caring about Lady Grainger." Lucy gave her head a sad shake. "How are the Ingram girls doing?"

We stepped into the drawing room for privacy. "Oh, they're broken up about their mum, but mainly they're quarreling with each other. Going after each other like cats and dogs. Miss Ingram blames Miss Mary, and Miss Mary starts to wailing something fierce."

"We all grieve differently," said Lucy.

"Yes, ma'am, that we do."

Dorsey had dark brown eyes and hair the color of wheat, a striking combination. A deep dimple at the side of her mouth created a charming parenthesis that emphasized her mouth. I could see she was a kind soul, and the acrimony between the sisters was bothering her.

"It'll be such a comfort to Lady Grainger that you're here.

You were always a great favorite of hers, ma'am. She loves you like a daughter. She's just there in her room, putting her feet up for a bit. Mr. Lerner gave her something to help her stay calm, and it makes her rather sleepy, it does."

"We can escort ourselves from here, Dorsey," said Lucy. "I'm sure you have more than enough to do getting the house ready."

"Aye, the young ladies' brother, Lord Ingram, will be arriving soon, and we're trying to get rooms ready for him."

As we stepped into the hallway, Blanche Ingram appeared in the doorway of her bedroom. Her face contorted in fury at the sight of us. "Go away. You are not welcome here!"

"I am sorry for your loss, Miss Ingram," said Lucy softly.

"As am I," I said. "Please accept our deepest sympathy."

"Get out!" spat Blanche. "This is my house, or it will be soon enough."

"Miss Ingram," said Lucy, "this house belongs to your aunt, and if she asks me to leave, I will. Until then, why trouble yourself? I am sure you have many letters to write, so do not let us disturb you."

"Letters? Yes, I have letters to write by the score. I am the daughter of Baron Ingram of Ingram Park. I am a peeress. And you two are nothing and nobody, not worthy of emptying my washbasin. How dare you show your faces here?" Blanche said.

If Lady Ingram's corpse had been in the house, her daughter's invectives could have raised her from the dead. In the event, we were lucky that the remains were still being prepared by the undertaker.

We tried to get by Blanche Ingram, but she planted herself with arms akimbo so that she blocked our way.

"Calm yourself, I beg you. We're here to offer comfort to Lady Grainger," Lucy said, taking two steps nearer the screaming woman. "Now please, let us pass."

"Comfort her? Don't make me laugh! Aunt keeps crying over that stupid dog, and it was already sick. I saw it retching in the garden."

"The dog became sick when you and your mother insisted on giving her milk, even though your aunt asked you not to," said Lucy, with a shake of her head. "Now, I'd like to see my friend. Come along, Jane."

"You think you're society, Lucy Brayton? My aunt dotes on you, doesn't she? But just wait. They will all turn their backs on you and your husband's bastard child!"

Lucy staggered under the weight of this verbal assault. I slipped my arm through hers in a gesture of solidarity. Blanche Ingram knew exactly how to hurt my friend, and I struggled to restrain my anger. The woman had lost her sense of propriety.

"Is your sister about?" I reasoned that the other Ingram daughter might be more conciliatory to our visit.

"Mary is down in the conservatory among the plants." Blanche tossed her head in a gesture of indignation.

I spoke in a gentle voice. "Miss Ingram, please let us pass."

"No." She pouted as petulantly as a schoolchild.

Lucy dropped her chin and locked eyes with Blanche Ingram. "I am asking you politely to please move. I have no quarrel with you. Lady Grainger is my friend. I merely wish to go to her."

Blanche Ingram snarled. "You'll do no such thing."

"Oh, bother. I really don't want to do this. But you leave me no choice," said Lucy.

To my utter astonishment, at that moment Lucy hauled off and punched Blanche right in the gut, causing the young woman to fall to her knees, groaning.

"You'll get over it, Miss Ingram. I've only knocked the wind from you. Believe me, I wanted to do more. Really, Blanche. You try my patience. I suggest you crawl off to your room, lock the door, and don't come out."

Chapter 37

Lucy led the way to Lady Grainger's chambers. The woman was in bed, curled up into a ball. In that careless world of slumber, she had no worries, and her relaxed face looked decades younger. Clutched in one hand were two small tufts of hair; a thoughtful person had clipped a bit of Mags's fur as a remembrance. Lucy leaned over her friend, lightly brushing a palm across the older woman's forehead to check for fever. In response, Lady Grainger sighed and murmured but remained asleep.

The chambers were spacious, in colors of muted yellow and bluebell, accented with judicious touches of white. Her furnishings included a large bed, a dresser, a low table, and two chairs sitting across from the fireplace, which was surrounded by shelving filled with books. Someone had started the coals on the hearth, and the heat they gave out was most welcome. A deeply cushioned navy blue chair sat next to the fire, waiting for a reader to curl up in it, with a footstool nearby.

Lucy crawled up onto the bed beside her friend and assumed a watchful attitude.

I took the deep chair near the fire and rested my feet on the footstool, taking care that my boot soles did not soil the fine needlework surface. It had likely been done by Lady Grainger, as the subject matter was a dog resembling poor Mags. Thus comfortably ensconced, I took time to enjoy my surroundings. The room was pleasant and quiet, except for the soft sound of Lady Grainger's breathing. "Lucy? I hope you didn't take Blanche's threats to heart. She can't possibly think people will really shun you."

"No, I'm not worried. I think she'd been drinking. I could smell it on her breath, couldn't you?"

"No, I wasn't close enough."

Lucy laughed. "Lucky you. Or lucky her. I could use a glass of gin right now."

"Where and how did you learn to fight like that?"

"I have an entire life history to tell you, but this is not the time. Suffice it to say, even as children, Bruce and I quickly learned the natural desire for self-protection. After our mother died, this was strengthened by my recognition that if anything happened to me, Bruce would be all alone in the world."

"But what about your father?" I asked.

"Some other time, Jane," she said with a sigh and a frown. "But as for what you called fighting, that was nothing. Over time, I learned what I could about self-defense. Sad to say, I had many chances to hone my skills and pick up pointers."

I thought back to my life at Lowood, the charity school I had attended. On occasion, girls fought, but the scuffles were short-lived. Usually, the end result was a scratch, or slap, or pulled hair. Nothing more. What sort of scenes had a society lady like Lucy witnessed, to have learned a more brutal method of fighting? I was intrigued to see this uncouth side to my friend. While Lady Grainger slept on, I decided to pursue the topic.

"I know nothing about defending myself, and clearly such knowledge could prove useful. Can you share any tips with me?" I asked Lucy. In truth, I expected her to demur, but Lucy warmed to the subject immediately.

"You noticed, I am sure, that Miss Ingram did not expect my attack. Surprise is paramount, especially for us females. It is best if you are underestimated. Let your opponent think you are defenseless or at the very least bewildered. Blanche was so occupied with her insults that she forgot I might stand up for myself. Note that before I struck her, I did not betray my moves. That is critical in such instances. If you tense up or flinch or divert your eyes, you warn your opponent. You must stay relaxed and nonthreatening so that the blow you deliver is shocking."

That much was true. Lucy's punch to the gut had seemed to come out of nowhere.

Lucy paused to think. "The best way to induce someone to start talking and forget everything else is to antagonize them. When we are angry, we become blind and deaf to everything around us. Ironic, isn't it? Our anger inflames the situation, yet distracts when one should best be attentive!"

She continued, "The location of the strike is critical. I hit her high and between the ribs. Right here," said Lucy as she touched the inverted V where the ribs parted above her waist-line. "Essentially, my blow forced her to exhale mightily. She had no choice. I knocked the wind out of her. Very effective because your enemy cannot chase you or retaliate. It takes a while for someone to recover. Fortunately for me, she was wearing a morning dress and not much of a corset under-neath."

"What would you have done if she had advanced on you?" For a moment, I had thought Blanche might do exactly that.

"The human body has many spots without natural armor," said Lucy, "where it is not protected by bones. Any soft spot is vulnerable, as are the arches of the feet, the eyes, ears, nose, and face in general. Also, anytime you exert a pressure that forces a body part to move opposite to the path decreed by nature, you can inflict damage. So, for example, our elbows bend thus"—she raised her arms to illustrate—"and to force them to bend the other way is to inflict great pain. This is particularly, spectacularly true with fingers, I might add. They are very easy to bend and break."

I winced, not liking to think how Lucy could know all this. "What if one's assailant has a weapon?"

Her expression turned grave. "Of all the weapons one might use against you, a knife is the most treacherous. A person can inflict so much damage, so quickly. Even in the hands of an amateur, a knife is deadly. The best result in most such attacks would be to come up with a distraction. There are always weapons at hand if you take advantage of their natural properties and the element of surprise. I once tossed a bucket of cinders in a man's face when he came after me with a knife. Naturally, he raised both hands to rub his eyes and dropped the blade. Then I kicked it away."

I struggled not to show my surprise. How could such a situation have occurred? Surely not in a drawing room while making calls. Perhaps while she was visiting Augie in India? I opened my mouth to ask, but having warmed to her subject, Lucy continued her lecture on defense.

"So, if I were to advance upon you right now, how could you defend yourself?" she asked me.

"I'm not sure."

"Think, Jane. Look around. You are a naturally observant person. What nearby object might inflict a painful blow?"

"The oil lamp?" One sat on Lady Grainger's bedside table next to Lucy.

"Yes, good choice. Furthermore, if it broke, the oil and fire would consume your opponent. That would definitely slow him or her down. Consider also that you are surrounded by books. Imagine slamming one down on a person's hand or head. Very painful."

"However did you come to learn all this? To think this way?" I asked. "What on earth made it a necessity for you?"

But Lady Grainger interrupted by rolling over and finally blinking open her eyes.

"Olivia, dear?" Lucy spoke to her softly. "It's me, Lucy, and my friend Mrs. Rochester."

"Mags?" asked Lady Grainger.

"I am sorry," Lucy said, leaning down to plant a kiss on her friend's cheek.

Levering herself into a seated position, Lady Grainger looked around. Lucy gave her a hug and climbed off the woman's bed. After gathering herself, Lady Grainger lifted her chin, and through a veil of tears she said, "Where is Mags? Her . . . body?"

"Stanton has her. He wrapped her in a favorite blanket."

"Good." The woman seemed to pull herself together. She turned to Lucy. "Tell Stanton to prepare a grave between the holly bushes, so that all will know that my affection for her is evergreen, and that my heart bleeds over her loss. Call Dorsey. I want her to help me dress. And Lucy, retrieve the Book of Common Prayer from my library. You know where it is. I shall ask Stanton to read from it. That's not blasphemy, is it?"

"Jane is the cousin to a clergyman." Lucy deferred to me.

"God made animals before he made man. Surely they are precious in his sight," I answered, although truly, I had no formal training and could not recall my cousin St. John's position on such matters.

Lady Grainger seemed relieved.

"Should I ask your nieces to join us?" Lucy's face held no animosity, no sarcasm.

"Absolutely not. They are in mourning for their mother and have no room in their hearts to spare for my Mags." Lady Grainger sighed. "And in truth, I have no wish for their ill will to corrupt my memorial."

Chapter 38

Blanche had retreated to her room, where I could hear her slamming around. Mary was nowhere to be found. Lucy quickly plucked the Book of Common Prayer from its accustomed home, and we descended the staircase to the foyer where Stanton and Dorsey stood at attention. She told them what Lady Grainger had asked. Dorsey hurried upstairs to help her mistress dress.

"I have already made preparations, ma'am, for Mags to be put to rest," said Stanton. "I had guessed where Lady Grainger would want the dog buried." He blushed. "My mistress and I have had many occasions over the years to share our thoughts on life after death, and I know she considers the holly bush to be symbolic of this world and the next. The glossy leaves attract, but like so many of life's experiences, they hide a prickly thorn that can also wound."

Barely a few minutes passed before we heard Dorsey clear her throat. Lady Grainger stood at the top of the stairs. Obviously, she had done much to dress herself, because it had taken her no time at all to get ready, and although her dress was rather haphazard, a thin shawl cast over her shoulders did something to disguise her general disarray.

The lady of the house smiled down at her butler, a long, tender gesture of appreciation. "Thank you so much, Stanton, for all you've done for me. Rest assured, I know who my friends are. All of you prove your affection for me with your good offices."

"It is always my pleasure to serve you, ma'am. May I offer you my heartfelt condolences. Mags was much loved. We all enjoyed her. This has been a very sad time for the entire household." He spoke with great dignity.

Lady Grainger stood a little taller and pulled her shawl close around her shoulders. "I can also count on you, I hope, to make sure that we are not interrupted."

With that she descended the stairs.

Once they were eye to eye, Stanton gave her a brisk nod. "Dorsey consulted with me, and as you know, we took the liberty of saving two little locks of Mags's tail. So she sewed this little purse for you." He passed Lady Grainger a small silk pouch.

Lady Grainger slowly opened her fist and stared at the two hanks of hair. Dorsey opened the purse, and reluctantly the lady pressed the tokens inside.

"Also, I retrieved Mags's favorite blanket and wrapped her remains in it. Along with that old silk stocking of yours that she loved so much."

"How incredibly thoughtful of you." Lady Grainger looked relieved. "Thank you so much for thinking ahead."

He inclined his head. His eyes were full of emotion. "My duty, ma'am. Only my duty. As I told the ladies, I have opened a shallow grave in a secluded spot by the back wall between the holly bushes. You see, as I told the ladies, I guessed that would be a fine resting spot. It's rather at the back of the garden so Mags won't be disturbed by visitors. You know what a light sleeper she always was."

Lady Grainger's eyes sparkled with tears, and she smiled at him tremulously. "What would I do without you, Stanton? Dorsey, will you take my arm? I'm feeling rather unsteady."

We followed Dorsey and Lady Grainger out into the soft morning air.

As Lucy had promised, Lady Grainger's garden was a delight. The mix of colors and textures caused my fingers to ache for my watercolor brush. The far edges, left and right, were deep shades of blue, larkspur, phlox, and forget-me-nots. These merged with the blue reds of roses and the clearer red of poppies. This slowly changed to white blossoms, foxglove, and Queen Anne's lace, and finally in the center was a circular herb garden. Although this occasion was solemn, my heart danced with happiness at our surroundings, so obviously planted with love and an artistic eye. Instead of dwelling on this sad day, I jumped ahead to imagine one day having tea out here.

A fresh pile of dirt rimmed a tidy hole in the rich soil at the center of the beds. Stanton came from the shed with a small bundle cradled in his arms. When he arrived at the graveside, he paused, waiting for Lady Grainger's direction. We bowed our heads and waited while Lady Grainger pulled back the blanket. She cried softly as she stroked Mags one last time.

"Dear, dear Mags. You never had a cross look for anyone. You were always thrilled to see me even if I only left the room for a moment. You woke up every morning excited about the day ahead. I shall miss you with all my heart, faithful friend, and I pray that you will wait for me on the other side."

She replaced the blanket over the dog and nodded to Stanton. He gently lowered his parcel into the grave.

Lucy passed him the prayer book, opened to the burial ceremony, and Stanton read in sonorous tones a fitting message of thanksgiving and hope. At the end, we joined in saying, "Amen."

"Please take care of . . . putting her to bed," said Lady

Grainger to her butler. She turned on her heel, unwilling or unable to watch dirt falling on her friend. As she walked, she paused to talk to her plants. "Coming along nicely, I see. Oh, I see that bit of bonemeal did you good. Dear, dear, you need more water, don't you?"

She stopped at a spot where stems had been cut almost even with the dirt. "Stanton?"

"Yes, ma'am." He put down the shovel and came to her side.

"What on earth?" She pointed to the shortened stalks. "Someone has been chopping at my foxglove."

"I believe Miss Mary has been helping you with your gardening," he said in such a way that suggested he thought little of the girl's efforts.

"She's hacked them nearly to the ground! If you see her out here, let me know," said Lady Grainger. "I shall put a stop to that right away."

Lucy and I walked her back toward the house. We were almost there when she turned to her lady's maid. "Dorsey? Instruct Cook to prepare tea—and summon my nieces to join us. It's high time I made some changes around here."

Chapter 39

When we returned, Blanche and Mary Ingram were in the drawing room waiting to be measured for their mourning clothes. Both young women wore fashionable dresses and lace-trimmed mobcaps, typical society attire for mornings at home. Blanche's muslin of lively pink with sprigs of blue red roses seemed to be particularly unsuitable given her recent bereavement, while Mary's pale blue was at least somewhat more somber. Although both girls showed signs of weariness, only Mary's eyes were red rimmed. She kept mopping at her nose.

The seamstress had uncoiled her measuring tape, and now she stood expectantly. "Which lady would like to go first?"

Neither girl looked up to greet us or acknowledge their aunt's entrance. Blanche mumbled, "I suppose I shall," while Lucy helped her friend into a chair beside the tea table. I waited until the older woman was seated and then took a chair on the periphery.

In short order, Blanche's measurements had been taken, and it was Mary's turn. When the seamstress turned to Lady Grainger, she demurred. "I still have what I wore when my husband died. It will be fine. Thank you, Mrs. Hutton. When can we expect these to be finished?"

"Tomorrow, ma'am," said the woman, hungrily eyeing the tea tray that the parlor maid set on the tea table. Evidently the Ingram girls had ordered tea while we were in the garden.

"Lillian? Please see that Mrs. Hutton has a cup of tea before she leaves," said Lady Grainger. "And wrap up whatever pastries are left from breakfast for her. I'm sure she and her sewers will be working late tonight."

"Thank you kindly, ma'am, and I speak for all of us when I say we are sorry for your loss." With that the seamstress followed Lillian from the drawing room.

That small gesture, I thought, spoke volumes about Lucy's friend. Despite her losses, despite being distracted, despite the vast differences in their stations, Lady Grainger had taken note of the woman's lean expression—and took the time to do the woman a good turn.

Blanche's actions were also illustrative—but not in a positive manner. Lillian had refreshed the hot water, and Blanche reached over and helped herself to a fresh cup of tea without offering to pour for her aunt. Lucy's nostrils flared with suppressed indignation, but instead of reproving the girl's bad manners, she said, "May I serve you, Lady Grainger?"

Then she did the woman's bidding and offered the same courtesy to me. The strong black tea was most welcome and revived my spirits. Lucy and Lady Grainger also took obvious pleasure in the brew.

Blanche glared at Lucy but otherwise ignored my friend's presence. The punch to the gut must have worked some magic, because Blanche seemed unwilling to further harass Lucy. Instead she was keeping her distance.

It was only after I set my teacup down that a shiver reminded me there was a poisoner in our midst, and we might be at risk. I glanced up, wondering if anyone other than me even harked back to that sad event of two days ago. How fickle is the human mind! How easily we discard self-preservation when it becomes inconvenient! We had each fallen on our drinks and pastries like a hungry horde without a second thought.

"I'm glad you are up and about, Aunt Olivia," said Blanche. "Someone needs to order mourning cards and put an ad in the *Times*. I cannot bear to visit the undertaker and select a coffin for Mother. You'll do that for us, won't you? And another thing, Aunt Olivia. You'll need to hire a midwife to sit with Mama's remains. When she's back from the undertaker, that is. Do find someone who looks reputable, won't you? That woman who kept watch at Uncle's visitation was a disgusting creature. I was surprised you let her into your home. Oh, and I think poor Mama should be wrapped in a black silk shroud rather than wool, don't you? Oh, I do hope we have a good representation of the ton for the visitation."

She continued, "I wonder if the Earl of Sessingham will visit. He's rather dashing, and I know he was interested in me. Need I wait a full six months to marry?"

These were the first words out of Blanche Ingram's mouth. I glanced sidewise at her sister, Mary, and watched the younger sister shift her weight uncomfortably on her chair. Mary had kept her eyes downcast. She hadn't touched her tea, and she'd wrapped her handkerchief so tightly around her fingers that they turned white.

Lady Grainger squinted at Mary. "Did you sleep at all last night?"

"No," she said, adding eagerly, "perhaps you could send a footman for Mr. Lerner."

I kept my eyes on my tea. The girl simply refused to accept the man's word that he was uninterested. I wondered what more he would have to do to be convincing. How would he be able to carry out his responsibilities in the same county as the Ingrams' estate if she continued with this nonsense? There was only one solution: We would have to hope that he would marry

Miriam quickly. Surely that would put an end to Mary's fantastical imaginings.

"I kept thinking about Mother," said Mary, and her voice broke under the strain of emotion. She used the end of her handkerchief to dab her eyes, and she appeared to be on the verge of losing herself to grief. "I miss her already."

"So do I, of course," said Blanche. "But we must go on. Oh, Aunt, I told that woman I need several dresses in lavender and gray as well as the black bombazine. That reminds me . . . I'll need a new bonnet as well. Something in dove gray that can be perked up with ribbons at a later date."

"Blanche," said Lady Grainger sternly, "black is de rigueur. Unless you want people to speak ill of you, you will wear it. Girls, I know you both have something you can wear until your mourning clothes arrive tomorrow, because the dresses from when your father died are still in my trunks. Remember? I shall instruct Dorsey to ready them for you, and I expect you to change immediately."

"I'll go up directly." Mary's lower lip trembled, and a fresh fountain of tears spilled down her cheeks.

"You are right, Aunt. This is a house of mourning. We must comport ourselves accordingly. So should your staff. Do you know that someone was out there digging in the garden? How unseemly. Really, Aunt Olivia, you must speak to your servants. They need to be taken in hand. If this were my house—"

Lady Grainger set down her teacup and cleared her throat. "I have been meaning to talk to you about that. Given the loss you have both endured, I know this timing is awkward, but if I wait to speak on this matter, you might embarrass yourself by saying something that later haunts you. Especially since your mother's passing will have naturally brought such concerns to scrutiny."

"Pray, what is it?" Blanche put down her teacup. "You sound very serious."

"It's about my will."

Blanche beamed as if someone had lit the wick in her oil lamp.

"I believe we should go." Lucy pushed back her chair, and I immediately followed suit.

"No. I wish you wouldn't," Lady Grainger said firmly.

I continued to gather my skirt, but our hostess stayed me with a wave of her hand. "Please, Mrs. Rochester. You are dear to Lucy, so you might as well hear this, too."

I folded my hands in my lap and waited. To disobey Lady Grainger would have seemed rude, so I stayed. I noticed that Lucy also lowered her eyes. It was as if we were trying to disappear, even though we'd been asked to stay. There was tension in the air—and we wished to avoid another scene with Blanche.

"Blanche, Mary," Lady Grainger began, "while your last visit was fresh in my mind, I met with my solicitor. Please know that I gave myself several days' worth of prayers and thought before proceeding. As you both are well aware, your father, my brother, was very dear to me. My husband and I always longed for children, although God deemed it best we not have them. When the three of you were born, I hoped you would become as daughters and a son to me, and I told your mother as much. Over the years, I have tried to make you welcome here."

"Everyone knows we're here for the holidays and for the Season," Blanche said.

"Yes, it has been your wont to use my home as your own. As a consequence, people have formed the assumption that you will inherit everything from me."

Blanche struggled to restrain herself, although the hint of a smile threatened to overcome her efforts. Mary's eyes, although still red and puffy, also grew round with expectation.

"Obviously, your brother had already inherited your family home and property. But your father was unable to make provisions for the two of you. He asked that I care for you financially. Your mother made it abundantly clear that she expected for me to give you, Blanche, this house, as the older daughter, and to leave Mary a dowry and an income."

"You are so kind, Aunt Olivia. Believe me, I shall never forget you, no matter how long I live. No matter what changes I make, I shall think of you. Dear, dear aunt." Blanche clasped her hands to her breast.

"Blanche, you are putting the cart before the horse," Lady Grainger warned.

The younger woman lowered her eyes and attempted to look chastised. "Of course, I am. Only because you brought up the subject. Otherwise I would have never said anything. We are obviously talking about the future—and certainly, a long time from now. A while, at least."

"Yes, well, that's why I want to talk with you. Things have changed."

Avarice triumphed over grief in the faces of the Ingram girls.

Lady Grainger continued, "I have decided not to do that. Instead, I am leaving the bulk of my wealth and my property to Evans Forrester."

Chapter 40

"Aunt Olivia!" Blanche slammed both palms against the table-top, which caused the silver to jostle. "You can't! You cannot do that!"

Mary started crying louder than before.

"Blanche, that's where you are wrong. I not only can do as I please with my money and property, but I *shall* do as I please. In fact, I already have."

Lucy's mouth had fallen open. "Olivia? Are you sure? I mean, that's terribly kind of you, but wholly unnecessary."

"I know, but it's my pleasure." The older woman grasped Lucy's hand and squeezed it. The two exchanged looks of purest affection. "Remember? I mentioned at the opera that I spoke to Claymore, my solicitor," said Lady Grainger. "Really, Lucy, my mind is quite firm on this. I have prayed over it for many hours, and I think it best for all involved. While Silvana walked this earth, she determined that Mary couldn't find a husband until Blanche was wed—and she delighted in seeing Blanche's triumphs. As a consequence, neither of my nieces has moved on with her life. Now things have changed, and I am even more confident I have done what's best for all concerned."

"How can you say that? You've impoverished us! First our mother dies and then you cut us out of your will!" said Blanche.

"Niece, you did not listen carefully. I said that I was leaving 'the bulk' of my earthly riches to young Evans. There remains money set aside as a dowry for you and your sister. I will also support you for one more Season, but that is it. This cruel charade must end. You have rejected many wonderful men with sterling qualities, and in my heart of hearts, I do not believe you do so because you care about love. You do so because you are caught up in being the belle of the ball, and that must stop. Now."

Lady Grainger sat with her hands folded loosely and regarded her niece. There was no malice in her eyes, only regret. "I have long thought that you were on the wrong path. You trifled with the affections of the men who have shown interest, because you enjoyed the thrill of the game, just like you enjoy a good hunt. Your mother supported you in this. Had she stopped such foolishness early on, you would have been happily married."

"Happily married? My mother sat alone at Ingram Park while my father had dalliances. That's not what I would call a happy marriage. Perhaps you think it so, but then—" Wisely, Blanche stopped. But not before I finally understood my adversary's motives: To her, marriage was a jail term, not an invitation to a more fulfilling life. Suddenly, I felt sorry for Blanche. As time worked against her, she struggled harder and harder to escape a future devoid of happiness. At least, that was her prediction for the years ahead. That she could be wrong never occurred to her. She was far too busy fleeing her presumed fate than examining it closely and weighing its accuracy.

Blanche was still sputtering. "But how can you leave your

estate to the bastard son of a man who's not even a blood relative? You can't do that! What about our father? We are your brother's rightful heirs!"

"Your father died without tuppence to his name. All he had left was his title and the deed to your home. If you'll recall, the bulk of my fortune is from my husband's family. Since the Graingers are not your blood kin, you have no legal claim to it. Please remember that out of the goodness of my heart, and because of my love for my late brother, I have propped up you and your mother and brother for years. Several times I have handed over money to erase gambling debts that your brother incurred. However, as of today, that comes to an end."

Mary sniffled into the damask cloth that she held to her mouth. "I miss Mama . . ."

"Oh, hush," said Blanche. "I miss her, too. If she were here, you would never dare to do this, Aunt Olivia!" Any semblance of good manners had flown out the window. Blanche spoke with all the brash intonations of a common fishwife. Her aunt's pronouncement thwarted all of Blanche's ambitions, and the girl was not about to give up on her hopes and dreams. Not yet.

"That is another reason that I must do as I have said. I can no longer countenance your behavior, girls. You have been unceasingly rude. You have taken liberties."

"Liberties?" Blanche looked askance. "Whatever are you talking about?"

"You came into my home and ordered around my staff. In fact, your mother even slapped Dorsey."

"But that was our mother! I didn't touch your servant!"

"No, but you have bullied them and brought them to tears with your accusations and demands. Somewhere along the way you and your mother forgot that this is my home. All three of you seemed to have misunderstood that you stay here by my grace and favor. Let me offer a simple example: Mary hacked away at my flowers. Without my permission. Without a word to me. And you both know how much I cherish my flowers. You see? You have made it clear to me that I am nothing more to you than a purse of coins. And that must stop," said Lady Grainger. "Without gratitude, you have nothing, because everything will never be enough."

Olivia Grainger's words of wisdom were lost on her nieces. Blanche fumed, her pretty face turning redder by the minute. Mary simply continued crying and repeating, "I want my mother."

My discomfort grew, as did Lucy's. My friend stared at her empty teacup, while she drummed her fingers on the arm of her chair. This habit, I had noticed, was a way of coping when she was upset.

"This is all your fault, Mary." Blanche spat the words out. "You had to go out there and putter around, didn't you? Cutting flowers and messing about in the kitchen. As if you knew what you were doing."

Without waiting for Mary's response, Blanche turned her attention to Lady Grainger. "Dear, dear Aunt! I am so sorry for what my sister has done. I promise you it will never, ever happen again. You can depend on it. I shall watch her like a hawk. But please, think carefully before you cut us off. At the end of the day, we are family, and blood is thicker than water."

"Your actions do not support your words," said Lady Grainger. "I've heard enough for one morning."

I realized that not once during this entire meeting had either girl shown any compassion for Lady Grainger. Not only had our hostess lost her sister-in-law, but she had suffered this tragedy in the confines of her home—and she had lost her beloved companion, Mags, as well.

Taking this opportunity to effect our exit, my friend said, "Olivia, there was a purpose to our visit. We were wondering how we could help. I am sure you have cards that need to be written. Jane and I would be happy to do that for you. Then you can sign them and send them on."

"That would be incredibly helpful," said Lady Grainger, as she rose from the tea table. Leaving the Ingram sisters behind, Lucy and I followed our hostess to her library. Once she'd given us a sample of the message she wanted to send and a stack of black-bordered cards and envelopes, Lucy and I were ready to return to #24 Grosvenor. My friend hugged the elderly woman, and I again offered my condolences for her losses.

"Thank you both for coming," said Lady Grainger. "Now I think I shall go back to my room and lie down. I've found this whole ordeal incredibly tiring."

Lucy and I were almost out the front door when Blanche pushed Stanton aside and blocked our way.

"You," she said, jabbing a finger at Lucy, "took full advantage of an old woman's friendship."

"You know that's not true," said Lucy. "Now, please, step aside."

The memory of Lucy's swift punch in the stomach must have given Blanche pause. Although she hesitated, she did move out of our way. "Oh ho! It becomes clear. This is all up to you, isn't it? This was your plan from the start, wasn't it? You are nothing more than a common murderer. You killed our mother—and I shall see you hang for it!"

Chapter 41

My much-subdued friend and I trudged along the pavement back to her home. A light rain had begun, and as we walked, others flagged down hackney carriages so that they could find shelter. But the rain was more of a mist than a downpour, and I found it oddly refreshing, as if it washed away some vestige of Blanche Ingram.

Upon reflection, I had no idea how Blanche might accomplish such a dire conclusion as a hanging, because I knew that there was no way to link Lucy to Lady Ingram's death. Still, I had seen firsthand how much damage a mere snub could cause. How much more would Lucy suffer for an unjust accusation?

I imagined it would create great harm. Especially if Blanche put any effort into it, which she undoubtedly would. Her grievance against Lucy was fresh, and while nothing could change history and erase my marriage to Edward, Blanche *could* potentially force Lady Grainger to change her mind about her will. This prize was both attainable and worthy of effort.

When we arrived home, Lucy tracked down Rags and then

went to her room with a sick headache, forgoing her noontime meal. Ned was napping, so I had a quick lunch during which Adèle and I conversed for a while in French. We talked about the paper dolls, the weather, and the story of St. Jerome from *A Child's Book of Martyrs*. The idea of being skinned alive had appealed to Adèle's innate sense of drama, and I regretted having selected it. However, she had been a good girl and read the entire piece, even though certain English words represented challenges to her vocabulary. There ensued a lively discussion, one that I could have avoided with a more judicial choice of reading matter.

After allowing Adèle to prance around in my feathered headpiece as a reward for her good effort, I left her to play with her paper dolls.

My children were fine, my husband was healing (or so I hoped), but my friend was at risk. Inside me there arose a restless feeling such as happens before a thunderstorm. I could not help but stop and peer out the window on my way downstairs from the nursery. The young conkers on the chestnut tree were hidden by pentagon-shaped leaves that had turned over, a sure sign bad weather was to come. I didn't doubt it. I could feel the storm gathering, although I could not see it. The hairs on my arms bristled with electricity.

I found my husband and Bruce Douglas sitting in the library, huddled over the day's newspapers. "You are home earlier than I supposed. What is the latest?" I asked Edward after planting a kiss on his cheek. A bit of road dust smudged his forehead, but I quickly cleaned it off with my handkerchief. Both men wore the coating of soot so common to anyone who spent time out of doors in the city, especially when the trip involved travel in the crowded streets and shopping stalls.

"I ordered a new pair of boots, Hessian style with white cuffs, because my friend here tells me they are all the rage. They and my old ones will be ready next week."

"That is good news, but I was actually wondering what Mr. Waverly had to say."

"We have been fortunate," my husband said. "Waverly is a friend to us, indeed. Although someone leaked word that there are questions surrounding Lady Ingram's death, Waverly has refused to confirm that he has opened a murder investigation. So at least we don't have the newspapers to deal with. Not yet."

"Oh!" I had forgotten all about the papers and their ongoing desire to print anything remotely salacious or inflammatory. This added a new and troubling dimension to Lady Ingram's death—and Blanche Ingram's threatened accusations.

Mr. Douglas added, "Waverly has confirmed that the woman had long-standing heart problems. I believe the receipt of Lady Ingram's obituary sparked an interest—and then the tittle-tattle that followed whetted the newshounds' appetites."

"Who would have talked to the papers? I can't believe that anyone from Lady Grainger's staff would. They are devoted to her," I said as I took my accustomed place on the hassock near Edward's feet.

"I would surmise that one of the undertaker's men has been paid to keep his eyes open. Would that make sense?"

I remembered that Mr. Lerner had stayed with Lady Ingram's body, and that during that time, he had procured the leftover coffee. A sharp observer might have put two and two together. Mr. Douglas straightened and rubbed the back of his neck. "The question is, how long will Waverly be able to hold them off? Especially once the magistrate reads Lerner's report?"

"Meanwhile," said Edward as he tamped the medicinal herbs down in his pipe, "I told Waverly that I had offered young Lerner a job, and that I personally vouched for the man's character. While the constable did not credit Mary Ingram's rambling accusation with much reliability, it was troubling to him. My faith in the young man's character gave Waverly yet another reason to disregard her nonsense."

I told them about our visit with Lady Grainger and shared the news about the change in the woman's will. The men were surprised by the woman's generosity, although Mr. Douglas said, "Lucy has been wonderful to the Dowager Lady Grainger. My sister has the knack of nurturing friends, just as some people are good with their gardens."

I finished my narrative by describing how Blanche had threatened Lucy.

"Blast," muttered Edward.

"Good Lord," said Mr. Douglas. "That woman will stop at nothing! I've never heard of a person so greedy. Blanche Ingram would destroy Lucy's reputation and endanger my sister's life to get her hands on Lady Grainger's fortune? That's unconscionable!"

"It's more than the money to Blanche. It's the end of her life as she knows it." I explained what Blanche had said about her mother being held captive by the late Lord Ingram.

"I had never thought of it that way," said Edward, "but now that you explain it, I can see why that would be an unhappy fate."

I shrugged. "Most marriages do not enjoy the sort of compatibility ours does. But even still, Lady Ingram could have taken matters into her own hands. She could have done charity work, or read books, or pursued other arts, or visited with neighbors. Anyway, all that is in the past. We must deal with what lies ahead, and I know of nothing that Lucy can do to save herself from Blanche's fury."

"Is it possible that Miss Ingram killed her own mother?" Mr. Douglas wondered. "What if Lady Grainger told Lady Ingram how unhappy she was about paying for endless balls and parties? And then Lady Ingram had a talk with Blanche, telling her that she must find a husband and give up her gay life?"

"So you are suggesting that Blanche murdered her mother, not realizing that the directive to get married came from her aunt?" I concluded.

That required conjecture, and as I applied my thoughts to the problem, I decided it was possible but unlikely. "Blanche Ingram's mother was her foil. Lady Ingram reflected her daughter's glory, the way a magnifying glass amplifies an image for the viewer. I doubt that the Dowager would have dampened down her daughter's enthusiasm for such a desultory life. Besides, Blanche also drank the coffee. Why would she drink a beverage to which she had added poison?"

"Then who did it? Her sister?" asked Mr. Douglas.

"Mary was brokenhearted," I said. "As much as Blanche was uncaring, Mary evidences the very heart and soul of grief. I cannot believe she would hurt her own mother."

"Whom does that leave us with? The staff?" asked Edward. "Lady Conyngham? Lady Grainger?"

"Or Mr. Lerner," I said. "Mary has accused him. She seems to know him better than any of us. Perhaps we've been too quick to dismiss her claims."

Chapter 42

The gentlemen turned their attention to news of the day, while I worked on my pen and ink for Evans. Thus the time passed pleasurably until Higgins announced that our tea was served, and we all proceeded into the dining room.

"Well, you shall have your chance to know Mr. Lerner better," said Edward, "because I have invited him and Mr. Carter here to discuss particulars of the young doctor's employment."

"Mr. Carter is in town?"

"He sent word this afternoon. This is one of his regular visits to London, I take it."

Polly conveyed the message that Lucy's head was still bothering her. "Changing weather, I s'pect. It hits her hard," she said. So we went on and supped without her. The day had wearied me, and I allowed the men to take the lead by discussing a boxing match to be held in Hungerford. Although organized fisticuffs had been illegal for seven decades, they still drew crowds. When I asked what kept the constables away—since a large gathering might surely be a tip-off that there was some mischief afoot—both men laughed.

"Members of the gentry pay constables to stay clear," said Mr. Douglas. "And the bouts are held on private land."

"Peers are willing to bribe the law? But why? Who would want ruffians from all over to congregate on their property?" I wondered. "It seems like they are taking a huge risk."

"They are, but the reward is worth it," said Edward.

"Many lords of the realm sponsor the boxers, owning and promoting them just as they might own a racehorse," explained Mr. Douglas.

"But we're talking about human beings!" I protested.

"Yes, and men have owned other men for centuries. That's how the pyramids were built," Edward reminded me.

It was gone eight when Mr. Lerner and Mr. Carter arrived. Mr. Douglas instructed Higgins to bring the men into the library, since Lucy's large desk could be used for note taking if necessary. After our visitors had said their hellos, the ever-efficient butler offered to relieve the young doctor of his satchel. Once again, I noticed how the papers threatened to spill out of it. This time, a glance told me the reason why: The latch was broken.

"No, thank you," said Lerner, holding the leather bag as if it were his most precious possession. "I keep all my important notes in it," he explained. Although his method did not inspire confidence, Higgins took the man at his word.

"Higgins, can you scare up a bottle of brandy? Perhaps some port for my wife?" asked Edward.

I excused myself long enough to check on Ned and Adèle as they prepared for bed. Ned wanted to cling to me, a new habit of late, but I gently transferred him to Amelia's welcome arms. Adèle stumbled over a few words as she read a portion from the Bible in English, but I praised her effort anyway and tucked her in. I looked in on Lucy, as well, and found her sound asleep with Rags curled in the crook of her legs.

In the library, Higgins poured brandy for the men, and a small glass of port for me, as Mr. Lerner watched Edward pack the medicinal herb in his pipe.

I thought back to Lady Grainger and her kindness toward the seamstress. There was a lesson there that I could happily absorb. "Mr. Carter and Mr. Lerner? Have you had your tea?"

"Yes, thank you, Mrs. Rochester," said Mr. Carter. "I ate at a pub near the inn where I'm staying."

But Lerner was slower to answer. "Um, no. No, ma'am. I usually only eat but once a day."

I did not press him for the reason why. His clothing showed signs of excessive wear. When he crossed his legs, I saw the soles of his boots were worn through. Excusing myself, I went downstairs to the kitchen and asked Cook if she might prepare a tray with a selection of sliced meats, leftover aspic, cheeses, and fresh bread.

Back in the library, Mr. Douglas was querying Mr. Lerner about his method for proving that Lady Ingram's coffee cup had held poison. His questions were interrupted by a knocking on the door. In short order, Higgins returned with a highly agitated Mr. Waverly.

"So, Lerner, you ran here to hide. Well, I have a bone to pick with you. Tried to pull the wool over my eyes," he said, yanking at his waistcoat.

Mr. Carter puckered his brow. "This young man did nothing of the sort. I've been with him all day, and we are here to keep a standing appointment with Squire Rochester."

"Mr. Waverly? May I introduce you to my doctor and long-time friend, Mr. Carter?" Edward said. "Carter, this is the man from Bow Street whom we all admire so much."

My husband's compliment flummoxed Mr. Waverly, as it is terribly hard to maintain ruffled feathers when one is being praised.

Sadie carried in the tray. I watched Mr. Waverly's eyes follow the food. So did the parlor maid, who set down the repast and then whispered to me, "I'll bring more right up."

"Have a seat, Mr. Waverly, your charges can wait a moment," said Edward. "Help yourself to the food."

"Brandy?" asked Mr. Douglas, offering a glass to the man from Bow Street. Mr. Carter passed the decanter to Lucy's brother.

"I, er . . ." Mr. Waverly seemed flummoxed as he stared at the liquid. At last, he answered, "No, thank you, but I would be grateful for even a thimbleful of that whiskey. The one we had the other night?"

"Of course." Mr. Douglas rang Higgins and asked that a bottle of the spirits be brought up from the cellar. "Now, you were in the midst of calling Mr. Lerner and Mr. Rochester 'two of a kind,' I believe. Care to pick up where you left off?"

At last Mr. Waverly slumped down into a chair. His glasses rested crookedly on his face, and his boots—always polished to a fine shine—were scuffed and dull. "In all of your visits to me, neither of you happened to mention this group that Mr. Lerner's a member of. Completely slipped your minds, didn't it? So then Miss Mary Ingram stomps into the magistrate's office—apparently, she wasn't satisfied with our response to her last visit, since I didn't arrest the doctor, so she went on and on rehashing her accusations about Mr. Lerner and his character, saying how he poisoned her mother and I'm caught completely off-balance. My supervisor had a go at me. He cuffed my ears. Well, verbally at least."

I thought to myself, *Of course she's striking out. Blanche now blames Mary for the loss of their fortune! And without their mother to intercede, Mary is on the receiving end of all of Blanche's fury!*

Edward looked amused. "You mean you didn't realize Mr. Lerner was a Jew?"

But a quick glance at Mr. Lerner affirmed that he was not laughing. No, he was terrified. The blood was draining slowly from his face. As I watched, he looked over at Mr. Carter, and the older doctor turned pale, too. I thought this a curious reaction, indeed.

"You know very well what I'm talking about, Mr. Rochester. You've got my head in a vice, and I'm not happy about it.

I trusted you when you vouched for this man's character. Now Miss Mary has made it clear that she has no compunctions about taking this up with the bishop. None. She's more than willing to keep talking to anyone who might listen."

"The bishop?" Mr. Douglas leaned forward in his chair, so that his elbows were on his knees. "Because Rochester is hiring a Jew, she thinks the bishop will interfere? Hasn't he got better things to do, such as memorize his portion for the coronation?"

Again, I looked quickly at the two doctors. Both wore a sheen of perspiration on their foreheads. Mr. Lerner sat with shoulders stooped and his head bowed, while his older mentor emptied the contents of his glass.

"Tell him, Lerner," said Mr. Carter.

What on earth was this all about?

"It's true," said Lerner. "I don't know how she found me out, but it's true. I am a Lunartick."

Chapter 43

"A lunatic, you say?" Edward looked as confused as I felt.

"A Lunartick. I am a member of a scientific community called the Lunar Society that meets once a month during a full moon, hence our name from the Latin word 'luna.' The timing of our meetings became important because early members gathered in Birmingham, and on the road to the meetings they found themselves set upon by highwaymen who stole their purses. When traveling by the light of a full moon, such misadventures were less likely to happen."

"A sensible precaution, but still . . ." mused Mr. Waverly.

"And you keep this a secret because your members fear being robbed?" Edward rubbed his jaw thoughtfully as he tried to make sense of this.

"No, Mr. Rochester. It's more complicated than that," said Mr. Lerner with a sigh.

"The Lunar Society began in 1765 when a group of like-minded individuals gathered to discuss ideas. Over the years, the membership has grown. On occasion, it has also shrunk when arguments occurred and men disagreed about fundamental principles or methods. But the meetings have long offered a time and place for men of science to put forth, discuss, and defend their ideas."

"Why would the members want to hide that?" I wondered.

A surprised Mr. Carter turned and stared at me.

"There are those in the Church of England who think science is blasphemous," explained Mr. Lerner. "They see it as a wrongheaded attempt to question what should be accepted on faith. In the past, members of the clergy have threatened to have Lunarticks rounded up and burned as heretics. As a matter of prudence, it was decided that we should continue our discussions in secrecy. Regrettably, to some, any attempt to understand the secrets of the Universe is an affront to our Creator. Rather than rely on scientific advancement, they counsel that all of men's woes can be solved with prayer."

"Considering the level of risk you are describing, you must value this group very highly. Otherwise, it might be more expedient not to belong," said my husband.

"I do value it," said Lerner. "That is why I agreed to serve as the recording secretary. I have learned a great deal, most importantly, how to think critically so I can make good decisions. As members, we seek to further our knowledge by sharing what we learn in our areas of specialty. For example, one of our number is working on a way to capture light on paper to make a permanent image. Two members are working together to make steam-powered engines even more efficient."

"But why do these engineering advances interest a man of medicine, such as yourself?" Edward mused. I could see that this captured my husband's imagination, but as he is a very practical man, he also wondered what benefits were accrued.

"Oh, there are many applications! Others are also involved in the field of health, and one of our colleagues has since catalogued many helpful plants with curative powers. Another is working on an instrument that can increase magnification hundreds of times. He theorizes that tiny organisms invade open wounds and cause sickness." Mr. Lerner talked faster and faster as he became more excited about these ideas. His energy was contagious.

"Did you learn about the efficacy of rose hips from your friends in this society?" I asked.

"No, that I learned from Miss Goldstein. Her father was also a doctor, and he shared much of his hard-won knowledge with her. She is exceptional. She speaks seven languages: English, of course, but also Hebrew, Greek, Latin, Italian, French, and German. Her knowledge of botany, mathematics, and healing would be put to good use with your tenants."

"But you did not tell me all of this," said Mr. Waverly. His voice quivered with indignation. "As a result, I could not defend you properly. Miss Mary pleaded with the magistrate for us to lock you up. She suggested your religion drove you to want to harm good Christians."

"Rubbish," said Mr. Carter. "She knows better."

"Is that why you are here, Mr. Waverly? To arrest Mr. Lerner?" I was happy for Mr. Carter's loyalty, but still worried about the reason for Mr. Waverly's visit.

"If I were going to arrest Mr. Lerner, I would not have wasted time explaining myself," said Mr. Waverly. "No, I came to satisfy myself that I had not been hoodwinked. I do not like to play the part of the fool!"

I found myself marveling at Mary Ingram's tenacity—and her boldness. Earlier this morning, I had felt sorry for her, thinking how forlorn she looked. I would never have guessed that she could have gathered herself up and visited the Bow Street Runners.

She must have hailed a hackney, as she had threatened to do when in Hyde Park with Mr. Lerner, and traveled to Bow Street all alone. Undeterred by her grief, she had found the strength to complain about her errant suitor. And to what end? Did she truly think she could change his mind?

No, she had wanted to punish him.

It struck me as terribly sad that this young woman could

be so vengeful that she would want to strike back and harm the man she professed to love, simply because he did not love her in return. How on earth had both of Lady Ingram's daughters come to believe that self-interest should trump all other concerns?

Mr. Carter shook his head slowly. "I believe I can prevent Miss Mary from taking her concerns to the bishop."

We all stared at him expectantly. Finally, Mr. Douglas said, "You have a suggestion for countering Miss Ingram's charges?"

"Not a suggestion. A revelation. I, too, am a member of the Lunar Society. If Mary Ingram insists on persecuting us, the entire county will be without a doctor."

Both Mr. Douglas and my husband raised their eyebrows at this admission. Waverly shook his head and huffed softly, as if to say, "More lives ruined."

However, I realized the courage it had taken for Mr. Carter to admit this, and the resilience that Mr. Lerner had shown in not betraying his friend. But before I could congratulate either of them, my husband said, "And you believe this will dissuade her? Because so far neither Mary nor her sister has proven herself amenable to reason."

"Yes," said Mr. Carter. "I know my admission will. You see, Lord Ingram stays at home for many reasons, not the least of which is that he has a hemorrhagic disposition, meaning that he bleeds easily, at the slightest blow or injury. It is a condition both extremely painful and dangerous. I am called to Ingram Park frequently to care for him. Have done for years. I shall leave here directly and point out to Miss Mary that if she continues with this folly, there will be no one available to help her beloved brother when he is suffering," he said. "Now, since I have another visit to make yet tonight, shall we discuss the particulars of Mr. Lerner's employment?"

Chapter 44

The next day was Sunday, and all of us, except the servants, slept late. After checking on the children, I went downstairs for breakfast where I found my hostess staring at a note.

"Lucy?" I went to her side.

She sighed and began to rip the letter into shreds. "A street urchin brought this. From Blanche Ingram."

"What did the letter say?"

"She suggested that I speak to Lady Grainger and convince my friend to address this grievous error in her will." Lucy went to the hearth and fed the paper to the coals.

"Is that all?" I measured loose tea into the pot.

"Not entirely." My friend took her seat at the head of the table. "Care for butter? My! Those crumpets smell wonderful! Oh, and the candied ginger scones are still warm."

"While I share your desire for a pleasant morning, it will do you no good to keep this a secret. I believe I'm in too deep to ignore the repercussions of any threats lobbed by Miss Ingram."

Lucy set down the tea caddy. She did not look at me when she said, "You are too intelligent for me to trick, and strong enough that I need not struggle to protect you. Blanche Ingram was not specific. She concluded with a vague 'you'll be sorry.' "

"How unoriginal."

"It was her postscript that causes me to feel . . . cautious." Lucy's thumb traced the gold rim of her saucer. "Her addendum states that if I am unwilling or unable to convince Lady Grainger to make a change in her will, I shall bring disaster raining down on all those who know and love me." She lifted her damask serviette and dabbed away a tear. "Oh, Jane. This should be a happy time in my life. I am so looking forward to Evans's arrival. Why does this have to happen now?"

"Because a calamity has struck the Ingrams," I said reasonably. "They have lost their past and their future all at once. Neither can run to her mother for solace. Neither woman can attend the coronation parties. Neither can count on an enticing dowry. Consequently, they must have someone to strike back at. It has not—and will never—occur to them to make the best of things. They have had no guidance in the art of resilience. So they will continue to strike out blindly until . . ."

"Until what?" asked Lucy. Her pretty blue eyes were now a misty shade of gray blue.

"Until they either achieve satisfaction or destroy themselves in the process."

Edward's appearance caused a change of subject. By unspoken accord, neither Lucy nor I mentioned the latest volley in our ongoing feud with the Ingram sisters.

"Mr. Douglas and I ventured out to collect the day's newspapers," said Edward, as he and Lucy's brother joined us. "What a glorious day this looks to be! The spring breezes are delightful."

His enthusiasm was infectious.

"Let's go for a carriage ride in Hyde Park," said Lucy. "All of us—the children, too. I'll instruct Cook to make up a picnic basket. All the ton will be out today, since it's sure to be one of the last fine days before hot weather sets in." Lucy told me in an aside how once the weather warmed, we would be forced to stay inside to avoid the smell of horse urine, horse droppings, human refuse, and garbage. Imagining all that, I found myself longing for Ferndean again, with its clean, fresh smell of wild honeysuckle on the vine.

Upon hearing our plans, Adèle hopped up and down, exclaiming, *"Moi aussi? S'il vous plaît? J'aime bien un pique-nique!"*

Lucy laughed. "You, too, little poppet."

A short time later, Polly selected for me a brightly patterned green muslin dress with a matching green spencer jacket. From Lucy's vast selection of bonnets, the lady's maid had discovered one of cream and green that matched my clothes splendidly. Adèle was determined not to be outdone, and she'd cajoled Amelia into letting her wear her finest party frock. Ned realized something wonderful was about to happen, but he couldn't tell what, so his dark eyes followed our every move until at last he, too, was in the carriage.

I thought an outing would do all of us good. I couldn't imagine how we could avert the catastrophe promised by Blanche Ingram. I wondered if Lucy considered asking Lady Grainger to amend her will, but my question would have to wait for later.

Lucy had been correct: Hyde Park was a veritable beehive of activity. Carriages of all shapes, colors, and sizes paraded around up and down Rotten Row, showing off for one another. There were phaetons, broughams, tilburies, and britzkas. Because the weather was mild, many paraded with their tops neatly folded down, and eventually Lucy acceded to Adèle's request to lower our roof as well.

There had been a shower overnight, and for the most part, the air was clear. Of course, other park-goers stared at us, and we stared at them, but that was the sport of it. Adèle kept up a running commentary, judging the apparel of all the ladies we passed. Her fashion sense was undeveloped, so Lucy happily offered guidance.

Along the way, we encountered several persons whom Lucy knew and one gentleman who was a member of the same club as Mr. Douglas. We climbed out, found a quiet spot under a tree near the Serpentine, and waited as Williams spread a blanket for us to sit on. Lucy and I handed out ham and Stilton cheese sandwiches on sliced bread slathered with butter. Cook had wrapped these in oil paper and thoughtfully included pickled cucumbers and eggs. Mr. Douglas uncorked a bottle of wine for us.

"I shall miss all this." Lucy spoke in a dreamy voice.

"Whatever do you mean?" I asked.

"If Blanche succeeds in blackening my reputation, I shall be driven out of London. No decent person will speak to me." With a brave smile, she added, "Here I'd thought I'd be able to offer so much to Evans, but instead he and I will have to run away. Isn't that ironic? Worse luck, there's nothing I can do about it."

"Lucy," said her brother sharply. "You don't know that. You are borrowing trouble. Perhaps Blanche will think better of it. Or she'll launch her war of accusations and no one will believe her. Besides, so what if the ton no longer invites you to tea? You're worth ten thousand of them."

Lucy laughed. "That's easy for you to say. Bad behavior may be overlooked in men, but it is deadly for women."

"So come back with us to Ferndean. Edward will build a wing for you onto Thornfield Hall," I said. "Won't you?"

"Of course I shall," he said. "Lucy, you are giving in too easily."

She sighed. "No, I am not. I am merely planning ahead. I had also thought that we might go live with Augie in India. That way Evans could grow up with his father."

That idea, of course, did have merit. But before I could give it more thought, a woman came running over the hill. "Hallo! Lucy Brayton? Is that you?"

The newcomer was nearly as tall as Edward, and her build was as robust as a man's, but as she came closer, I saw one of the sweetest countenances I'd ever encountered, framed in tight curls.

"Maria? Is that you?" Lucy stood to greet her friend. The two embraced.

Over the same hill came a second woman, a younger version of the first. As her skirts flew up, it was impossible to ignore her finely shaped calves.

"Minney? How you've grown!" Lucy let go of the older woman and embraced the younger one. "Come! I have to introduce you to my friends."

Turning to us, my friend said, "Allow me to present you Maria Fitzherbert and her daughter, Mary Georgiana Emma Seymour."

"Call me Minney," said the young woman.

So this was the King's true wife and his much-loved daughter, I thought.

Introductions were made all around, and for some time there was nothing but the most banal of conversations about the weather, the park, and, of course, Adèle's talents, since she insisted on singing a hymn—"Onward, Christian Soldiers"—that Edward had recently taught her. Both women admired Ned and asked for turns holding him. Maria asked Lucy about Evans, and Minney claimed that her mother had crocheted an adorable blanket for the child.

By the time we said our good-byes, I was thoroughly charmed. Both Maria and Minney proved themselves to be wholly original women, without artifice, and delightful companions. I could see why George IV had fallen in love with Mrs. Fitzherbert, and why he would care enough about both women to want to protect them.

Moreover, I could also better understand why Lucy refused my offer to give the letter to Lady Conyngham. These two charming women would bear the brunt of any repercussion that followed—and they deserved better. As I watched Mrs. Fitzherbert smile at her daughter, I made a vow that neither would come to harm by my actions.

It was a vow that would prove hard to keep.

Chapter 45

Later that evening at Lucy's house, Edward dictated to me two letters, one to Mrs. Fairfax at Ferndean inquiring again about John's recovery and one to Augie telling him about Blanche's threat.

"I am not sure it will do more than make him feel helpless," Edward said about the latter as I guided his hand to the spot where he could put his signature. "But if I were he, I'd want to know what my wife was facing."

I agreed. "Do you really think she'd go to India? Would that be so bad for her?"

Edward considered my question carefully. "I don't know. I can't answer that. I haven't visited the country."

We climbed into bed and I took solace in my husband's arms. The thought of a forced separation seemed inhumane to me, and I told him so.

"That is the prerogative of the King, to move us all around like chess pieces on a board."

"But we are not his possessions! We have our own wills, our own dreams and desires!"

"As long as men have minds, they will want to determine their own destinies," Edward said as he kissed me. "They will also want the freedom to marry whom they choose. That, dear heart, is a right our sovereign does not enjoy. Nor do most of his citizens."

After Edward fell to sleep, I clambered out of bed and sat looking out the window at the twinkling lights of candles and torchères all over the city of London. I imagined that each light represented one soul. How could it be that an accident of birth gave one man the power to make such important decisions for all of us?

The next morning, while Ned was still sleeping and Adèle was eating porridge with Amelia, Edward and I were at breakfast when Higgins announced that Mr. Waverly had arrived.

Edward raised an eyebrow to me by way of wondering why the man had again joined us, and I murmured, "I don't know."

"If you are looking for Mrs. Brayton, she isn't up yet. You are making quite the habit of visiting us," I said. "We've become a regular stop on your daily rounds. Tell us, what have we done now to warrant such interest?"

"Could I trouble you first for a cup of tea?" One side of his waistcoat hung lower than the other, as the result of being wrongly buttoned. The lapels of his jacket were dusty, and he needed a fresh shave. The past few days had taken their toll on Mr. Waverly.

"Of course." I poured for him. "Please help yourself to the rashers and eggs. I'm sure Mrs. Brayton won't mind."

"I will at that."

We ate in expectant silence. When Mr. Waverly finished most of his food, he said, "I am not a fool."

Of course, we had no idea how to respond. Neither of us thought of him that way. In fact, we'd come to appreciate the man and his unending desire to uncover the truth.

"Mr. Waverly," Edward said, "rest assured that my wife and I have only the highest opinion of your talents. Furthermore, Mr. Douglas told us early on that you were the best of your lot. And we all know the Bow Street Runners to be courageous as well as intelligent. If you think we have overlooked the fact that you have a good head on your shoulders, you are sadly mistaken."

Mr. Waverly sagged in his chair. "I resent being ordered to carry out ridiculous orders simply because a young woman has convinced my superior that she is right and I am wrong."

"Mary Ingram again?" I asked with exasperation. "Will she not put this fantasy of hers to rest? Why does she refuse to leave Mr. Lerner alone? Did Mr. Carter's intervention mean nothing to her?"

"Not Miss Mary," said Mr. Waverly. "Her sister, Miss Blanche Ingram. She has now changed her story and determined that it was Mr. Rochester who poisoned her mother."

"Ho!" Edward coughed. "It's a bit early in the day for such joking around." My husband peered at Mr. Waverly, straining to discern the other man's expression. "Come now, Waverly. Such antics are beyond the bounds of good taste."

"I couldn't agree more, sir, but there it is. She swears up one side and down the other that you poisoned Lady Ingram."

"This grows entirely too tedious," I said through gritted teeth. "Pray tell me, how could my husband have accomplished such a dastardly deed? What access did he have to poison? How could he have killed her when they weren't even in the same room?"

Waverly shook his head. "I have no idea, but the Honorable Blanche Ingram has convinced the magistrate that all of this is not only possible but likely. She says that she was drinking coffee when Mr. Rochester arrived earlier that morning to beg her forgiveness. She wrote in a statement that she was briefly alone with him because her mother and sister tarried. According to Miss Ingram, Mr. Rochester must have added the poison to the tin of coffee sitting on the tray when she got up to see her sister."

"The woman talks nonsense," I said. "At this rate, they shall next blame me."

Edward put his hand over mine. "Except that they know that by blaming Lucy and me, they are causing you to suffer greatly. My dear wife, it is abundantly clear that you fear nothing—except harm that comes to those you love."

In truth, though, Edward was right—and I was frightened. This continuing persecution by the Ingram sisters had begun to wear me down. I had been concerned when they blamed Lucy, but I knew their accusation was impossible. I had been there, I had watched the proceedings, and, if necessary, I could proclaim my friend's innocence. Besides, it had been early days back then. I thought that the Ingrams would retreat as time went on and their malicious ideas gained no traction. Instead, they kept launching salvo after salvo. This new claim shocked me to my core. I fought the urge to retch as I imagined Edward, crippled and almost blind, being arrested and taken to Newgate. How would he survive among thugs and killers?

He would not have a chance.

"If that was how it was done, why didn't the coffee have a deleterious effect on Miss Ingram?" Edward seemed outwardly calm, but I knew him well enough to know he was livid.

"That's the point. She says it did. She states—and others can confirm—that she was taken ill after Mr. Rochester's visit. That had she not purged herself of the poison, she, too, would have died."

"When Lucy and I visited, shortly after Edward and Mr. Douglas left, Lady Grainger told us that Miss Ingram had been under the weather. It certainly did not sound like a recent bout. It sounded as though she had been unwell for some time. In fact, when we saw her at the opera, her color was unusually pale," I said.

"Look," Mr. Waverly began in a peevish tone, "I am here, presenting this to you, because I hope one of us can answer this charge. I know it to be unfounded. All of this nonsense keeps me from finding Lady Ingram's real killer."

I understood the selfish purpose behind Blanche Ingram's bold falsehood. The Honorable Blanche Ingram thought that by accusing Edward of this crime, she could put pressure on Lucy to force Lady Grainger to readjust her will.

"The answer is simple. Go fetch Mr. Parmenter. He'll inform your supervisor that Edward's eyesight is so impaired that such a move, an action requiring a great deal of finesse, would have been impossible," I said.

"Better yet," suggested Edward, "I shall accompany you to speak to the magistrate. When I stumble into his office, trip over his furniture, and plant my face in his carpet, he will see the light!"

Chapter 46

Luckily for us, Mr. Douglas sauntered into the dining room. "What ho! Look at all these gloomy faces. And here I came to brag about my winnings at the card table last night."

I poured his tea while Edward and Mr. Waverly filled the man in on Miss Ingram's latest antics.

"Silly chit. People had already begun to talk about her becoming a spinster. If word gets out of these scurrilous remarks, she'll be a laughingstock," Mr. Douglas said as he helped himself to the last of the bacon, folding it inside a piece of toast and taking a bite.

"We should all hope word doesn't get out. Your sister will suffer, as will your new nephew, just because she has opened her home to us," I said.

Sadie brought in another plate full of sliced ham, a fresh selection of cheeses, and a hot loaf of bread. Mr. Waverly proceeded to eat like a starving man. Mr. Douglas was only a little more moderate in his consumption.

"Look," said Mr. Douglas, "I'm happy to go with you two down to Bow Street. I don't have much influence, but I do have a little."

"Gads, that's right. You helped the Bow Street office during the Cato Street riots, didn't you?" Mr. Waverly now looked much livelier. "Magistrate Birnie is bound to recognize you."

"Yes, indeed, and I can talk to him on Mr. Rochester's behalf. On the way back, I'd like to stop by Hatchards. There's a book by William Blake that I want."

"You sound confident that my husband won't be charged. Are you really so sure?" I tried not to let my worry show. "Perhaps I should come, too, in case I am needed."

"No," said Mr. Waverly, tucking his truncheon under his arm and standing at attention. "I beg you to stay away, Mrs. Rochester. Once Mr. Rochester has shown my superior how ridiculous this matter is, I hope the magistrate will no longer waste my time or his listening to the imprecations of young women with bees in their bonnets. This is nothing more than a distraction, and while I am a party to it, a real killer escapes justice."

My hands knotted into fists as I watched the coach drive off. How I wished I had an opportunity to punch Miss Ingram in the stomach just like Lucy had! As if responding to my thoughts, my friend appeared at the top of the stairs. "I have a horrible headache," she said, as she pinched the bridge of her nose.

"Let's get you a cold cloth and a nice cup of tea. I'll see if Polly has any remedy for your condition."

Once Polly and I had seen to Lucy's comfort, I checked on the children. "Young Master is awful cranky, ma'am," said Amelia. "Those little teeth of his are trying to break through the skin." While she ran downstairs for brandy, I carried my son into Adèle's room. The French girl sat in her chemise in the middle of a circle of dolls. "Adèle! You need to get dressed *tout de suite*," I said, before I further instructed her to read another story of a saint.

"Which one?" she asked.

"You choose." I joggled Ned and tried to distract him from the pain.

Amelia took my son from me. "If the rain holds off, I'll

take the children to the park this afternoon. Maybe we can get Young Master to forget how badly his mouth hurts."

I thought this a good idea and told her so.

A little later, with help from a tisane that Polly brewed, Lucy felt much better. Rags stretched out next to his mistress and licked her hand. "Dear, dear Rags. If the world turns its back on me, you'd still think I hung the moon, wouldn't you?"

"Lucy, I am loath to call you overly dramatic, but you are tipping the scale in that direction. Whatever abuses Blanche Ingram heaps upon you, there will be plenty of us who know how truly wonderful you are. Stop letting her destroy your happiness. In a few days, Evans will be here—and he won't care one iota if you are invited to Almack's or not. Come now. Let's get you up and about."

I told her about Mr. Waverly's visit.

"Oh! I despise that woman more and more each day! I do not know who poisoned her mother, but I think the killer cut down the wrong Ingram!"

I tugged the bellpull for Polly. "Once you are dressed, we can discuss a strategy for dealing with this plague. Boils, locusts, and Ingrams!"

In short order, Lucy came down the stairs looking like her lovely self. We repaired to the drawing room for tea and a planning session. "We could always drop by and see Minney and Maria," said my friend as Higgins appeared with a card on a tray and once again bypassed Lucy. He held it out for me to take. "The courier is waiting for a response, Mrs. Rochester," said Higgins.

Although not a muscle moved in his face, he still seemed somewhat impressed.

The note was of thick ivory stock with a red embossed crown on the flap. I peeled off the wax seal and opened an invitation to visit the King at Carlton House, right away.

I put the card back on the tray and said to Higgins, "Please tell the courier that I have other plans."

Chapter 47

Higgins looked aghast but turned to go.

"Wait!" Lucy stopped her butler. "Jane, have you gone mad? This only *looks* like an invitation. It is in fact a royal summons. You may think you have a choice, but you don't. You must go or risk the King's displeasure."

I had no idea what that might mean, but the tone of her voice caused me to recognize she was deadly serious.

"Don't risk it," she whispered. "You think you are safe because you are blameless, because you are a loyal citizen. But can you say the same for Edward? Can you be so confident that nothing in his past might come back to haunt him?"

"Such as what? His marriage to a madwoman?" I scoffed, certain my husband had withheld no secrets from me.

She sputtered and stomped her foot and finally spat out, "Such as a duel? Did you not ever wonder why his father was so eager to pack up his son and marry him off? Why it was important that Edward marry a woman of vast means and resources? Are you ignorant of the fact that the penalty for dueling is to be hanged to death?"

I sank slowly into a chair, a little stunned by the realization that she was right. "Mrs. Fairfax had told me some of the particulars, but she edited her version quite skillfully." A sick chill started in my fingers and quickly traveled up my arms. Was it possible my husband was at risk? Lucy had suffered from the King's revenge, and now she hoped to spare me similar misery. Her husband might never come home, if His Majesty had his way.

I turned to Higgins. "Please tell the courier that I am delighted to do the King's bidding. I won't be but a moment."

Polly helped me into my claret-colored silk. Lucy oversaw my toilet, suggesting one of her bonnets and a spencer that would look well with my dress. When I was suitably attired, Lucy and I went downstairs to the entry hall where there stood a man in livery, his red jacket covered in an excessive amount of gold braid.

"Really," I said with a smile to him, "this is most unexpected and—"

The young man bowed deeply, a motion causing the multitude of frothy ruffles around his neck to flutter like white butterflies. "A carriage awaits you."

I gave Lucy a quick hug good-bye, and she whispered, "You'll be fine."

"Thank you," I said. "I wish you were coming with me."

She smiled. "I shall go and visit Maria Fitzherbert. I know she'll be happy to see me."

By the time I stepped outside onto the pavement, rain had begun in earnest. The equerry and a footman helped me into the King's carriage, and I tried to brush off the water as we rode through the streets of London at a faster pace than strictly necessary, pulled by a pair of ivory-colored horses. Even if bystanders had not caught a glimpse of the King's new crest, with its addition of the blue garter, they would know the conveyance was his simply by glancing at the matching horses, the Royal Hanoverian Creams. I told myself I should at least enjoy the view as we circled St. James's Park on our way to Carlton House.

We arrived at the hexastyle portico flanked by Corinthian columns. One of the footmen ran up with an umbrella, which he held over my head as I climbed out of the carriage.

Once I was inside the front door, I was greeted curtly by a maid of honour who introduced herself as Lady Pamela Gordon. Although she could not have been more than sixteen, she acted supremely bored. She was here to learn court manners and to make a good marriage, not to think deep thoughts.

I did my utmost to pay attention and observe my new environs, as I thought it highly unlikely that I would ever be invited back. Carlton House was different from most of the finer homes in London in that the visitor entered an enormous foyer on the main floor, rather than climbing up a set of stairs from the area into the living quarters. Lady Pamela escorted me through an octagonal room with a vast winding staircase at one side. From there we proceeded into the main anterooms and turned left.

"Lady Conyngham asked to speak with you first. Then you will be taken to His Majesty." Lady Pamela did not indicate what she thought about this diversion.

Being waylaid should not have surprised me. This was exactly the sort of control that Mr. Waverly had suggested the Marchioness held over the King. We processed into an ornate sitting room, decorated in the French style, using pale silk as a foil to ornately carved woods. An exquisite painting on the wall stopped me.

"Beautiful, isn't it?" Lady Conyngham spoke from an elaborate chair near the window. "It is a Rembrandt."

"It is masterful," I said. I had heard much of Rembrandt's genius, but I had never seen any work of art that matched this in conveying such a sense of intimacy with the subject.

With effort, I tore myself away from the painting and approached Lady Conyngham. I sank into a deep curtsy. This time, she did not offer to embrace me. That fulsome affection she had offered at Lady Grainger's home was nowhere in evidence. As she had been every other time I saw her, Lady Conyngham was opulently dressed in lush fabrics, with deep ruffles of lace surrounding her face and hands, and gros de Naples under the bust of her gown. Jewels hung from her ears and peeped out from her fichu.

"Pamela? Bring us tea."

The Marchioness remained seated in a deeply cushioned chair, and I took the straight-backed chair across from her. The calculated discomfort of my seat was not lost on me, and I marveled again at the Marchioness and her ability to knock others off their game. The maid of honour left, and Lady Conyngham stared at me, hard, letting silence drag on.

Lady Pamela returned, struggling under the weight of a heavy tea tray. The tea set was silver, but the cups and pot were fine porcelain, nearly translucent, with gold trim. The serving plate was piled high with candied ginger scones, crumpets with ripe currants, and an assortment of iced biscuits. Pots of jams, clotted cream, and butter waited to be slathered onto the pastries.

"So, let us go immediately to the heart of the matter. You are here to see the King?" asked the Marchioness.

"At his request, yes, ma'am."

"Well, I thought this a wonderful opportunity for us to have a small tête-à-tête." She smiled but did not bare her teeth, which Mr. Douglas had told me were as false as her friendship. "You are familiar with the word, are you not? Ah, that's right. You were a governess, weren't you?"

I could see where this was going.

"Yes, ma'am. I have been a schoolteacher, and I once tutored Mr. Rochester's ward, Adèle Varens."

"The daughter of the French opera dancer."

"Yes." I felt as though she was toying with me, the way my cat Mephisto does when he finds a small lizard, before he kills it. My adversary wanted me to know she was familiar with domestic aspects of my life. I wondered why she'd gone to such trouble. Several days had passed since the Marchioness and I had last spoken, and in the interim, I had largely pushed Mr. Waverly's warning about her to one side. Now her intensity brought back all of his concerns about her tenacity of purpose—and her ruthlessness.

Perhaps I should not have come here alone.

Lady Conyngham prepared the tea, measuring into the pot three spoonfuls of fragrant leaves. A pile of cubes was heaped high in the sugar bowl with a set of tongs resting on top. Likewise, the cream pitcher was full to the brim. She poured a cup of tea for me, and I added the sugar and cream.

"So," she said, "Lady Ingram was murdered, and the Bow Street office believes that she was killed with poison." This was not the topic I thought she'd introduce. I had expected her to ask me about the letter.

In light of her pronouncement, I thought it needed amending. "Mr. Lerner's experiments seem to have proven as much. At least to him."

"Who is responsible for Lady Ingram's death?"

"I have no idea, ma'am."

"Well, I do. The Honorable Blanche Ingram visited me yesterday. She had the most amazing story about your husband! Oh dear, I could scarcely credit it, but she assures me it is all true and that she has proof. My, my, but Miss Ingram is very . . . shrewd."

With both hands, I lifted my cup to cover my face and forced myself to drink more tea. I needed to play for time. At last I said, "Indeed."

"Yes, evidently Squire Rochester paid a visit to Miss Ingram at Lady Grainger's home before the rest of us arrived that afternoon. Miss Ingram swears to me that he slipped a toxic substance into her tin of coffee."

"How?" I told myself that I must remain calm. That any

sign of weakness would surely serve to encourage the Marchioness in her quest.

"She did not go into particulars, but she assures me that her sister can support her in this."

I said nothing, although I fought many emotions. Fear, most of all, and dread.

"Then, too, there's the matter of a duel. Your husband had quite a temper when he was younger."

I continued to stay silent.

"Have you ever visited Newgate Prison, Mrs. Rochester? Or seen a felon die by hanging? Oh my. It fills the mind with nightmares that cannot be erased." As she spoke, Lady Conyngham watched me, her face glowing with self-congratulation. I did my best to keep from showing how frightened I was, but I know I wasn't terribly successful.

"Mr. Waverly underestimates me," she said at last.

"How so?" I managed with difficulty. Her abrupt shift of topic had caught me unaware.

"He thinks that I don't know what he is about."

I drank even more tea, as I tried to sort through my options.

"He thinks I don't know the real reason he's been assigned to me." She sighed. "I know very well that His Majesty has ordered Waverly to keep an eye on me. That the Bow Street Runner hopes to uncover any wrongdoings on my part and report them to the King."

"Why would His Majesty order Mr. Waverly to do that?"

"Please, Mrs. Rochester," she said with a smirk. "Do not act a part to which you are not well suited. You are plain and unassuming but tolerably intelligent. More so than most. You can very well guess at what his intentions are."

"I have met the King but once, and I can assure you that I do my utmost to ignore gossip. As one who has been on the unhappy receiving end of such slander, I am eager to discount what I hear. Instead, I tend to believe what I see, and even that I temper with skepticism. Therefore, I am singularly unqualified and too uninterested to even hazard a guess at any such motives."

She sat back, crossed her arms over one knee, and puckered her mouth at me. "Well, well, well."

I kept a bland expression on my face.

"You don't make this easy, do you? I might as well speak frankly with you, as one woman to another. You see, I know the King. Intimately. He is fickle, and he is manipulative, and he tires of women easily. I pamper him, I wait upon him, I coddle him, and tell him what a god among men he is. In return, he frets and stews and thinks of nothing but himself. Typical of the gender, wouldn't you say?"

"Not of my husband."

"Ah. Lucky you. But then your husband is half blind and crippled. That does rather take the spirit out of the stallion, doesn't it?"

This brought the heat to my face. Then I remembered Lucy's advice: To get a person to talk, incite anger. And every bit as quickly, I cooled off.

"Actually, my stallion still can kick out the slats in his stall. However, Edward Rochester is exceptional, and I do recognize my good fortune. I am sorry for you that His Majesty does not properly appreciate your . . . service to him."

She chuckled. Her next words were pitched very low. "The King instructed Mr. Waverly to keep an eye on me, because he enjoys having leverage over others. When a man is weak, he enjoys the weakness of others because it makes him feel less alone. I am not weak. Miss Ingram thinks that I am easily led. In truth, I am neither. I think you know that."

I waited.

"Miss Ingram has her own motives for suggesting that your husband is to blame for her mother's murder, doesn't she?"

"That's right. She does." Relief ran through me, and I felt the tension leave my body. I sat back a little in my chair, as I offered a prayer of thanksgiving.

Lady Conyngham smiled at me. "See? I am neither weak nor foolish. No, I have not advanced this far in life because I have let others run over me. Miss Ingram thinks she can influence me to help her. But she has nothing I want. Nothing. However, you do. I want that letter. If you do not turn it over to me, I shall have to tell Mr. Waverly what I saw."

"What do you mean?"

"I shall have to tell him that I saw Lucy Brayton put something into Lady Ingram's drink."

Chapter 48

✤

"You did not," I said quickly. "You couldn't have, for it never happened."

"Really?" The Marchioness raised her eyebrows at me. "You are the one who told Mr. Waverly that Mrs. Brayton held the tin before passing it to Miss Ingram. That's when your friend Mrs. Brayton took the opportunity to poison Lady Ingram. Not only did she have the means, Mrs. Brayton has a strong motive for killing the Dowager. Mrs. Brayton coveted Lady Grainger's fortune for her new son. Oh yes, I have my spies. Nothing escapes me. I know all about the new will. It gives Mrs. Brayton every reason to want Lady Ingram out of the way—getting rid of Lady Ingram brings her son one step closer to a grand inheritance."

"But there was no time for Lucy to do anything—and she had nothing on her person to add to the coffee grounds. I know because I was there. The tin passed by quickly. I saw it!"

Marchioness Conyngham smiled. "Ah, so it would be my word against yours."

"Yes." I felt a trickle of perspiration run along the seams of my corset. My heart hammered in my chest like a blacksmith at his anvil.

"Whose side do you guess the Ingram girls would take? Mine or yours? Especially with all that I can offer them? Even though they are in mourning, they could still attend the coronation and the celebration. After all, a royal invitation cannot be ignored. True, it wouldn't be proper for them to dance, but they could still be in attendance. I could introduce them to powerful people. And that's only the beginning. There are positions at court. Alliances. Marriages." She smiled patiently at me. "When Miss Ingram railed about her changed pecuniary fortunes, she convinced me how malleable she really is. On the other hand, I can best be described as . . . intractable. So it's really no use. I want that letter and I shall have it."

I tried to swallow, but my mouth was dry. Even a sip of tea did me no good.

She raised one eyebrow, speculatively. "So you see, this is a lost cause. You have one course of action, and only one: Hand over the letter, or your friend will suffer the consequences. Is that what you want? Is a silly piece of paper worth destroying the life of someone dear to you?"

"No," I said, and I meant it with all my heart. "No, it most certainly is not."

"Too right, Mrs. Rochester. That letter is cursed! It brings sorrow to all who own it. Look at what happened to that poor Biltmore girl. Now you possess it and your friend is in a precarious position. If I were you"—she leaned forward to speak in a faux whisper—"I would waste no time getting rid of that communication. It harbors ill will. If you give it to me, there might still be time to save yourself and your friend more heartache."

All of that was true, but she had artfully skipped over an important point: While the letter had caused nothing but grief to all involved, letting go of the papers would not insure Lucy's safety.

"If I hand you the letter, what assurance do I have that you will not blame my friend Lucy Brayton for Lady Ingram's death and tell the King about Edward's duel anyway? I would be foolish to take your word as your bond."

"True enough." She sat back in her seat as her face took on a pensive expression.

"I believe I would need a written statement from you, Lady Conyngham. An assurance that could withstand scrutiny."

"You surprise me, Mrs. Rochester. You push your advantage here, but I'm happy to exchange such a document for the letter you have."

"That's not enough," I said, struggling to keep my voice even.

"Really? My, my. What more do you want? A peerage for your husband?"

"Nothing for myself or my husband. All that I want is for Lucy Brayton to continue to enjoy her status as part of the ten thousand. Even if you don't accuse her, Miss Ingram has done and will do. Therefore, Mrs. Brayton is still at risk. For me to give up the letter and lose all advantage would be shortsighted if I can't walk away with confidence that my friend is secure in her position."

"You are annoying me, Mrs. Rochester." Lacing together her plump fingers and resting them in her lap, she glared at me. "First you set a condition that I am willing to meet. Next you suggest that you require more. Quit playing games. I am a busy woman and a powerful one. What is it you want? Say it clearly."

"I want you to take Mrs. Brayton and her son, Evans, under your protective wing."

"And how do you propose I do that? It's a bit late for me to introduce her as my own flesh and blood."

I stared at the Marchioness and delivered my ultimatum with clarity: "I ask that you and the King serve as Evans Forrester's godparents."

I was fairly certain that having the King and Lady Conyngham serve as Evans's godparents would secure Lucy's place
in society. Standing up at a baptismal font and swearing to
be responsible for the moral rectitude of the child being
blessed would constitute an alliance between the palace and
the Brayton family. The names of the King and the Marchioness would go down in the record book of the Church for all
and sundry to see, for decades and possibly centuries to come.
Furthermore, their oaths would be given as part of a holy
sacrament.

By the very public nature of the deed, I could rest assured
that the Marchioness had done as I asked—and that she could
not at some later date withdraw her patronage.

All in attendance would grasp the significance of this time-
honored rite. To participate in the holy sacrament of baptism
would require that the King and the Marchioness confer their
unequivocal approval of the boy and his "mother." Once they
stood at the altar and pledged to safeguard the child's immortal soul, they committed themselves to a lifelong spiritual
guardianship.

I waited for the Marchioness to catch up with me, which
she did in short order.

"Well played, Mrs. Rochester. Well played," said Lady
Conyngham, setting down her cup and narrowing her eyes at
me. "Yes, I underestimated you. That's a mistake I won't make
again." She reached over and yanked the bellpull.

As we waited for the maid of honour to appear, the Marchioness said, "Once you and I have effected an exchange, I
will send Mrs. Brayton a letter confirming that the King and
I will take on the spiritual responsibility for her child. At the
conclusion of our dealings, I would have no reason to speak to
Miss Ingram or to repeat her slanderous accusations."

"Agreed."

"Then we are done here." Without a good-bye, the Marchioness stood up, turned her back on me, and walked away.

I would have breathed a sigh of relief, except the reason for my presence at Carlton House had not changed. There was still my audience with the King.

Lady Pamela led me back the way we came, but this time when we reached the anteroom we turned the opposite way. I walked behind her, the way a diligent schoolgirl follows her instructor.

Had this been any other sort of visit, I would have enjoyed George IV's collection of artwork immensely, especially the extensive Dutch and Flemish landscapes. These depictions of rural life enchanted me, and I moved slowly to better appreciate a scene of peasants in the midst of haymaking, and another of a shipbuilder and his wife.

Lady Pamela coughed, a polite signal that I was taking too long. "His Majesty's private apartments," she said, sotto voce.

Chapter 49

Two guards eyed me cautiously, while a footman announced me. When I was invited to enter, I found King George IV sitting in a huge chair by the fireplace with his feet propped up on cushioned ottomans. Two courtiers waited to do his bidding, dozing while seated on hard chairs against the wall on either side of the door.

The King did not look well. No amount of costuming could disguise his extravagant bulk. The grotesque nature of his elephantine feet suggested he was in great pain, for surely they were swollen with fluid. His eyes seemed unfocused, so I walked to where he could see me without turning his head, and then I curtsied and dropped my gaze to the floor. Behind me, the sound of rustling silk told me that Lady Pamela had also curtsied. Light footsteps suggested that she had left me.

George IV did not invite me to take a seat. Instead, he stared at me warily, barely acknowledging my curtsy. Without pleasantries, he demanded, "Lady Elizabeth wants the letter, doesn't she?" His wig sat crookedly on his head, and his diction suggested that he was not wearing his false teeth.

"Yes."

"Did she ask you for it? Just now?"

"Yes."

"I thought she might. She is crafty. I have always recognized that in her. Have you met Mrs. Fitzherbert?"

"As a matter of fact, I did meet her and her daughter just yesterday. Although our meeting was brief, both women impressed me greatly."

"I am not surprised." Lifting a hand, King George IV gestured around him. "See all of this splendor? Magnificent, isn't it? I can own anything I want. I can commission artists to make whatever I desire. I can change out the fabrics as often as the whim strikes me. I am master of all I survey, sovereign and ruler. But I am also a captive slave to my birthright. Yes, I can have anything a man can buy, but I cannot have the one thing a man cannot buy: his one true love. What profit does all this confer on me if I am doomed to loneliness?"

A pain crumpled his face and he moaned.

I turned around, looking for help. Neither of the two gentlemen of the chamber noticed their patron's whimper of pain. Remembering Lucy's admonition not to touch the sovereign, I said, "Your Majesty, is there anyone I should summon or anything that I might do for you?"

"The only thing you can do for me, young lady, is to keep me in your prayers," said the King, with slurred pronunciation.

"I will do that. You have my promise."

"As I was saying, my position is one of supreme irony. I can command an army, but I cannot command fate. I can protect this green island, but I can't protect my own daughters. Poor Charlotte married at my command, and now she is gone."

He rummaged deep in his waistcoat and withdrew a silk handkerchief to wipe his eyes. "Would her fate have been different if she had married the man she wanted? I cannot say. Now poor Minney wants to marry a sailor. Her mother and I are against the match, but it weighs upon me heavily, because

I think about Charlotte and wonder, 'Was she happy? Did I do right by her?' I know I did right by the Kingdom, but what of my child?"

I could imagine a day when Ned wanted a wife. What would I want for him? Was it right to have one's own desires and preferences? Surely all parents wanted the same thing: a happy child. But did we truly know what was best for our children?

"That must weigh heavily on you, Sire."

"It does, and so do the futures of Mrs. Fitzherbert and her daughter."

Groaning, the King attempted to make himself more comfortable in the chair, but he was wedged tight. In fact, in various places the architecture of the chair cut into his mounds of flesh. The effort of rearranging his bulk caused beads of sweat to form along his hairline, and under the rice powder on his face, his pallor increased.

His suffering was clear. By all outward signs, the man was incredibly ill, so much so that I wondered if he would live long enough to ascend the throne. The irony was inescapable. Despite his position and vast inheritance, George IV was nothing more than a man struggling to grasp what none of us can have: a respite from our own demise. Suddenly, his passion for collecting art, for having his portrait painted, for planning an unforgettable coronation—an event that all said would be remembered throughout the decades—made sense to me. He was aiming for some sort of immortality. Not by deeds or descendants, but by the sheer drama of his existence.

"Lady Elizabeth wants the letter you have. Of all I have ever written, it is both the most heartful and the most damning. If you give it to her, she will hand over the letter to my brother Prince Ernest Augustus, Duke of Cumberland. He will whip up the population in such an anti-Catholic fervor that Minney and Maria will be hunted down and killed. Of that I am quite sure. Imagine! At my coronation, I am to be the Supreme Governor of the Anglican Church, but I had the audacity to love—and secretly marry—a Roman Catholic woman! That taken with the never-ending tides of Roman Catholic Irish immigrants who come to England, hoping to flee the ongoing problems with potato crops, and instead take jobs away from the common man, and I would be viewed . . . harshly. Very harshly, indeed. All because I had the temerity to love—rather than scorn—a woman of another faith. Is that such a misdeed? I ask you! But I would suffer. The attempts on my life would increase. Of course, I am well-protected, but Maria? Minney? The objects of my affection? They would be lambs to the slaughter, Mrs. Rochester."

He added, "Their deaths will be on your head."

A clock chimed down the hallway.

"You may go."

One of the sleeping courtiers stood up and stuck his head out the door, and Lady Pamela reappeared. Once outside his chamber door, Lady Pamela led me down the hallway. When we arrived at the entry hall, she sent a footman to hail a hackney for me. From my dry place inside Carlton House, I watched the rain come down in heavy sheets.

The jarvey who drove the carriage-for-hire did not offer to escort me to his conveyance with an umbrella. Neither did the footman lounging at the door of Carlton House. Now that I was no longer of interest to His Majesty and his paramour, I was on my own, so I picked up my skirts and hurried as fast as I could. When I got to the coach, I struggled with the door. The driver paid me no heed. By the time I was safe inside and out of the rain, I was soaked to the skin and shivering. My mind was whirling, turning all this over, concentrating on these ideas, when the carriage door flew open—and in jumped Pansy Biltmore.

Chapter 50

"Do not shout or I shall be forced to stab you," she said as she poked the tip of a knife against my waist.

A small gasp escaped my lips before I could restrain myself. Then the recriminations began. Why hadn't I been more prudent? I had been so busy turning over in my mind the problem of keeping Maria and Minney safe, that I had walked headlong into danger. "I tried to persuade you with reason, but you paid no attention to me. I want that letter. I need it! I lost my daughter over it. I am not going to lose my home," she whispered, leaning close, her hot breath tickling my ear. "If you think you can overpower me," she said, "think again. I hired the man who is driving this coach. You can't get away. Now tell me where the letter is."

I shivered, not from the rain that soaked my clothes, but with fear. I thought quickly about my position. Here on the streets, I did not have a chance. But I might back at Lucy's house. "I have it in a strongbox at Lucy Brayton's home."

"Exactly where in the house is it?" she demanded.

"Behind a painting in the library."

Then with a start, I realized my mistake: Ned and Adèle were likely to be home! Since it was raining, Amelia would not have taken them for a walk in the park. I clenched my fists in irritation. This would never do. I had to think quickly, review what options were left to me. I thought back to Lucy's sermon on how to defend oneself. I needed to plot my course. Lucy had said I should catch my opponent off guard. I had to take advantage of the fact that Mrs. Biltmore was convinced that I had bowed to her wishes. I wanted her to think me too meek and mild to put up a fight.

"There will be children in the house." Lucy, I hoped fervently, would still be away visiting with Maria Fitzherbert. Perhaps my husband and Mr. Douglas would take their time at Hatchards. That would leave me only the staff to contend with, and they would do my bidding. So presumably they could stay safe, if I could manage to issue orders that they leave us alone.

"Well then, if you do not want the children to be at risk, you must follow my directions carefully. I don't want to cause them harm, but of course, what happens is entirely up to you."

On that score she was right: Their fate and mine was in my hands. I would do anything—anything!—to make sure my family and friends were unharmed. And I would begin by encouraging the woman to underestimate me, to think me too timid and frightened to rise up against her.

"M-m-m-my husband is blind. P-p-p-lease don't mistake his actions for aggression. If he comes too close to us, it's because he must . . . to make us out." I sounded appropriately scared, but I had a plan behind my disclosure. I needed to protect my husband, and I could best do that by emphasizing his deficiencies. This was my most pressing worry. Edward and I had always enjoyed a connection, some sort of understanding between us that alerted us to each other's needs. It now occurred to me that if he sensed I were in danger, he might rush to my aid—and the consequence could be deadly.

"He's blind? What a pity, although that might make a man more . . . amenable. Is that why he married you? Someone every bit as small as a child and just as plain?" She sighed. "Because he could not see what he was doing? What a shame.

Mrs. Biltmore leaned close, in a menacing way. "When the coach stops, you and I will exit together. I have a firm grip on your waistband. If you try to jerk away from me, if you lunge or scream, I shall draw back my arm and jab you."

For effect, I whimpered. "Please, please don't!"

"Do you want to feel the edge of this blade?" She sounded almost triumphant. "No, I thought not. Know that I had it sharpened this morning by a butcher, and it is exceedingly sharp. Together you and I will make our way up the stairs to the front door. You will ring the bell and greet the butler as if nothing is amiss. You will quickly dispatch him, telling him we need privacy, and thus the two of us will go together into the drawing room."

"The library," I corrected her. "It's in the library."

"Good, you see? It is so much easier to be cooperative. So we will go to where the strongbox is hidden behind the painting. If anyone interrupts us, you will tell them we need to discuss a sensitive matter—a very private matter—and that we wish to be alone."

"Yes," I said. "Yes, of course." Rivulets of sweat ran down between my shoulder blades. I nodded briskly, concentrating on playing the part of a tame little mouse.

I thought it best to preempt any problems. "What if someone approaches us? What should I do?"

"You will greet them and say we have reconciled our differences. That you realize now you were wrong about me. You can do that, can't you?"

"Of-of course." I stuttered so as to maintain the illusion that I was scared witless.

"Good, because I would hate to have to hurt one of the servants, but such things happen. As for your high-and-mighty friend Mrs. Brayton . . ." Her face broke into an ugly smile. "Let's just say I have no use for her."

I came to a swift and unequivocal decision: If I had to give over the letter to Mrs. Biltmore, I would. While I regretted any problems it might cause Minney and Maria, I could not risk having my family harmed.

The carriage rolled to a stop. "Remember, I have a knife. You cannot run from me. Do as I have told you and all will be well."

"I understand. I shall move slowly so that you can stay near me," I said. The jarvey did not jump from his perch to help us. Realizing this, I twisted the handle, put my shoulder into the door, opened it, and stepped out on the carriage block. Mrs. Biltmore moved with me; soon we were on the paving stones leading to Lucy's front door.

After I rapped the door knocker, Higgins opened the house to us. "Ah, Mrs. Rochester. Welcome home. Young Master has been keeping us all entertained. I believe he is learning to walk. Been pulling up on furniture and such."

"How delightful! I want to see his progress. But first, Mrs. Biltmore and I are going to the library and I need privacy. Please make sure that we aren't disturbed. Oh, and we shall keep our outer garments." I knew this would seem curious to him; however, I could not chance him reaching for Mrs. Biltmore's wrap and getting stabbed by her knife.

"No tea?" His face was as bland as usual.

"Thank you, but no. However, I might ring for coffee later." I smiled at him.

I never drank coffee—and I counted on Higgins to realize that.

"Indeed? Oh yes, quite right." There was a flare of understanding in his eyes and a slight change in his gaze, so subtle that Mrs. Biltmore could not have detected it, but I did.

What he would do next, I did not know and could not guess. However, if he made any attempt to interfere, I would surely feel the tip of Mrs. Biltmore's knife. I needed him to give me time, so I added, "But the coffee can wait. I have business to attend to first. I want privacy."

"I understand. Yes, ma'am." Although Higgins did not betray anything, I could tell that he realized there was a problem.

"I assume Mrs. Brayton is still out on her morning calls?" I wanted to be sure that Lucy did not walk in on us, lest it endanger her.

"Yes, ma'am. Quite right. The gentlemen are still out on their errands as well."

"Well, go on then," I said, in a brusque tone. I gave him a brisk nod of dismissal, something else out of keeping with my behavior.

"I think we'll dry ourselves in front of the fire in the library," I said to Mrs. Biltmore as we resumed our slow climb of the stairs. But one look over my shoulder told me that Higgins knew something was amiss from the slow way he started toward the back stairs. Otherwise, why hadn't I requested that Polly come and assist us? Mrs. Biltmore and I were both soaked, with water dripping off our skirts and onto the floor.

"You've done well," Mrs. Biltmore whispered as we gained the top of the landing. "Just keep it up, and I shall be gone from here with the letter in no time."

Chapter 51

As we walked into the library, I thought back again to Lucy's lecture that day in Lady Grainger's room. What I needed was a weapon. Something within reach. Something unexpected. I surreptitiously glanced around. Immediately my eyes went to the hearth, as I remembered Lucy's story about having thrown cinders at an attacker. But when I glanced toward the bucket of ashes, my heart sank. Lucy's maid of all work, Sadie, had already removed all the leftover grime and grit from the night before.

I would have to come up with something else to press into service.

"That is the painting I told you about." I tipped my head toward the landscape. "First I must lift it down. Then I must retrieve the key."

"Where is it?"

"Mrs. Brayton has told me it's in the desk, but I don't know which drawer."

"Move that way slowly," Mrs. Biltmore said. "I shall stay at your side—and don't forget this blade is very sharp. I only need to stab you once and you won't live to see another day."

You must prevail! I told myself. *And you can only prevail by thinking clearly and calmly.*

To further put Mrs. Biltmore at ease, I began to narrate my actions. "First I shall unhook the painting."

The seascape was on a wall perpendicular to the desk. With both hands, I struggled to lift the heavy painting, freeing the wire on the back from its hook.

"Now I shall set it down." Moving slightly past Mrs. Biltmore and facing the piece of furniture, I rested the painting at one end of the blotter. From the vantage point of someone behind the desk, the Turner now occupied the upper left hand quadrant, while in the right hand quadrant sat all the necessary writing accoutrements: inkwell, box of blotting sand, and slotted letter holder filled with fresh stationery.

I turned back to face the bare wall. "As you can see, the box is exposed, but it is locked. I must remove the container from its hidey-hole to gain access."

The oak strongbox was securely wrapped with brass straps. A heavy lock dangled from a D-shaped ring on the front, where all the straps met. To set the heavy object in the middle of the desktop, I needed to maneuver around Mrs. Biltmore.

My goal was to force the woman to become accustomed to my movements. Lucy had counseled me to put distance between myself and the knifepoint. To do so, I needed Mrs. Biltmore to let down her guard.

During all my machinations, she had remained right with me, glued to my side. Now, to get a better look at the strongbox, she stepped back a foot or two. But the distance between us worried her.

With a quick move, Mrs. Biltmore yanked me close to her. Since she was a big woman, she had the advantage of me, and I stumbled. But she had a good grip on my arm with one hand, and the other kept the knife pointed at my waist. She put her mouth to my ear and hissed, "Beware! That key better be there. You had better not be lying to me!"

"I am not lying about the key," I said. I felt a burning sensation along the back of my waistband—and when I touched that spot, my hand came away covered in blood. Fresh crimson.

"I only pricked you." She wore an expression of contentment. "Dear, dear."

I stood staring at the bright red blood coating my fingertips. Curiously, the jab had not hurt as much as I would have reckoned, but I knew from previous injuries that the body has a strange way of forestalling pain until later. I pulled out my handkerchief and scrubbed my fingers, while growing keenly aware that my side was bleeding profusely. There was a curious gathering of dampness along my waistband, a mix of hot and cold, as the hot blood leaked out and then cooled when it touched the air.

"Hurry up," she snapped at me. "I don't have all day."

I put my handkerchief back in my pocket, and while doing so, I felt such a pinch of pain that I fought the urge to retch. I swallowed hard and said, "I'm going to open the desk and search for the key. Lucy told me that it's in the top drawer, but as you can see, that could be any one of these three, and I don't know which one."

This was a lie. I knew perfectly well which one held the key: It was inside the bottom right-hand drawer, behind the secret compartment. But I recommitted to my goal of lulling Mrs. Biltmore into false security. I wanted her to think she had total control of me, so I added, "Please don't stick me again," in a plaintive voice.

"Then get to it," she said.

"I need to switch sides," I said. Mrs. Biltmore followed my lead around the desk. But our half circle ended when we came to the ottoman that Lucy used for propping up her feet. I stepped over the low footstool, but Mrs. Biltmore did not. That put the hassock between us.

"Go right ahead. You're doing fine," said Mrs. Biltmore, her voice sounding confident.

I was facing the kneehole when I opened the drawer on my far left. Mrs. Biltmore stood as close as possible to watch what I was doing, but she did not step over the hassock. I rummaged through the drawer, making much of my effort and muttering, "Where is it?"

I moved on to the middle drawer. The clutter in this drawer allowed me to slow down as I murmured, "She said it was here," but I did not dare to drag my charade out too long. With each minute that passed, the pain below my ribs hurt more. My waistband grew steadily colder, as it became wetter and wetter with blood.

"It must be in the third drawer," I said, for effect.

The far right top drawer was my last chance, or so I would have Mrs. Biltmore believe.

"Hurry up," she said.

"I'm trying." I managed to sound frightened, knowing full well that I would have to act soon—and act decisively.

Footsteps echoed outside the door.

Mrs. Biltmore half turned to listen.

In her distraction, she allowed the knife to stray away from my ribs.

This was my chance. I grabbed the box of blotting sand and tossed it in her face.

Chapter 52

"Ouf!" Pansy Biltmore sputtered as her hands flew up to her face. Her knife clattered to the floor. With a swift kick of my foot, I shoved the ottoman as hard as I could. The footstool screeched away from me, hitting Mrs. Biltmore right around the knees, and propelling her backward. Her arms circled in a windmill-like motion as she fought to regain her balance, but the urge to brush the sand from her eyes was equally compelling, and she lurched to one side, crashing against the brass fireplace fender. The loud crash startled both of us, and she blindly groped toward me, but I shied away, staying just out of her reach.

"Jane!" Edward came through the library door with Bruce Douglas right behind. Higgins followed closely.

"Grab her knife," I yelled to Mr. Douglas. "There! On the floor!" I pointed as he followed my fingers with his eyes.

"Got it!" He snatched it up even as Edward ran to me, instinctively shielding me with his body.

"Darling! Are you? Good Lord! What is this? You're bleeding!" Edward's hand recoiled from its purchase on my waist.

Mr. Douglas now turned upon Mrs. Biltmore. In a swift and graceful move, he grabbed one of her flailing arms, twisted it behind her back, and smashed her facedown onto the desk. She screamed and shouted obscenities at him, but he held her steady.

"We need rope," he told Higgins. "Plenty of it. Get Williams. He'll have rope and he can help. Then go and fetch Mr. Waverly at Bow Street."

"Let me go!" screamed Mrs. Biltmore. But the words were muffled because her face was turned to the desktop.

"Unhand me!" snarled Mrs. Biltmore.

Edward had one arm around my waist. He touched his fingertips together, tentatively. "Blood? Jane! You're hurt."

"I'll send someone for Mr. Lerner," said Higgins, coming back into the room with Polly, Williams, and a length of rope.

"I've got you." Edward scooped me up and carried me to the settee. Mrs. Biltmore kept screaming, her cries becoming louder as she discovered that Mr. Douglas was not to be swayed.

Under Mr. Douglas's direction, Higgins and Williams soon had Mrs. Biltmore trussed up against a straight-backed chair. The whole time, she gnashed her teeth and tried to slam her head into her captors. She continued to caterwaul, so Higgins untied his cravat and stuffed it into her mouth.

Polly had dropped to her knees to get a good look at my wound. Her expression turned grave. "I'll go get towels and water. Perhaps it looks worse than it is." As she peeled back the fabric at my waistband, her face went white with worry. She turned to Edward. "Sir? I hope the doctor hurries. This don't look too good to me."

In an attempt to free herself, Mrs. Biltmore began to rock the chair she was in back and forth. The scheme did not work. When Mr. Douglas noticed the trajectory of her struggles, he and Edward repositioned the woman and her chair in the far corner of the room where her gymnastics could not have much effect.

Mr. Waverly arrived shortly thereafter. The man from Bow Street took one look at the blood seeping from my wound and started swearing under his breath. "How did this happen?"

"The King summoned me to Carlton House," I said, although I was panting with pain. "When I was leaving, Mrs. Biltmore jumped into my hackney and held a knife to my side. She told me she had been in league with the jarvey. I presume they were watching me and chose that time for an attack."

"Was she after the letter?"

"Yes," I said. "As is Lady Conyngham. She diverted me on my visit to the King. Unless I give her the letter, the Marchioness told me she plans to claim that Lucy poisoned Lady Ingram."

"Blast her to Kingdom Come," said Edward.

"Mrs. Biltmore accosted you at knifepoint, demanded entrance to a home that isn't hers, and wanted you to open a strongbox that isn't yours on penalty of your life?" Mr. Waverly summed up the crime. "And then she stabbed you."

"Yes." I grew weaker by the minute.

"The doctor has just arrived," said Higgins.

As Mr. Lerner approached, Polly ceded to him her position at my side. When he crouched down, papers fell out of his bag. *We need to buy him a bag that closes properly.*

After a quick exam, he said, "I would appreciate better light. Any chance we could move Mrs. Rochester onto a bed in a room with a west-facing window?"

Edward and Mr. Douglas used their arms to fashion a hammock. As they carried me down the hall, I rested my head against my husband's chest, letting the beat of his heart soothe me. "You will be fine, darling Jane. You have to be, because I cannot live without you," he said as he kissed the top of my head.

Polly brought more towels and a fresh basin of hot water. To a glass of water, the doctor added several drops of laudanum and then suggested that Mr. Douglas leave the room. Asking for Polly's help, Mr. Lerner cut my dress away from my body.

I regretted that. The frock was ruined, but I had rather liked the color. I said as much to Edward, and he responded with, "I would be happy to buy you an entire warehouse full of silk for more dresses."

Rolling me onto my uninjured side, Mr. Lerner said, "Next to the drops, distraction seems to help my patients deal with pain. Therefore, I suggest you talk to me about anything, anything at all that suits your fancy."

"Why?" I gasped.

"Because this is going to hurt like the dickens."

Chapter 53

He was not lying. A white-hot splinter of pain jabbed me in the side. Edward offered his hand for me to grip, which I did. I winced and said, "Mr. Lerner, tell me more about your studies as a Lunartick. What sort of things have you found most intriguing?"

The doctor's forehead creased in thought. "Recently I did learn from one of my fellow society members how a simple garden plant can help a weak heart. The tincture could have helped Lady Ingram, for example, live more comfortably. But it would have required careful monitoring."

"So you could have helped her?" Edward asked.

Mr. Lerner nodded slowly. "I think so. It would have taken daily visits and much attention, because of the precise calibration necessary. Too much would have caused her heart to stop, but a small amount would have helped regulate it. Rather a tricky balance was needed."

"Then you are saying that this tincture could act both as a poison and as a cure?" I found this idea fascinating. Typically, I thought of poisons as only hurtful.

The doctor said, "Yes," before instructing Polly to bring a lamp closer to give him even more light.

"So the trick would have been making sure that Lady Ingram received neither too much nor too little of this cure," Edward continued, more to keep me occupied than from real interest.

"Absolutely. First it must be prepared properly, and those calibrations made, and then administered in minute doses, while recording the patient's response. You see, it could encourage a weak heart, but too much would be like giving a stallion a sharp jab with spurs. He would run away and perhaps kill the rider." The doctor stood to talk, and now bent to resume his probing of my wound.

"But if you treated Lady Ingram, it would not have saved her from poison," I stated the obvious.

Despite my pain, or maybe because of it, my mind functioned with unusual clarity. Suddenly, I could postulate a theory as to what happened to Lady Ingram. But first I needed to ask a few more questions. "Did anyone know about the use of these common flowers?"

The pain was a living creature, a green dragon loose inside my skin.

"I told the Ingram daughters about the remedy in general terms," he said. "Lady Grainger was not a party to the discussion. Do try to remain still for me, as I have a bit more digging to do."

"All right."

The pain worsened, and I found it hard not to pull away from its source, but Mr. Lerner murmured encouragements and Edward gripped my hands with all his might. "How does one prepare this tincture?" Edward asked.

"First the leaves must be picked on a dry day. They must be allowed to dry further, and then an extract is prepared. A small amount of the leaves will go a long way. At each step, one must take careful notes. As the tincture is administered,

more notations must be made, so that the dosage and prepara-
tion are precisely monitored."

"But you did prescribe rose hips," I said, although the effort
cost me dearly. "To help Lady Ingram."

"Yes, roses are another common garden flower with medicinal
uses. However, rose hips are not harmful in any dose. But this
other flower I'm speaking of has long been thought to be toxic.
Only after my friend diluted it, could he see its beneficial use."

"But that's the rub, right? Finding the right dilution," said
Edward. "Not much longer now, Jane."

"Right. If the dosage is wrong, obviously the patient could
die, but otherwise a person might feel nausea. He or she might
faint and have bouts of dizziness. At times it could be difficult
for the person to catch his or her breath. The heart might race
or alternately slow down."

"Uh." I allowed myself a small gasp of pain. Tears welled
up, and I bit back the urge to cry.

"Very good. Very, very good. We are all done with that,"
he said, and he waved a small pair of bloody tongs near my
face. "See? The tip of her knife rammed a bit of fabric into
your flesh. If I had not found it, it would surely have festered
and given you a fever. Fortunately, the wound gaps such that
finding the cloth was none too difficult. I would have hated
to poke and prod at you much longer."

My eyes had grown so heavy that I could barely stay awake.

"Does it have a common name?" I wondered.

"Does what have a common name?" He was sewing my
wound closed.

"That plant. The one that could have . . . helped . . .
Lady . . . Ingram . . ."

"Several common names. Some call it lady's glove. Others
call it fairy thimbles. We are done here. He's there."

"My brave, brave girl," whispered Edward.

Chapter 54

I woke a short time later to the sound of Lucy humming a sweet tune.

"Hello, dear heart," she said, as she tucked a stray lock of hair behind my ear. "How are you feeling?"

"Hurts." That was all I could say.

"Cook has made a lovely beef tea for you. We'll have Sadie bring it up. Mr. Lerner says you must take as much of it as you can." She smiled at me and stroked my cheek. Turning toward the windows, I realized it was nearly dark outside.

"Ned? Edward? Adèle?" The names came out in a rush.

Despite the drawn look of her features, she laughed, and a brilliant white ruffle framing her face swayed gently. "Bruce will be hurt when he hears he was forgotten. All are well. You've been asleep for hours. The men are downstairs. The children are asleep."

"Lucy, I have good news," I said. My mouth felt as though I'd been chewing on a strand of wool, but I told her about my visit with Lady Conyngham. "I know it doesn't sound promising, but I have her word that she and the King will stand up

for Evans at his baptism. They'll serve as his godparents . . .
if you want. And if you agree that I should turn over the
letter."

She marveled at me. "You are amazing. After nearly losing
your life, you cannot wait to share a plan for protecting me!
But that's enough about the letter. We can talk about it later."

"But it is safe, isn't it?"

"When I returned home and heard about your altercation
with Mrs. Biltmore, I checked on it. The letter is inside the
strongbox, behind the painting, and that horrid woman has
been incarcerated."

She filled a glass with water, put in two drops of laudanum,
brought it to my lips, and helped me drink. After I did, I said,
"I know you worry about Maria Fitzherbert and Minney, but
if I don't give the Marchioness the letter, she and Miss Ingram
will work together to ruin you!"

Lucy gave me a tender look. "Hush, Jane. Do not distress
yourself so. I spoke to Maria about the letter. That was one
reason for my visit."

"You did what?"

"She already knew about it. Carlton House is full of courtiers who have no loyalty to the King. They will report anything they hear to anyone who offers them a coin or two. The
Duke of York has several persons there who work for him, and
he told Maria what was happening."

"And what did she say?"

"She, more than anyone in the world, knows the King. She
had expected something like this. Maria is no fool, and she
had sensed there was danger in the air. With the populace
already angry about how the King has treated Caroline of
Brunswick—and with word coming daily of the tremendous
sums he is spending on his coronation—they could easily be
convinced to riot against him in the streets."

"But she came here to London and appeared openly with
her daughter!"

"Yes, she did. She came to meet with the Duke of York to beg his assistance. If the letter is made public, she plans to flee the country." Lucy spoke with such calm and such resolution that I knew she and Maria Fitzherbert must have discussed this at length. My friend was far too settled in her discourse for me to believe that she harbored any questions as to the correctness of this plan.

"And she is happy with this course of action? This resolution?"

Lucy had been staring down at her fingers. Now she lifted her chin and fixed her gaze on a spot outside the window, someplace far away from here. "She is at peace with her decision. It is the only way."

"But?" I heard the hesitation in my friend's voice.

"But Minney refuses to go along. She will not leave the young man she wants to marry. He is in the Army, and if he were to quit the country, he would be a deserter."

I had thought the matter was settled. I had worked it out in my mind. I planned to hand the letter to Lady Conyngham and free Lucy from this curse. And now, once again, I was confused—and the laudanum made matters even worse, as I struggled against it.

I knew that I must weigh my loyalty to my friend against fairness to a young woman I had met only once, a young woman in love.

"But Lucy, if I don't give Lady Conyngham the letter, she and Miss Ingram will conspire to ruin you."

"They can only ruin me if I care about being accepted by the ton." She stood up and began pacing the room, a habit she indulged when she was thinking through a problem. "Your visit has forced me to reevaluate all that I once thought important. When I came back from a morning call and discovered my dear friend had been stabbed, my conversion was complete. You must understand, Jane, I turned to the ton for entertainment, affection, and companionship when I recognized that

Augie might never be allowed to leave India. But since you and your family have welcomed me into your lives, I have come to realize that I don't care about the ton. They mean nothing to me. You and Edward and Adèle and Ned do! My true friends won't desert me, no matter how society shuns me."

When she returned to the chair beside my bed, her face was calm. I could tell she had given this much thought, and I was glad she found resolution.

"What about their accusations?" I asked.

"They cannot prove an action that never happened. They might try, but they can't. And thanks to Mary Ingram's accusation of Mr. Lerner, the whole of Bow Street knows the Ingram girls are prone to making spurious assertions. No, I say either give the letter to Lady Conyngham or burn it. That wretched pile of papers has caused too much grief for you . . . and for me. It's a cursed thing; Maria feels the same. Minney and her young man will have to work out what they want to do. There is the possibility that the Duke of York can secure for him a foreign posting. We shall see. But again . . . I counsel you to burn it. Or do what you will with it. But you cannot protect me. Or Maria. Or her daughter."

Sadie brought in a tray loaded with tea, wafer-thin crackers, and a tureen of wonderful-smelling soup. "Mr. Rochester asked me to fetch him when you were awake, ma'am."

"I'll go get him." Lucy planted a kiss on my cheek before she left.

Moments later, my husband came to the door, holding Ned in his arms. "Look, little man. There's your mother! You have a surprise for her, don't you?"

"Ma-ma!" said Ned. I almost melted with happiness.

"I taught him that." Adèle peeped out from behind them. "I was very worried about you!"

The French girl launched herself at me, but Edward caught the back of her sash and stopped her in her tracks. *"Faites attention! Doucement!"*

"Just for a while, *ma petite*," I assured Adèle. "I am hurt, but I will heal."

Amelia appeared in the doorway. "Time for your bath and bed, Young Master. You can come and help me, Little Miss. I'm awful glad you weren't hurt too much, ma'am. Awful glad."

When the door closed behind her, at long last, my husband and I were alone.

"How are you?" He uncurled my fingers and kissed the palm of my hand.

"Weak. My head is muddled. My side hurts, and I am confused. Edward? Why did you not tell me that you once fought a duel?"

"Oh? So you heard about that." I had caught him off-guard. He did not drop my hand, but he relaxed his grasp. "It is one of the many foolish incidents of my youth. One where my temper prevailed upon my good sense, and I paid the price for it."

"So . . . did you? Fight another man?"

"I did not. I was waiting there at dawn, hands shaking and knees quaking, wondering what I had gotten myself into when John crept up behind me and threw a potato sack over my head. Oh, I railed and struck out at him, but all the while I secretly blessed him for saving me from myself. Why do you ask?"

I explained about my worries when the King summoned me. I also told him about Lady Conyngham's promise that she and the King would stand up as Evans's godparents in return for the letter.

Edward's mouth puckered with surprise. "Did she really?"

"Wouldn't that make a difference to society?"

"It certainly would. A child is to have three godparents, so the King, the Marchioness, and Mr. Douglas could all stand up for Evans. By the laws of the Church, the godparents are auxiliary parents, whose charge is to assure the child a proper spiritual upbringing. No one could argue that Evans wasn't desirable after that sort of public commitment. Actually, dear girl, it's a brilliant idea," he said, stroking my jawline with the knuckle of his good hand.

"But Lucy says she doesn't care," I said, and I told him how she had decided the ton did not matter to her.

"Ah," said my husband. "But when Evans arrives, she may change her mind. A child forces you to consider your life in context. At least, that is what Ned has done for me."

I related what Lucy had told me about Maria Fitzherbert and Minney Seymour. "So you see, dear husband, I cannot help Lucy without hurting them. Nor can I be assured that Lucy will not be charged with the Dowager Ingram's death. If it were up to Mr. Waverly—"

"It would be disregarded summarily as ridiculous. He knows what the Ingram daughters are about," Edward finished for me. "But if the chief magistrate is pressured, who knows what might happen?"

"Edward, I have no idea what to do. None." I gripped his hand hard, hoping that his strength would transfer to me.

"Then let it rest, Jane. For this evening at least, let it go." And I did.

Chapter 55

The next morning, Sadie brought me a poached egg, toast, beef broth, and tea. Although I still felt weak, the breakfast was a help. Polly, that mistress of fashion and of aid to the injured, came a half hour later. "Mr. Lerner told me to check your wound and see how it's doing. I'm going to dab it with honey. Me mum says it helps with the healing."

Polly was nearly done tending to me when Lucy rapped lightly on the door. "How are you this morning?"

"Better, and I'm determined that there has to be a way around these accusations of murder, as well as the difficulty with the letter. While I am confined to lying down, I plan to apply my mind to both problems. Would you be so kind as to bring me my pencil and sketch pad? It might help me to think. Oh, and can you bring me that book on flowers from your library? The one I was looking at before?"

All morning I worked on adding vines and blossoms to the piece I was doing for Evans. After puzzling over the letter and devising no solution for dealing with it, I decided that solving the mystery of Lady Ingram's death would at least go a long way toward safeguarding my friend's reputation.

I decided I should review the facts, in case we had all overlooked some fundamental bit of logic. Some discrepancy. Something out of place. Something missing that should be there. *"Qui bene?"* I asked myself. Who stood to benefit from the Dowager's death? If the Dowager Lady Ingram was an impediment, whose way did she block? How would her death benefit anyone? And why did she need to die right now?

What did the Dowager Lady Ingram represent? Why was she perceived as an insurmountable threat?

To Lady Grainger's staff, the Dowager Lady Ingram and her daughters presented a short-term inconvenience. There was no reason to kill Lady Ingram, because eventually the Ingrams would move on.

To Lucy, Lady Ingram was an obstacle, regarding her social standing. But Lucy derived no benefit from killing Lady Ingram. My friend was hoping for a truce with the Dowager. And Lucy knew nothing about the changes to Lady Grainger's will. Furthermore, Lucy never had the opportunity to poison the coffee. She had held the tin but briefly before passing it along.

To Lady Conyngham, Lady Ingram was simply another visitor. The Marchioness had engineered the visit at Lady Grainger's as an opportunity to take my measure. She had no reason to poison Lady Ingram.

To Lady Grainger, her sister-in-law and nieces were an annoyance, but nothing more. She exerted control over her brother's family, because she held the purse strings. So she had no reason to poison her sister-in-law.

To the Honorable Blanche Ingram, her mother was her ally, her help in continuing her whirlwind life as an unmarried member of the ton. As long as Lady Ingram was alive, mother and daughter could share in the excitement of Blanche's popularity.

To Mary Ingram, her mother was the facilitator of a fantasy. As long as Mr. Lerner treated Lady Ingram, Miss Mary could continue to see the young doctor—and hope that one day he would fall in love with her. Therefore, she had no reason to poison her mother.

All right, Jane, I said to myself. *You have run into a dead end. What would you advise a student working on a maths problem?*

I would suggest that my student approach the conundrum from a different angle.

What if . . . ? I knew these to be the two most powerful words in any creative person's vocabulary. What if I paint the sky like this? What if I add the sound of bells to this piece of music? What if I carve around the flaw in this piece of marble?

What if . . . ?

What if the poisoning had been accidental? What if no one had ever intended for Lady Ingram to die?

Chapter 56

I allowed this question to take up residence in my mind. I did not try to shoo it away or force it to bear fruit. I simply allowed it tenancy as I continued to work with my pencil, occasionally switching to my pen when the results were pleasing. After a while, I grew tired of the daisies and roses that I was adding. My artwork demanded a different shape, so I flipped through Augie's wonderful book on garden plants. I considered this blossom and that, rejecting each in turn, until I happened upon foxglove. The slender thimble-shaped flowers would contrast nicely with the others I had drawn.

Foxglove. Also known as fairy caps, fairy bells, fairy fingers, and lady's glove. The selfsame biennial herb that Miss Mary had hacked to the ground in Lady Grainger's garden.

Why would she have done such a thing? Although I had visited many rooms in Lady Grainger's house, I had not seen one bouquet of fresh flowers. Not one. So what had happened with all those plants? The stubble left behind suggested a fulsome harvest. Where did they all go?

And what was it that Polly told me? Something that

Dorsey had said about the younger Miss Ingram leaving a mess in the kitchen.

Why would Miss Mary do such a thing?

Miss Mary, who followed Mr. Lerner around like a lovesick puppy. Miss Mary, who wanted to prove to Mr. Lerner that she would make a good doctor's wife. Miss Mary, who craved her mother's approval. Miss Mary, who badly needed her mother to put down her foot, to demand that her sister quit shilly-shallying around and at long last marry someone. Why would Miss Mary cut down an entire stand of foxglove and take it into Lady Grainger's kitchen?

Unless . . . unless she planned a use for it!

Then I realized what if Miss Mary picked up errant papers from Mr. Lerner's satchel? She might have read his notes concerning the titration of foxglove, otherwise known as digitalis. And thinking she could follow the instructions, she might have tried to brew a tincture herself. What better way could Mary prove her potential as a doctor's wife, much less win her mother's affection, than to cure the woman of problems with her heart?

Chapter 57

Despite my excitement at having pieced together a possible solution to the puzzle that was the Dowager Lady Ingram's death, my wound tired me so much that I took another nap. I had only just awakened when Polly came to say, "Mr. Waverly is here to see you, ma'am. Should I send him away? Your husband warned us not to let you become too tired."

"No, I'd like to speak to him. Could you help me dress?"

"Of course."

"Are the others here? Where is Mrs. Brayton?"

"No, they are all out. The children are walking in the park with Amelia, and Mrs. Brayton is out ordering a funeral wreath to be sent to Lady Grainger's house for Lady Ingram's viewing tomorrow. Finally! That coroner's had her body nearly six days! Anyway, Mrs. Brayton said she'd be back in a tick. Oh, and she's just had word that her little boy and his nanny have crossed the Channel and are on British soil. Won't be but a day or two before they're here. Mrs. Brayton is over the moon about it!"

"That's wonderful news. And my husband and Mr. Douglas? Where are they?"

Polly smiled. "Them two. A right couple of boys, they are. They're off to pick up Mr. Rochester's new boots, I heard. Should be back soon enough."

"Good. Could you send for Mr. Lerner?" Noting the worried look in her eyes, I hastily added, "I am on the mend. It's another matter I wish to discuss with him."

After I was suitably attired, Higgins carried me into the library. Polly saw to it that I was comfortable with my feet propped up as I sat in a wingback chair in front of the fire. She tucked a crocheted lap blanket around me as tenderly as any mother would and positioned a small silver bell near at hand.

"Ring it and Sadie or me, we'll come running."

"Would you be so kind as to retrieve a book for me? The one I was perusing on gardening?" I asked. "I want to show Mr. Waverly something in it. I should have remembered to bring it along."

"Certainly, ma'am," said Polly. She turned to do my bidding and nearly bumped into Mr. Waverly as he entered the room.

"Thank God, you are all right." The Bow Street man stood there staring down at me. His fingers turned his hat 'round and 'round in his hands as he looked me over.

"Please sit," I said and rang the bell. "Sadie will bring us tea. I have a theory regarding who killed Lady Ingram, but I should like to wait and try my thoughts out when everyone is present."

Just then, Edward and Mr. Douglas joined us. The men had accomplished their errands and seemed quite pleased with themselves. I had to admit that my husband's new boots looked very dashing. Lucy arrived a few minutes later.

"What's all this? Are you feeling better?" she asked, as she bent to give me a kiss on the cheek.

"I am," I replied, just as Higgins announced Mr. Lerner's arrival.

Once everyone was assembled, I handed over to the constable the gardening book Polly had fetched for me, and I instructed him to look at the page I had marked.

"I see a flower called foxglove and its description," Waverly said, "but I cannot see its relevance to Lady Ingram's death."

I explained my thought process to my audience, who listened carefully. I summarized, "I believe it was Miss Mary Ingram who killed her mother. But not on purpose. She tried to make a healing titration that she'd heard Mr. Lerner speak of. She attempted to concoct it herself, from foxglove plants in Lady Grainger's garden. It wasn't that she wanted to poison her mother. Quite the contrary. Mary hoped to cure the woman and to win her affection, plus the admiration of Mr. Lerner. But she miscalculated. Badly. She made the dose far too strong."

"Oh!" said Mr. Lerner. "You could be right in your theory, Mrs. Rochester, though I feel horrible that Miss Mary might have done this because of me! I guess that when she heard me explaining how digitalis worked, it piqued her interest. I didn't give her any instruction, though—she must have tried to create the potion by looking over my papers. I keep meaning to have the latch on my satchel fixed, but there's never enough time."

"While I'll agree you need to repair the lock, I hardly think that most reasonable people would have taken it upon themselves to play at being a doctor," said Edward, kindly. "Mr. Lerner, you have no reason to castigate yourself for such an extreme reaction to a few loose papers."

"But Miss Blanche Ingram also said that she felt ill. How do you explain that?" asked Mr. Waverly.

"I suspect that Miss Mary was testing the dosage on her sister," I said, "figuring that since her sister was healthy, she could refine her experiments without any deleterious effects. Or at least, not too much of an adverse response."

"Exactly," said Mr. Lerner. "Since Lady Ingram had a bad heart, the medication had a more radical and immediate impact on her than on Miss Blanche Ingram. Of course, it also overpowered Lady Grainger's poor dog."

"I had not given the decimated patch of flowers much thought, but it makes sense," said Lucy. "Otherwise, why would Miss Mary have cut down those and left everything else standing?"

"And there's the reported mess in the kitchen," I reminded her.

"Even if you're onto something—and I think you are, Mrs. Rochester—we lack proof," said Mr. Waverly as he adjusted his spectacles.

"But we can't sit by and do nothing. Miss Mary and her sister have threatened Mr. Lerner, my husband, and Lucy in turn. If we don't at least try to prove my theory, the Ingram girls will continue to blacken our names. Miss Ingram has even gone to Lady Conyngham, hoping to strike a bargain that would benefit her at our expense."

"The devil you say!" Mr. Waverly slapped the arm of his chair.

"Miss Blanche Ingram would certainly be likely to stop her rumormongering if she knew her mother had been killed by her own sister," said Edward.

"Mrs. Rochester is right. If word spreads that one of the sisters poisoned her mother—even by accident—Lady Conyngham would have nothing more to do with either of them," said Mr. Douglas. "We must encourage Miss Mary to confess. Although for the life of me, I can't imagine how."

"Not only that," said Lucy, "but the confession must be public. Otherwise, the Ingrams will pretend it never happened. We know from experience that they are practiced liars."

"If we're aiming for a public display, the visitation is to be tomorrow afternoon at Lady Grainger's house," said Edward. "That would surely be our best option."

The group murmured in agreement.

"Now that we have the time and the setting, what we need is a lever," said Mr. Douglas. "An instrument to put pressure on Miss Mary."

I mulled this over.

And suddenly, I had a plan.

Chapter 58

Everyone agreed that my plan might work. We would want to keep Mrs. Biltmore's attack on me a secret, otherwise my presence at Lady Ingram's viewing might seem suspicious. Lucy was dispatched immediately to talk to Lady Grainger about our scheme. "I think she'll go along with it, if only to have the matter settled."

Only my husband had misgivings. Later that evening when we were in bed, he questioned me. "Are you up to this? It could mean being on your feet a long while at the visitation, as there's sure to be a lengthy receiving line."

· His unruly hair had grown long during our visit, but I rather enjoyed the way it brushed his nightshirt collar. I touched a strand lovingly as he said, "There has to be a way around having you at the viewing. I shall go and offer our sympathy, but you don't need to come. We must be able to gather Miss Mary's confession some other way."

"I can't think of one. Neither could anyone else," I said. "Besides, I am the squire's wife and it is my duty to attend as well as yours."

"But you are injured," he said. "I shall tender your regrets. Today I saw a bit more color in your cheeks, and I hope to continue to see such progress."

"You will."

He smoothed my hair and kissed the top of my ear, and I thought I could smell green traces of the medicinal herb he'd been using as Mr. Lerner had recommended. "When I see the progress, I really mean that. I *see* how you are coming along."

"Really?" Joy bubbled up inside me.

"You are not wholly distinct, but I can discern more detail. More substance. There are edges around objects. A bit of acuity has returned."

"Oh, Edward!" I threw my arms around his neck and felt the pinch of pain as my reward. "Oh!"

"See? You are in pain. You need to stay here. Lady Ingram was nothing to you—less!—and I can share your regrets. We will manage somehow without you."

"No," I said. "I shall heal better knowing we can put all this behind us."

"Jane," he said, as his lips teased my throat, "you try my patience."

"Oh, sir . . ."

Chapter 59

The next day, I rested until the last possible moment. Edward had won a concession from me: I agreed to let Mr. Lerner check the progress of my healing and decree if I was well enough to execute my plan. When the doctor pronounced me "coming along nicely," Polly helped me dress in my finest black silk, and Edward and Mr. Douglas carried me downstairs and into the carriage.

Once we arrived at the Grainger house, I insisted on walking into the building as though nothing were wrong. It pained me, but I felt it necessary to maintain the illusion of health. I did not want to draw unwarranted attention to myself—at least, not until the right time. I did not want Miss Mary Ingram to wonder why I'd bothered to make an appearance after I had been hurt so badly. Any sort of suspicion on her part might spoil the impact I hoped to have on the young woman.

No one could mistake Lady Grainger's home for anything but a house in deep mourning. Black crape covered every window and all of the mirrors. The staff wore soft mourning slippers to muffle their footsteps. The hall clock had been stopped, as a reminder that time stands still in that world beyond this. The cloying fragrance of lilies perfumed the air.

Because Lady Ingram's body had been given over to the coroner, her remains were now six days old. The smell of the corpse could not be disguised, no matter how many fragrant bouquets of flowers were on display throughout the house. The horrid smell of decay triumphed over all else. Lucy had suggested that we all carry perfumed handkerchiefs, and I blessed her silently for thinking ahead as I held mine to my nose.

Lucy, Mr. Douglas, Edward, and I took our places in the receiving line. The queue moved slowly forward and up the staircase to where Lady Ingram's mortal remains rested on the dining room table. I knew there would be a lot of mourners, but I had not anticipated so many. I could only believe that word of the Dowager's sudden death and the girls' many accusations might have made their rounds. The crowd seemed unusually chatty for a group of mourners, so I assumed that many here were hoping for a choice bit of gossip. As we mounted the last of the stairs, the entry hall began to spin. Black encroached on the edges of my vision. Edward slipped his arm around my waist, but I was quickly growing weak. I grabbed Edward tightly and struggled to stay on my feet.

"This is too much! Let me find you a chair," he whispered.

A stray lock of his hair tickled my face and caused me to smile. "No. It will only be a little longer, and then my mind can rest as well as my body." Sheer force of will kept me standing and gave me strength. I was determined to do this for Lucy. If this scheme worked, her reputation would be spared. *Not much farther now. I can do this!*

I could hear Miss Blanche Ingram holding court as the line moved forward, out of the hall and into the dining room. Those paying their respects first greeted Miss Mary, and then Miss Ingram, and finally Lady Grainger. Young Lord Ingram was not in attendance. During her visit with Lady Grainger the past evening, Lucy had learned that he was taken ill and could not leave his bed at Ingram Park.

After offering their sympathies to the Ingram daughters and Lady Grainger, mourners made a clockwise procession around the coffin in its place of honor on the dining room table. Floral tributes of every color and size lined the perimeter of the room. Guests paused to read the cards offering condolences. It was expected that they would also gaze on the face of the departed, as a gesture of respect and a reminder to us all that we would share the same fate.

My friend and her brother had moved along in the line so that they were face-to-face with Miss Mary. But before Lucy could share her condolences, Miss Ingram turned on her with a fury.

"How dare you?" she said to Lucy.

"Stop it, Blanche." Lady Grainger put a hand on her niece's shoulder.

All the other mourners turned to watch. After a calculated pause, Miss Ingram turned to her aunt, and in a loud voice said, "But Aunt! Lucy Brayton poisoned my—"

"Stop it!" Lady Grainger's command was more forceful this time. She reached past her niece to bundle Lucy into an embrace. "It is so good to see you."

This was our cue. Edward and I pushed our way forward, rather rudely, I admit, while Lucy extricated herself from our hostess. Then Lucy and Mr. Douglas stepped to one side.

My husband took Miss Mary's hand. "Mr. Lerner sends his regrets, but he is busy with his fiancée making wedding plans."

"You lie!" She gasped, yanking her hand out of Edward's grip.

The other mourners stopped talking so that they could listen in.

"No, Miss Mary," I said softly, "my husband is not a liar. But you are." I raised my voice. "It was you who poisoned your mother, wasn't it? You didn't mean to, but you did."

"I—I—I," she stuttered. "I never!"

"You were only trying to help. You thought you knew what you were doing—and hoped to prove to Mr. Lerner what a fine wife you would make. You thought if you could make your mother feel better, she would love you more." I paused. "Poor Mary. You were tired of being second best."

The blood drained out of Miss Mary's face.

A hush fell over the other mourners. The crowd surged forward, closing in on me, so that they could better hear what I was saying.

"Right now, Mr. Waverly is down the hall, searching your room. What do you think he'll find?" said Edward. "I suspect he'll happen on Mr. Lerner's notes concerning the use of digitalis, common foxglove."

"It's no use denying it, Mary," said her aunt. "Cook has already told us how you've been in her kitchen, soaking plants in hot water. Plants she's identified as foxglove."

Miss Mary's hands flew up to cover her mouth, and she teetered on the edge of a swoon. Lucy and Lady Grainger moved forward to shore the girl up. Miss Mary sobbed, "I didn't mean it! I didn't! I loved my mother! I didn't mean to hurt her!"

Now the quiet ended, replaced by a low roar of whispers as the visitors reacted to the young woman's confession. Their curiosity unleashed, they pressed even closer, a few elbowing me in their eagerness to eavesdrop. But they didn't have to strain their ears much, because Blanche now screeched, "What have you done? *You* killed our mother?" Miss Ingram turned on Miss Mary, grabbing her sister by the arms, and she would have given her a shake, but Mr. Douglas levered Miss Ingram away.

The mourners gasped in chorus, as if they had been

directed to do so. The sound echoed in the room, a mournful human empathy given voice. But the oneness did not last for long. The shock passed, and everyone seemed to want to share a question or opinion. The din was unbelievable, especially in a house of mourning where soft slippers are worn and bell clappers are wrapped in muslin to muffle sound.

The Honorable Blanche Ingram flew at her sister, even as Mr. Douglas tried to move Miss Mary out of striking distance. "It was an accident," he told Blanche. "Miss Mary didn't mean to do it."

"She only meant to help. You are feeling better now, aren't you, Miss Ingram?" I asked of Blanche. "Your sister had been dosing your coffee, trying to calculate how much of the tincture to give your mother. Of course, she never expected you to share it. That's how everything went terribly wrong. The small amount in the coffee had only made you slightly ill, but given your mother's weak heart. It was a fatal dose."

"I never intended . . ." Mary whispered. "Never . . ."

Chapter 60

Outside in the hallway, Mr. Waverly had been waiting for this confession. He walked past us, taking care that his black baton was highly visible under his arm. When he reached Miss Mary's side, he said, "Come with me, miss. You don't want to make a scene, do you?"

Miss Mary only cried softly and shook her head.

"You—" Blanche Ingram had been temporarily struck dumb, but as the man from Bow Street led her sister away, the older Ingram sister gave her sibling a withering look and called out, "I hope you rot in prison!"

Edward, Lucy, Mr. Douglas, and I accompanied Lady Grainger downstairs, leaving the rest of the mourners to console "poor" Miss Blanche Ingram.

"I feel sorry for Mary," said the Lady, as we watched Mr. Waverly help her niece into a waiting coach. "I hope they won't deal too harshly with her."

"Though her attempts to cast blame on innocents won't win her any favors, I believe she might get off rather lightly, since the poison was not a poison, per se, but rather a medicinal treatment misapplied," said Mr. Douglas. "Of course, the fact that she is the daughter of a baron will be helpful to her as well."

"Are you all right, Olivia?" Lucy asked her friend.

"I'm terribly saddened by this—and I wish things were different. Mary has lived so long in Blanche's shadow. Perhaps I should have reached out to the younger girl," said Lady Grainger. "Although in truth, I don't know what else I could have done. I did speak up on her behalf, several times. But Silvana was such a dominant personality. So confident as a mother. When I did make suggestions, she cast them aside with ugly commentary implying that a childless woman like me could not understand her role as a parent."

I shook my head in disbelief. "A child grows in a mother's heart, not just in her womb. Our love and concern can extend beyond blood ties, else how could a marriage last?"

"Well said, my darling." Edward squeezed my hand.

Lady Grainger turned to stare at me. "You are wise beyond your years, Mrs. Rochester. I suppose this is as good of a time as any to thank you for figuring out what really happened to my sister-in-law. My staff will be relieved to know that the murky cloud of suspicion has lifted from our household."

"You are very kind," I said.

"What will you do about Miss Mary?" asked Mr. Douglas, when we had reached the ground floor. "I hope you'll consider hiring a good barrister for her. If necessary, I can recommend several."

"Yes, of course, I will." With the recognition of that respon-sibility, Lady Grainger crumpled a little.

"And her sister? It will be devilishly hard for Miss Blanche Ingram to navigate the choppy waters of society after this," Edward said.

"Her marital prospects will have dimmed considerably." Lucy's tone was matter-of-fact.

"There's always an Italian count lurking somewhere, who

wants a peeress for a bride," said Lady Grainger. "I shall urge
Blanche in the strongest tones to travel the continent. Perhaps
I'll even go with. She still has a modicum of beauty, but I shall
impress upon her that the blush on her cheeks is fading fast."

Although I did not betray my emotions, I couldn't help but
think that with any luck, I'd never see Blanche Ingram again.
I should have to pray she found her Italian count—and that
he was a determined homebody.

"It must be a relief," said Lucy, hugging her friend, "to have
this over. I know it is for all of us.

"I've seen better days," Lady Grainger admitted. "But the
dog breeder sent 'round a message yesterday that he has a new
litter of pups that have almost been weaned. I'm to choose one
next week."

"Good for you," said Lucy. "I shall want to meet the newest
member of your family."

"And I shall want to meet yours when he arrives," said Lady
Grainger, as she gave Lucy one more hug before we departed.

The events at Lady Grainger's house had sapped all my
energy. As a consequence, I spent the next two days resting in
bed and working on my pen-and-ink piece for Evans, taking
my time as I drew in the foxglove stems with finger-shaped
blossoms.

I did my best to forget about the King's love letter. It was
locked away safely, and Lady Conyngham had lost her leverage
over me now that Miss Mary was in Newgate, as was Mrs.
Biltmore. Mr. Waverly had sent 'round a note that he would
need a formal statement from me, but that it could wait until
I regained my strength. He also thanked me for solving the
mystery of Lady Ingram's death. With any luck, we would
never cross paths again.

Mr. Lerner had accepted the position to assist Mr. Carter,
and he and Miss Goldstein were to be married later in the
summer. They had kindly invited all of us to attend, and I
was looking forward to the event and to meeting the young

lady. Meanwhile, as an early wedding gift, Edward and Mr. Douglas had located a new satchel for the doctor. One with a sturdy latch.

A letter from Mrs. Fairfax informed us that John was definitely on the mend, sitting up in his bed and grumbling about having "nowt to do." The roof was another story, as the builders continued to uncover more and more rot in the structure. However, our housekeeper thought that good progress was being made. Good progress was also being made with Edward's eyesight—though it would never return to normal, it was improving steadily.

As I recovered, the Brayton household was in happy chaos around me. Lucy put this unhappy passage behind her and turned all her attentions to preparing for Evans's imminent arrival.

On Saturday afternoon, there came a knock at the front door. When it was not immediately answered, it came again. This time Rags went wild with barking. I could hear the commotion all the way upstairs in the nursery, where I was reading to Ned, after instructing Adèle to translate a textbook passage from French into English, while Edward and Mr. Douglas were spending time together at Boodle's.

Voices drifted up, but they were indistinct, so I continued with the story about the golden goose from *Grimm's Children's and Household Tales*. I was explaining how the youngest son asked his father if he could cut wood when Amelia ran in. "Come quickly, ma'am. He's here!"

"He who?"

"The little boy. What's his name—Evans!"

I handed her my son and hurried to get Adèle. "*Vite!*" I told the young French girl, as she reluctantly put aside her dolls. She and I immediately started down the stairs all the while taking great care not to put stress on my wound.

Voices from the drawing room attracted me, so I hurried there to find Lucy. In her arms was an infant with a face as round as a soup bowl, bright blue eyes, and a tuft of ginger-colored

hair. Tears streamed down my friend's face. All she could say
was, "Oh, oh, oh, oh. He looks exactly like Augie!"

Seated across from her was a kindly looking woman with
gray hair slicked back into a neat bun. "Mrs. Wallander, I
presume?" I offered my hand.

"Ja," she said. Her sturdy shoes and simple traveling frock
spoke volumes about this no-nonsense woman.

She took my hand and shook it solemnly, giving me the
chance to take note of her button nose, her cherry-shaped lips,
and her ruddy complexion. One look in her eyes told me she
was a shrewd judge of character, and that she was taking
everything in, trying to decide if Evans would be happy here.

I could have told her that he would. Lucy would make his
happiness her mission in life.

I took Adèle by the hand and gestured for Amelia to follow
with Ned on her hip, so that we were approaching Evans with
great care, as I did not wish to overwhelm the boy. I moved
closer to the newcomer. "Adèle and Ned, this is Evans. Lucy's
son. Your new best friend."

The babies stared at each other, wide-eyed and curious
Adèle crowed with delight. A stream of French followed, but
the gist was, "Now I am the sister to two boys!" and then she
dropped to her knees to cover Evans's face with kisses. Rags
joined the throng, standing on his two hind legs and dancing
in a happy circle.

Amelia took Mrs. Wallander upstairs to get settled into
her new quarters. I sank down on the settee next to Lucy, as
she gazed on the baby in wonder. Adèle continued to murmur
endearments to her new friend. Lucy, for the first time since
I'd known her, seemed entirely dumbstruck. All she could do
was stare at the boy. At long last she said, "Is it true? Really
true? Jane, tell me, am I dreaming?"

"No," I said, and I carefully wrapped my arm around her
shoulders. "No, dear heart. You are fully awake, and your
dream has come true."

Chapter 61

The entire household was overjoyed to meet little Evans. Mr. Douglas doted on the child, and Edward declared the boy to be his father's mirror image. Over the next few days, the baby was passed from one set of arms to another as we took turns admiring the newest member of what we called "our family." As for Lucy, she was positively radiant. Happier than I'd ever seen her.

The arrival of Evans turned the household into a busy beehive of visitors and commotion, as Lucy received numerous well-wishers. In between visits, I tried to keep as still as possible so that my stitches would heal. My wound had turned a variety of colors, but thanks to Polly's daily applications of poultices and honey, the spot had not grown hot to the touch, and no infection had set in. Still, it pained me.

I sat in the library and worked on my gift for Evans by using my paints to add light washes of color to the piece. The effect had been very pleasing, as my touches brought out the tiny rabbit hidden in the bushes and the robin in the tree and the frog under a bush.

"This is magnificent, Jane," said Lucy. Her face beamed with happiness as she examined my work while Evans was upstairs napping. "You have done such an impressive job. He will treasure this forever. I know he will."

"Look who we found on the front doorstep," said Mr. Douglas, coming into the library alongside my husband, and stepping aside to reveal Mr. Waverly.

"My congratulations to you, Mrs. Brayton, on the newest member of your household," Waverly said to Lucy.

"Thank you." She smiled. "How kind of you to come in person to offer them."

"I wish I could say that had been my intention." He sighed, sinking into an armchair. "The truth is, however, that while the circumstances surrounding Lady Ingram's death have been cleared, there is still the matter of the letter Mrs. Rochester possesses, the one that drove Mrs. Biltmore to such extremes. Lady Conyngham continues to meet with the Duke of Cumberland," he said. "I've eavesdropped as often as possible. I don't know what they're up to, but it can't be anything good." Mr. Waverly took off his spectacles and cleaned them with his handkerchief. "She's playing both sides against the middle. Coddling the King whilst she plots against him. She's got a list of demands longer than my right arm. I can only guess they're trying to figure out some other way to pressure Mrs. Rochester to turn over the letter."

"The Duke of York has promised Maria Fitzherbert that he can smuggle her out of the country if need be, but Minney has told her mother in no uncertain terms that she will not leave her fiancé," said Lucy.

"Are they truly at risk?" I asked my friends. "If I hand over the letter, are they likely to be hurt?"

"I don't know." Mr. Waverly put his glasses back on.

"It depends," said Mr. Douglas, "on what the Marchioness and the Duke want, and whether the King is willing to give it to them."

"Then let us be frank with each other. As long as I have that letter and George IV is our Regent, we can safely presume that someone will want it. It's simply too valuable as a tool of persuasion."

"Aye," said Mr. Waverly. "As coronation day grows closer, the stakes get higher in anticipation of the King announcing his appointments and such. Believe me, everyone and his brother has his hand out. There's a regular parade in and out of Carlton House." He rose from his seat. "I can't tell you what to do with it, Mrs. Rochester, but I wish you the wisdom of Solomon."

After Mr. Waverly's departure, Edward and Mr. Douglas left Lucy and me alone in the library once again. I turned to her and asked, "Do you mind taking the letter out of the strongbox for me? I want to look it over. Perhaps some flash of an idea will come to me. Odd, isn't it? That correspondence purports to be a love letter, yet its purpose has nothing to do with love. The King wrote it to Mrs. Biltmore to get rid of her in the most expedient way imaginable."

"Have you decided what to do?"

"No," I said. "I only pray that I might be divinely inspired to come up with a solution."

After Lucy retrieved the letter, she went to check on her son. I stared at the six pages on royal letterhead. *What to do? What to do?*

Mr. Waverly had been right. I needed the wisdom of Solomon. I took down a copy of the Bible from Augie's bookshelves. Opening it, I read out loud: "And the king said, 'Bring me a sword.' And they brought a sword before the king. And the king said, 'Divide the living child in two, and give half to the one, and half to the other.'"

I shuddered, thinking of what might have happened if the child's true mother hadn't stepped forward. To divide a child? How horrible! Too ghastly to contemplate. But it did spur my thoughts. The idea of division stuck in my head, whirling 'round and 'round.

Then came my answer: I would divide the letter in two! But could I? First I would have to ascertain if my skills were up to the task. After tearing two sheets of paper out of my notebook, I went and sat behind Lucy's desk. Spreading all six pages out in front of me, I pored over the King's words, occasionally scribbling a phrase or two on my scratch paper. My artistic skills extended to mimicry, and at length, I decided on several simple phrases, concocted from the words he had written. These I copied over and over on my notepaper, using the King's handwriting as my guide. I took especially careful note of where his strokes began and followed their route to the end.

Next I applied myself to his signature. This proved more challenging, but a reasonable facsimile wasn't very difficult to create. I only hoped that no one would look too closely. After all, I reasoned, exposing the letter as a "fake" could even end up beneficial. But as I stepped away from my work, doubts plagued me. Yes, it was clear that I could produce a reasonable facsimile, but . . . should I? Was it morally right to do so? Or would I be telling a lie on paper?

This worried me. I thought about the King, about Maria and Minney, about Lady Conyngham and wondered, *Is it ethical to divide up this letter and forge the King's signature?*

My musings were interrupted by a visit from Mr. Lerner. After ringing for Polly, I put down my pen, and he examined my wound while I leaned against Lucy's desk for support. Once he pronounced it "very nearly healed," he noticed my scattered papers.

"I am glad you are not doing anything too strenuous," he remarked, as he turned his back on me so Polly could help me readjust my clothes.

"Polly? Could you ask Sadie to bring us tea?" I said, as a method of gaining us privacy. With a gesture, I indicated to Mr. Lerner to take a seat. Remembering how hungry he always was, I added, "And ask Cook to send up slices of mutton, cheese, and bread, please."

When she had left, I took a chair as well and said, "Mr. Lerner, what does your religion teach about ethics? I know very little about Judaism except from what I've read in the Bible, of course."

His eyes were lively with intelligence. "Why do you ask? Is this about the ethics of tricking Miss Mary into a confession?"

That might do for my purposes, but I was bound to say, "Not exactly. Although I am curious about that, too."

"Let us start there. The teachings are very clear that protecting and preserving life triumphs over every other consideration, including the Ten Commandments. You did save my life, in that, had Miss Mary's false accusations resulted in a trial, I might well have been hanged."

Sadie entered with a heavily laden tray of food. The steam rising from the teapot, the green scent of bergamot, and a delicate hint of ginger in a plate of fresh scones, distracted the young doctor and me. After the maid left, I served Mr. Lerner, pouring hot tea into his cup.

"Did you have other questions?" he asked, once he'd eaten a plate full of food.

"What if you aren't sure that the other person is in danger? Does your religion still call upon you to act?"

"Absolutely. We are commanded to protect each other, and not to leave each other in a condition that might be harmful. So, for example, if I see a man's cart about to overturn, it is my duty to warn him and give him aid. Especially if that accident would cause harm to him or even to his donkey."

As I sipped my tea, I reflected that Maria Fitzherbert's situation was not so very different from what he described. All my options came to this: I could not stand by and put Maria and Minney's lives at risk.

After Mr. Lerner left, I returned to my practice. When I was satisfied with my results, I separated the letter's fifth page from the sixth. To the bottom of the fifth page, I added my version of the King's signature. To the top of the sixth page, I added a phrase.

And now I had not one, but two letters written by King George IV.

Chapter 62

I came up with my plan not a moment too soon. The next morning, Higgins walked into the breakfast room, bringing me a note on a silver platter.

I opened it quickly. "It's from Lady Conyngham. She wants to meet with me, alone, in Hyde Park today. And she requests I bring the letter. She doesn't say what she'll do if I turn her down, but the threat is there all the same."

"Darling girl, are you sure you don't want me to come with you?" Edward asked.

"No, but thank you. I do not want her to be suspicious. If the Marchioness thinks she has bullied me into submission, if she believes I've come with my tail tucked between my legs, all the better. I shall rely on my insignificant size and unchallenging mien to lull her into her natural state of superiority. She will think she's put a scare into me and determine that I'm incapable of deception."

"Are you capable of lying? You are such a good girl, my love."

"You would be amazed at what I am capable of, Mr. Rochester. As soon as my stitches heal, I intend to show you."

A few hours later, Williams brought Lucy's carriage to Hyde Park, a place where the bushes were low and no trees blocked the view of us. Taking his time, he helped me out of the carriage, making sure I did not trip over the bright red shawl I had worn for the purpose of making myself more conspicuous.

A few minutes earlier, we had dropped Mr. Douglas off on the other side of the park. He planned to make his way across the acreage to a spot where he could observe my transaction unobtrusively.

The map enclosed in Lady Conyngham's note had indicated we were to meet at a bench close to the street. That was fortunate for me, although the purpose was surely to make life easier for the heavyset Marchioness.

I did not have to wait long. A handsome maroon cabriolet with a pair of matching black horses clattered down the street before coming to a halt. Twin footmen in maroon livery, with gold epaulets on their shoulders, opened the door and escorted the Marchioness out. This morning her age was obvious as she moved with the sort of hesitation common in older people. When she was close enough, I pushed myself to a standing position and did my best to curtsy, although my genuflection was incredibly painful.

The Marchioness took a seat, and I sat next to her. "Well, we aren't here to chat. I've heard that you managed to best Mrs. Biltmore, and she is locked up. You also managed to determine who actually killed Lady Ingram. One of her daughters is in jail, and the other is touring the Continent. I suppose you are congratulating yourself. I imagine that you think that I no longer have any influence over you," she said.

"Actually, that's not the case. I know better."

She raised an eyebrow at me. "Go on."

"I am fully cognizant that you can still ruin Lucy. Yes, her name is cleared as to the death of Dowager Lady Ingram. And Blanche Ingram won't be able to gossip about my friend or me. But you are still here. You still have the ear of the King. You have it in your power to do much damage to us all."

"My, my." The Marchioness sounded like a contented kitten. A genuine smile lifted the edges of her lips. "You are much smarter than I thought."

"Therefore, I have decided to give you the love letter."

Reaching into my reticule, I handed her the missive, folded with the King's own seal on the outside. She tore it from me and read it quickly:

My Darling Pansy,

I am sorry you find yourself with child; however, I cannot marry you because I am already married.

Pity the poor head that wears the crown! No one can imagine what dangers and pressures assail me on every side. The dreams I have of my time on the battlefield! The terror I relive! Sometimes I fear that I am every bit as mad as my father!

George

What she held in her hand was the last page of the love letter, to the top of which I had merely added a salutation and opening sentence.

Lady Conyngham stared at the single sheet and murmured as if to herself, "I recognize his handwriting and the paper. No other stationery could have that same provenance. But although it was clearly written when Mrs. Biltmore was pregnant, it does not state to whom he is married! It doesn't name Mrs. Fitzherbert as his wife! He could well be writing about Queen Caroline!"

I said nothing.

"Honestly," she said, as she pursed her lips, "to hear the

King speak of it, you'd think this letter proved he defied the Royal Marriages Act. I should have guessed he wouldn't do that. He was far too diffident to his father to risk his disapproval, although this does prove he committed adultery." She flicked the paper with a finger, "You have gone to a lot of effort to safeguard something with very little value. No one expects a King to be a saint!"

I shrugged. "I never suggested it had great value. Everyone else did. And I suppose to some, it might still. If you don't want it—"

"I shall keep it," she said quickly. "Though I am not sure it is worth standing up at a baptismal font."

"But I have done as you asked. Now you must keep your portion of our agreement!" Actually, Lucy and I had concurred that Lady Conyngham's patronage mattered very little to her and Evans. But I still thought it best to keep up appearances.

"No, I think not. Yes, you have turned this over to me, but it is a worthless piece of paper," she said. "It's clear to me that over the years the King has forgotten exactly what he wrote."

Yes, that was what I had hoped she might think. After all, she had no respect for the man, other than what he might afford her—and he had no respect for her. It stood to reason they would not credit each other with any sense.

I pressed my point. "But you told me you would stand up for Evans!"

"I think not. I am tired of you and your friend. Now that I have the letter, I have no need for either of you."

To my way of thinking, that was just fine.

Chapter 63

From my seat on the park bench, I watched her carriage drive away. Williams came to my aid. "You all right, ma'am?"

"Never better. Except for my side."

"Well done, Mrs. Rochester. Bravo!" Mr. Douglas stepped out from a stand of rhododendron bushes.

We returned together in the carriage to Grosvenor Square, where he helped me walk into Lucy's marble entrance hall. From the drawing room came the sound of happy female voices. I squared my shoulders and walked into the room, eager to join the gathering. The three women did not hear my approach, each was so absorbed in what she was doing.

My friend Lucy was pouring tea. Minney Seymour was cradling Evans and cooing to him. Maria Fitzherbert was marveling over a letter she held in her hands.

A letter that began, *"My Darling Pansy . . ."*

Author's Note

Dear Reader, I always wonder what is truth and what is fiction when I read. So come closer and I shall whisper a few of my secrets in your ear:

You are probably wondering if Minney Seymour actually was the illegitimate child of King George IV and Maria Fitzherbert? Scholars are divided on the subject. However, she was certainly the child of his heart. The King remained exceedingly fond of Minney his entire life, sending her small presents and settling upon her the sum of £20,000 on her twenty-first birthday.

Yes, there were only eight Bow Street Runners, and their primary charge was to protect the King. Given how disliked George IV was, that would not have been an easy task. As for the love letters, it is true that the King wrote them and bought them back . . . repeatedly. And the Marchioness Conyngham's family did prosper from her "special friendship" with the monarch.

Did King George IV really marry Maria Fitzherbert in secret—and then publicly marry Caroline of Brunswick? Yes. But his heart stayed true to Maria. In fact, he left instructions that he was to be buried with a miniature portrait of her that he wore around his neck, hanging on a tattered black ribbon. As for poor Queen Caroline, she was barred from attending her husband's coronation ceremony on July 19, 1821. Eleven days later, she suffered severe abdominal pains and finally died on August 7. Some suggest that she had been poisoned.

What about the Lunarticks? Did they really exist? Yes, and one of their number did recognize digitalis as a possible cure for heart problems. While the original society supposedly disbanded in 1813, they still meet today, which suggests they actually were driven underground.

Cannabis was first cultivated in 4000 BC in China and is considered one of the fundamental herbs of Chinese medicine. It can be effective in treating glaucoma because it lowers inter-ocular pressure. An Irish doctor in Calcutta published a paper about it in 1839, so it is reasonable to assume that word about its healing properties might have spread informally before that date.

The Great Famine occurred in 1845; however, in the years preceding there were many potato crop failures that sent the Irish to London hoping for jobs, including one in 1821.

For more information about King George IV, I suggest *Mrs. Fitzherbert and George IV* by W. H. Wilkins, *Prince of Pleasure* by Saul David, and *The Trial of Queen Caroline* by Jane Robins.